MARIO

BLOOD PACT
& Other Stories

Edited by
Claribel Alegría & Darwin Flakoll

Translated by
Daniel Balderston, Rachel Belash,
Jo Anne Engelbert, Darwin J. Flakoll,
James Graham, Maya Gross, W. Nick Hill,
Flaurie S. Imberman, Louise Popkin,
Gareth Price, Maria & Matthew Proser,
Tim Richards, Hardie St. Martin and
David Unger

CURBSTONE PRESS

Special thanks to Louise Popkin
for extensive editorial work on this book.

FIRST EDITION, 1997
Copyright © 1997 by Mario Benedetti
Translation Copyright © 1997 by the respective translators
All Rights Reserved

Printed in the U.S. on acid-free paper by Bookcrafters
Cover design: Les Kanturek

Curbstone Press is a 501(c)(3) nonprofit publishing house
whose programs are supported in part by private donations
and by grants from organizations, private foundations, and
government agencies. This book was supported by grants from
the Connecticut Commission on the Arts, a State agency whose
funds are appropriated by the State legislature, and from the
National Endowment for the Arts, a Federal agency whose
funds are appropriated by Congress.

Library of Congress Cataloging-in-Publication Data

Benedetti, Mario, 1920-
    Blood pact and other stories / by Mario Benedetti.
    p.   cm.
    ISBN 1-880684-39-X
    1. Benedetti, Mario, 1920-   —Translations into English.
    I. Title.
    PQ8519.B292A23   1997
    863—dc20   96-21343

published by
CURBSTONE PRESS   321 Jackson Street   Willimantic, CT 06226
    phone: (860) 423-5110   e-mail: curbston@connix.com
            http://www.connix.com/~curbston/

Contents

BLOOD PACT
& Other Stories

The Budget

The last time our office got a new budget was way back in nineteen twenty-something, when most of us were still struggling with geography and fractions. Nevertheless, the Boss remembered that event, and sometimes, when we didn't have much to do, he'd sit himself down on the edge of a desk, legs dangling, immaculate white socks peering out from under his trouser cuffs, and describe with all his old emotion and his customary five hundred and ninety-eight words, the magnificent day long ago when his Boss—ours was First Secretary at the time—had clapped him on the back and said, "My boy, we've got a new budget," with the satisfied air of a man who has already figured out how many shirts he can buy with his raise.

A new budget is any government bureau's highest aspiration. We knew that some other bureaus with larger staffs got new budgets every two or three years. And we'd watch them from our little administrative island with the same mixture of resignation and despair Robinson Crusoe must have felt as he watched all those ships sail over the horizon, knowing it would be just as futile to send up signals as to complain. Signals and complaints would have been just as useless where we were concerned, because we never had more than nine employees, and it wasn't very likely that anyone would pay attention to such a small department.

Since we knew nothing in the world was going to get us any extra perks, the best we could hope to do was cut expense, and to a certain extent we succeeded, thanks to a rather primitive system of cost sharing. I, for example, would pay for the *mate*, and the First Assistant, for afternoon tea. The Second Assistant would spring for the sugar; the First Secretary took care of the crackers, and the Second got the butter. The two typists and the porter were exempt,

1

but the Boss, who earned a little more than the rest of us, supplied the newspaper we all read.

Our entertainment allowance was also shaved to the bone. We'd go to the movies once a month, making sure we all saw different pictures so we could tell each other about them. That way, we kept up with what was playing all over town. We had developed a taste for games of concentration like chess and checkers, which didn't cost much and did a lot to keep us from yawning. We'd play from five to six, when we could be sure no new documents would be coming in because the sign in the window said no "transactions" after five. We had read that phrase so often, we couldn't remember who had invented it, or even exactly what a "transaction" was. Sometimes people would come asking for the number of their "transactions." We'd give them a document number, and they'd go away happy. So a "transaction" might be a document, for example. To tell the truth, our life there wasn't all that bad. From time to time, the Boss felt obliged to lecture us on the advantages of the public over the private sector, and some of us figured that by this time it'd be strange if he had any other opinion.

One of his arguments was Security: we could be sure we wouldn't be laid off. For that to happen would take a meeting of the Senate; and we all knew the senators only got together when they had to grill some Minister. So, in that sense, the Boss had a point: our job security was real. Of course, that wasn't the only kind of Security we could count on: we could be just as sure that we would never earn enough to pay cash for an overcoat. But the Boss, who couldn't buy one either, never thought it was the right moment to criticize his job, or ours. And—as always—he was right.

The resigned, almost definitive calm that had settled on our Office, leaving us reconciled to our lot and a bit lethargic for lack of insomnia, was broken one day by something the Second Secretary reported. He was the nephew of a high ranking official at the Ministry and it just so happened that this guy—no disrespect intended—had found out there was talk of a new budget for our Office. Since at that point we didn't know where the talk might be coming from, we just smiled with the special irony we reserved for such occasions, as if the Second Secretary had to be nuts, or thought the rest of us were morons. But when he told us his uncle had said it had came from the *alma parens* of the Ministry—namely, the Secretary himself— we suddenly felt that something was changing in our seventy-peso lives, as if an invisible hand had finally tightened a loose bolt, as if someone had come along and slapped us out of our passivity and resignation.

As for me, my first reaction was to visualize and even say aloud the word "fountain pen." Until then, I had never even thought about buying a fountain pen, but when the Second Secretary's news pointed our noses toward that vast horizon where anything is possible, even the tiniest whim, I immediately exhumed from who knows what cellar of my desire a fountain pen with a black barrel, a silver cap, and my name engraved on it. God knows how long it had been waiting down there.

I also saw and heard the First Assistant say he wanted a bicycle, the Boss stare absentmindedly at the rundown heel on his shoe, and one of the typists make snide remarks about the "dear old purse" she had been carting around for the last five years. And I saw and heard all of us go on and on about our plans, not because anyone cared what anyone else was saying, but because we each needed a safety valve for our pent up and unacknowledged fantasies. And I saw and heard all of us decide to celebrate the good news by dipping into our contingency fund to buy special pastries for afternoon tea.

That—buying the pastries—was the first step. Next came the pair of shoes the Boss bought himself. The shoes were followed by my fountain pen, to be paid for in ten installments. My pen was followed by the Second Secretary's overcoat, the First Typist's purse and the First Assistant's bicycle. Within a month and a half, we were all in hock and in agony.

Meanwhile, the Second Secretary had brought some more news. First, that the budget had gone to the Main Office. Then, that it hadn't: it wasn't in the Main Office, it was in Accounting. But the Head of Accounting was sick, and his opinion was crucial. So we all started worrying about the Head of Accounting, even though all we knew about him was that his name was Eugenio, and he was reviewing our budget. We would even have welcomed daily bulletins on his health, but all we ever got was the discouraging news that came from our Second Secretary's uncle: the Head of Accounting was getting worse. We were so sad for so long about that man's illness that the day he died we actually felt relieved—like the relatives of a critically-ill asthmatic must feel, when they don't have to worry about him any more. But most of all, we were happy for ourselves, knowing that with Don Eugenio gone, they might finally name a new Head of Accounting, who might finally review our budget.

Four months later, the new Head of Accounting was named. That afternoon we canceled our chess match, our break for *mate*, and all our office work. The Boss started humming an aria from "Aida," and between that and everything else we were soon so nervous that we had to go out for a little window-shopping. We came back to some shocking news: according to the uncle, our budget had never reached Accounting; that was a mistake. In fact, it had never even left the Main Office.

This news cast a dark shadow over our horizon. If the budget had been held up in Accounting, we wouldn't have worried. After all, we knew about the Head Accountant's illness. But if it had never even left the Main Office, where the Secretary—the man in charge— was in perfect health, then the delay was unexplainable and might drag on indefinitely.

Now our depression reached a critical stage. Each morning we looked at each other with the same pessimistic question in our eyes. At first we would ask, "Heard anything new?" Then we cut that down to "Anything new?" and finally, we just raised our eyebrows. Nobody knew a thing. And when somebody did, it was that the budget was being reviewed in the Main Office.

Eight months after the first bit of news reached us, my fountain pen was no longer working — it had quit two months earlier; the First Assistant had broken a rib riding his bicycle; the books the Second Assistant bought had been pawned to a Jew; the First Secretary's watch was losing a quarter of an hour a day; the Boss's shoes had been half-soled twice, stitched the first time and just tacked the second; and the Second Secretary's coat had threadbare lapels that stood up stiffly, like two tiny wings that didn't belong there.

One day we heard that the Minister had requested the budget. A week later the report was issued. We wanted to know what it said, but the uncle couldn't find out because it was "strictly confidential." We thought that was idiotic, since we treated documents with a card clipped to them marked "Extremely Urgent," "High Priority," or "Strictly Confidential" exactly the same way we treated all the others. But, apparently, at the Ministry they didn't do things that way.

Next we heard that the Minister had spoken to the Secretary about the budget. Since conversations don't usually come with little cards clipped to them, the uncle was able to find out that the Minister had concurred. Concurred about what, and with whom? By the time the uncle got around to asking, the Minister had changed his mind. And we understood, without further explanation, that he had once concurred with us.

Next we heard that the budget had been revised: it was on the agenda for next Friday's session. Fourteen Fridays later, however, it still hadn't come up for discussion. Then we started keeping track of all the meetings, and each Saturday we would say, "Well, now we'll have to wait till next Friday. We'll see what happens then." And nothing would happen then. Nothing ever happened ever.

By that time I was pretty upset over all the money I owed, because the fountain pen had thrown my finances off and I still hadn't managed to get them back on track. That's why I got it into my head that we should pay a visit to the Ministry.

We rehearsed our interview for several afternoons. The First Secretary pretended to be the Minister, and the Boss, who had been chosen by all to speak on our behalf, presented our request. When we felt we had done enough rehearsing, we asked for an appointment at the Ministry and were given one for that Thursday. So on Thursday we left one of the typists and the porter at the office, while the rest of us went to have a talk with the Minister. But a talk with the Minister isn't the same as a talk with anyone else. To have a talk with the Minister, you have to wait two and a half hours; and it sometimes happens, as in our case, that you can't have a talk with the Minister even when the two and a half hours are up. We never got past the Secretary, who took a few notes as he listened to the Boss, excused himself briefly, and returned with the Minister's response: the budget was on the agenda for the next day's session. As for the Boss, he didn't do nearly as well as he had done at our worst rehearsal: during rehearsals, at least no one stuttered.

As we were leaving the Ministry, relatively satisfied, we saw a car stop at the door and the Minister step out.

We found it odd that the Secretary had brought us the Minister's personal response, when the Minister hadn't even been there. But in fact, we all stood to gain by not asking too many questions, and so when the Boss suggested that the Secretary had probably consulted the Minister by phone, we were relieved and only too happy to agree with him.

The next day, at five PM, we were all pretty nervous. Five was the time they had told us we should call to inquire. We hadn't gotten much work done; we were too restless to do anything right. Everyone was very quiet. The Boss didn't even hum his aria. We waited a discreet six minutes before calling. Then the Boss dialed the number we all knew by heart and asked to speak to the Secretary. Their conversation wasn't very long. In between the Boss's responses— "Mmm, " "Mm-hmm," "I see,"—we heard the muffled drone of another voice. When the Boss hung up the phone, we already knew the answer, but just to confirm it, we listened: "It seems they didn't get to it today. But the Minister says the budget is definitely on the agenda for next Friday."

1949

Translated by Jo Anne Engelbert

Iriarte Family

There were five "families" who placed calls to the Boss. Since I answered the phone on the morning shift, I recognized all the voices. We all knew that each "family" was a liaison of his, and sometimes, we traded impressions.

To me, for instance, Calvo family was a plump, pushy little number, who widened the contours of her mouth with lipstick; Ruiz family was a clothes horse without much class, who combed her hair over one eye; Durán family was a skinny intellectual, one of those bored, anything-goes types; Salgado family was a full-lipped woman, the kind that gets by on pure sex appeal. The only one who sounded like an ideal woman was Iriarte family. Neither fat nor thin, with enough curves to make you bless the gift of touch that Mother Nature gave us; neither headstrong nor submissive, a real woman, one with character—that's how I pictured her. I got to know her spontaneous, contagious laugh, and invented a personality to go with it. I studied her silences, and used them to fill in her eyes, wonderful eyes, dark and melancholy. I listened to her warm, friendly voice, and imagined her as sweet and gentle.

As far as the other families were concerned, we had differences of opinion. For example, Elizalde thought Salgado was petite and unassuming; Rossi thought Calvo was a prude; Correa thought Ruiz was just another broad who'd been around. But when it came to Iriarte family, we all thought she was a knockout. We even agreed pretty much on what she looked like, just from the sound of her voice; we were sure that if she walked into the office one day and simply smiled, without saying a single word, we would all recognize her at once, because we had all endowed her with the same unmistakable smile.

The Boss, who was always shooting his mouth off about the confidential matters we dealt with in the office, was a pillar of discretion when it came to the five families. On that subject, our conversations with him were discouragingly brief. We would simply answer the phone, press his buzzer and say, for example, "Salgado family." He would reply, "I'll take it," or "Say I'm not here," or "Have them call back in an hour." Never a comment, not even a joke, even though he knew he could trust us.

I couldn't figure why it was that of the five, Iriarte family was the one who called the least, sometimes only once in two weeks. Of course, when she did call, the "busy" light stayed on for a good quarter of an hour. I would have given anything to spend a whole fifteen minutes listening to that lovely, sweet, self-assured voice of hers.

One time I got up the nerve to say something, I don't remember what, and she answered me, I don't remember what. What a day! After that, I kept hoping I'd get a chance to talk to her a little more, so maybe she would come to recognize my voice the way I recognized hers. One morning I had the bright idea of saying, "Would you mind waiting while I try to connect you?" and she said, "Of course not, if you'll keep me company while I wait." I know I must have come across as an idiot that day, because all I could talk about was the weather, work and a possible schedule change. But another time, I got my courage up and we really talked—about generalities, but with particular meanings. From then on, she would recognize my voice and greet me with a "How's it going, Mr. Secretary?" that absolutely bowled me over.

A few months after that new development, I went off to the beach on vacation. For years my vacations at the beach had been my best hope of meeting someone. I kept thinking that on one of those trips I would meet the girl of my dreams, someone I could lavish all my stored-up affection on. Because, to be honest, I'm as sentimental as they come. Sometimes I could kick myself for it. I try to tell myself that nowadays it's better to be cold and calculating, but I'm hopeless. I go to the movies and sit through one of those Mexican tearjerkers about fatherless children and penniless old men, and even though I know it's nothing but eyewash, I still get a lump in my throat.

As for this business about trying to find a woman at the beach, when I've searched my soul I've come up with a few less than sentimental motives. The fact is, all the women you see at the beach are wholesome, healthy, and well rested, ready to laugh and have fun. I don't mean there are no wholesome women in Montevideo— of course, there are. But the hassle of wearing high heels, riding the bus, and climbing all those stairs makes them tired, sweaty and irritable. In the city you practically forget what a happy woman looks like. That's more important than it may seem. Personally, I can tolerate just about any kind of female pessimism; I doubt there's a single type of crying, shouting or hysteria I can't handle. But I'm much more demanding when it comes to a woman's laugh. Some women have a laugh I absolutely can't stand. And at those beach resorts, where all the women are laughing from the time they get up in the morning for that first dip until the moment they lurch out of the casino late at night, you really know who's who, whose laugh is horrendous and whose is delightful.

It was precisely at a beach resort that I heard her Voice again. I had been dancing between the little tables on the terrace, by the light of a moon no one seemed to notice. My right hand was resting on a peeling back that was still warm from the afternoon sun. The owner of that back was laughing; and it was a good laugh, one to be reckoned with. Whenever I could, I stole a peek at the almost transparent tendrils of blond hair near my partner's ear, and to tell the truth, I was quite smitten. She wasn't much for talking, but when she did say something it was generally so dumb that I actually appreciated her silences.

It was during the agreeable span of one such silence that I heard someone ask, as clearly as if the question had been manufactured for my ears: "And what's your favorite drink?" A trivial question, then and now, but I remember it word for word. We were in one of those little traffic jams the tango has a way of creating. The Voice had come from nearby, but just then I couldn't relate it to any of the hips that had grazed my own.

9

Two nights later, at the Casino, I had just lost ninety pesos when I got the wild idea of playing fifty on one last ball. If I lost, well, that was it; I'd have to go straight back to Montevideo. But thirty-two was what turned up, and I felt infinitely relieved and hopeful, as I cashed in the eight orange chips I had bet on that number. Then someone said into my ear, as if into a phone receiver: "That's the only way to play; you've got to take chances."

I turned around calmly, knowing what I'd find; and, in fact, Iriarte family was standing right there next to me, every bit as delicious as we had pictured her back in the Office, from the sound of her voice. It wasn't very hard to pick up on what she had just said, invent a theory of risk and get her to take a calculated risk with me—talk a while, dance a little and agree to meet on the beach the next day.

From then on, we did everything together. She told me her name was Doris, Doris Freire. That turned out to be absolutely true (for some reason, she showed me her I.D. card) and very understandable; I had always suspected that the "families" were just telephone names. From the first day, this was the way I saw things: she obviously had a relationship with the Boss; just as obviously, that hurt my pride, but (notice what a good "but") she also happened to be the most delightful woman I had ever met; and I ran the risk of losing her forever (now that fate had put her within earshot) if I didn't bend a little.

Besides, there was another possibility. If I recognized her voice, why couldn't Doris recognize mine? Of course, to me, she had always been a marvelous, inaccessible ideal, while I was only just beginning to enter her world. Still, the morning I ran out to meet her with a cheery "How's it going, Ms. Secretary?" and she rolled with it, laughing, grabbing my arm, and starting to tease me about a brunette in a jeep who had just cut us off, I couldn't help noticing that she seemed nervous, as if some suspicion had been awakened. Not long after that, however, it looked like she was feeling more philosophical about the possibility that I might have answered her phone calls to the Boss. And what with all her sweet talk and the encouraging looks of complicity she kept sending me, I dared to hope for even more: she clearly appreciated the fact that I hadn't mentioned him; and while I couldn't be sure, she would probably repay my sensitivity by breaking off with him soon. I've always known how to read faces, and Doris's was particularly sincere.

I went back to work. Every other day, I did my morning stint at the telephone. There were no more calls from Iriarte family.

Almost every afternoon, I met Doris after work. She ran an office in the Justice Department, made a good salary, and everyone seemed to like her.

Doris had no secrets from me. The life she was living was an open book. But her past? As far as my feelings were concerned, I was just glad she didn't try to mislead me. Her fling, or whatever it was, with the Boss wasn't going to poison my share of happiness. Iriarte family had stopped calling. What more could I ask? Doris preferred me over the Boss and soon, all he would be to her was the one bad memory every young woman is entitled to.

I had warned Doris not to call me at work; I don't remember what reason I gave her, but frankly, I didn't want Elizalde, or Rossi, or Correa to answer, recognize her voice, and then make up one of their snide little stories. At any rate, she, as agreeable and unsuspecting as always, didn't seem to mind. I was glad that she was so understanding about this taboo, grateful that she didn't make me invent pathetic excuses, the kind that can leave a woman wondering if your intentions are honorable.

She took me home to meet her mother, a good woman, though a little weary, who had lost her husband twelve years earlier and had never quite recovered. She looked at Doris and me with an expression of gentle approval; but sometimes her eyes filled with tears, perhaps as she recalled some detail of her own courtship. Three times a week, I stayed till eleven; at ten she would say a discreet goodnight, so Doris and I still had an hour to cuddle, talk about the future, and estimate the cost of sheets and the size of the apartment we would need, just like a hundred thousand other couples all over the country, who at that very moment were undoubtedly exchanging identical cuddles and estimates. Doris's mother never mentioned the Boss, or anyone else who had been interested in Doris. I was always given the treatment respectable households reserve for the daughter's first suitor, and I was more than happy to accept.

Sometimes I couldn't help feeling a certain sordid satisfaction, at having acquired (for my own use and enjoyment, no less) one of those inaccessible women usually seen only on the arms of ministers, men in public office or important officials. I, a lowly administrative assistant.

Doris, I have to admit, attracted me more and more with every evening we spent together. She was sweet and generous with her affection. She had a way of kissing and stroking the back of my neck, of whispering tiny endearments while she kissed me, that left me reeling with happiness and, yes, with desire, each time I left her house. Back in my bachelor quarters, tossing and turning in my lonely bed, I would torment myself with the thought that her wonderful skills were proof of her expert training. But then (was this an advantage or a disadvantage?) I couldn't help thinking of the Boss, so straitlaced, so proper, so stuffy and respectable, and I simply could not imagine him as her enviable tutor. Had there been others, then? How many? Above all, who had taught her to kiss like that? I always ended up reminding myself that this was nineteen forty-six, not the Middle Ages, and that, now, I was the most important person in her life. And I would fall asleep hugging my pillow, a poor substitute for other embraces which figured prominently in my plans, and for which I would definitely have to wait.

Until November 23rd, it felt like I was drifting easily and inevitably toward marriage. And I was. All we had to do was find the kind of apartment I wanted, a place with plenty of windows, fresh air and sunlight. We had spent several Sundays apartment hunting but whenever we found something we liked, it was too expensive, or too far from a bus line, or Doris found the neighborhood too depressing, or too out-of-the-way.

On the morning of the twenty-third I was on duty at work. The Boss hadn't been in for four days, so I was relaxing by myself, reading a magazine and smoking a cigarette. Suddenly I heard the door open behind me. I turned around lazily and saw Doris's adorable and somewhat hesitant face peering in. She was looking a little guilty, because, as she explained, she was afraid I might be mad. The reason she had come down to the office was that she had finally found an affordable apartment with everything we wanted. She had drawn a neat little floor plan and she showed it to me, obviously pleased as punch. She looked stunning in her light summer dress, with that wide belt that hugged her waistline so perfectly. Since we were alone, she perched on my desk, crossed her legs and asked where Rossi sat, and Correa, and Elizalde. She didn't know any of them personally, but she knew all their quirks and foibles from the takeoffs I did of them. She had just lit up one of my cigarettes, and I was holding her hand in mine, when the phone rang. I picked up the receiver and said "Hello." Then the phone said, "How's it going, Mr. Secretary?" and life seemed to go on as usual. But in the few seconds that call lasted, during which I, half-stunned, mechanically asked, "Well, how are you after all this time?" and the phone answered, "I've been traveling in Chile," in fact, everything changed. Ideas whirled in my brain like the last thoughts of a drowning man. The first, "So, the Boss never had anything to do with her," did wonders for my pride. The second was, more or less: "But then Doris?..."; and the third was, literally: "How could I possibly have confused that voice with any other?"

I explained to the phone that the Boss was out, said goodbye, and put down the receiver. Her hand was still in mine. Then I looked up, knowing what I would find. There on my desk, still thinking only of her stupid floor plan, smoking a cigarette just like any other stuck-up little broad, sat Doris with a smile on her face. An empty, superficial smile, of course, the kind you can see on any face, a smile that threatened to bore me all the way to eternity. Afterwards, I would try to make sense of the whole thing, but at that moment, deep in some unknown place in my heart, I signed off on that little misunderstanding. Because the truth is I'm in love with Iriarte family.

1956

Translated by Jo Anne Engelbert

Lead Us into Temptation

Van Daalhoff? Pleased to meet you. So, Areosa gave you my phone number. How's he doing? I haven't seen him in years. It says here on the card that you're looking for an idea for a short story, and he thinks I can help you. Well, of course. Delighted to help, anytime I can. Any friend of Areosa's is a friend of mine. Ana Silvestre, you say? Sure, I know her. Since 1944, at least. She's engaged now. Who would have thought. There's a good story there, all right. But you must change her name. But anyway, you're not from here. You'll publish it in your country, of course. That's better, much better. Ana Silvestre. As a stage name, I don't much like it. I never understood why she refused to go by her real name: Mariana Larravide. (Ice but no soda, please.) In 1944 she was just a kid, only seventeen. Always skinny, restless, never combed her hair, but by that time she already had a certain something that would get the boys all worked up, and even older men, like me. How old do you think I am? Don't overdo it! The day before yesterday I turned forty-eight, yes sir. A Scorpio, and proud of it. So, sixteen years ago Mariana was just a kid. The best thing she had going for her were those eyes. Dark, really dark. Very innocent, while she was in her innocent phase. And then just as wicked, when she moved on to the next one. At the time, she was still in high school, planning to study law, of course. She was in the same class as the Zúñiga brothers, the Aristimuño boy, Elvira Roca and that Anselmi girl they called the "Bombshell." They were inseparable, a really close-knit group. When the six of them walked down the street together, you'd have to step aside, because nothing could pry them apart. I knew them well since I was a friend of Arriaga's, a philosophy teacher they worshipped like a god, because he was easygoing and came to class on a motorcycle. At least until he slammed into a number 22 streetcar at the corner of Capurro and Dragones. That landed him in the hospital with both legs broken, and forced him to retire permanently from active womanizing. But at that time Arriaga never dreamed he'd be on crutches. From time to time, he'd join me in the café and we'd watch them coming and going, jostling each other and cracking stupid jokes of the sort that only seem funny when you're in the acne stage. I could see that Arriaga really was infatuated with Mariana, but she didn't give an inch in the way he wanted. She admired him as a professor, and that was all. Elvira Roca and Anselmi the Bombshell, who were a year older, were already sleeping around; but Mariana kept herself intact, and dedicated herself to friendship and a little harmless necking now and then. Hers must have been the most publicized virginity in the Free World. Even the waiters were aware they were serving coffee to a virgin. The most remarkable thing was she insisted she had nothing against sex— she just wasn't interested in having it. I assure you, considering she felt no inclination, she did a pretty good job of getting people to look at her, with her plunging necklines and that strategic crossing of her legs. We never found out who was the first. Anselmi the Bombshell put it around that it had been an administrator at the Vásquez School, but one night when he he'd had a few (his name, by the way, was none other than Vásquez), he confessed he had been the second. (Thank you. One more ice cube. Perfect.) In fact, there were several candidates for that honor, and I was among them. What happened was that Mariana used to tell every man she went with that there had only been "one other man in her life." And we were happy, idiots that we were, since in her case being second was just about as good as being first, without any of the disadvantages of the premiere. One thing you have to recognize is that Mariana always had her own style, whether she was acting innocent or having a wild time, partying or feeling blue. She had absolute freedom, because her parents were in Santa Clara de Olimar, and she was living here in Montevideo with an aunt, who has her own glorious past for sure. The house was in Punta Carretas, near the jail. One of those fancy Bello and Reborati concoctions that have always reminded me of the building sets I played with as a child. The aunt would go off to Buenos Aires for weeks at a time, and Mariana was left with the house and its enormous assortment of hallways and balconies completely to herself. That was when she would throw incredible parties, where you could drink, fool around, and dance to your heart's content. Arriaga was a regular at those little soirées, and I began to go as his guest. At that time, I was fond of Anselmi the Bombshell. After the third drink she would get emotional and you'd have to rush her upstairs and console her. What a knockout she was back then, as shapely as they come! Nowadays, as the honorable wife of councilman Rebollo, she has shapeless blobs where those gorgeous tits used to be. But back to the point: at those private little bacchanalias of ours, most of us partied like it was our sworn duty. It was a party, and we had to raise hell. It was a dance, and we had to dance. It was the good life, and we had to live it to the hilt. All very predictable. But Mariana, who by then wasn't a kid any more, didn't meet us at the door with a big smile on her face, no sir. When we got there she was always serious, as it hadn't been her idea, and we were forcing her to have a good time. But we were on to her, we knew she just needed to create an atmosphere for herself, and be drawn into it slowly. So the younger Zúñiga boy would tell one of his intellectual jokes, one of those overworked ones that by the time you get it you're yawning from the wait. Aristimuño, who's from Bella Unión, would come up with some stories about the frontier types from around there; Elvira Roca would say she was too warm, and start taking off her blouse and a few other things; and Arriaga, who had studied phonetics and rhetoric, would recite highly cultured indecent lyrics from Classical Antiquity. And in the process Mariana would begin to loosen up slowly, with a real sense of rhythm, letting herself laugh. When Raimundo Ortiz, a guest of honor at one of those blowouts, witnessed that buildup to what he, as a true man of the theatre, called Mariana's "climax," he asked her to join his independent theatre group, "La Bambolina." What an eye for talent! From the outset—I seem to remember her début was in a short play by O'Neill—Mariana was the darling of the critics, who at that time were neither numerous nor particularly astute. First Ortiz, and then

Olascoaga (Mariana left Ortiz's troupe for Olascoaga's, after Beba Goñi scratched her face the night she wrested from her the role of Whore IV in a play that was then avant-garde but is now considered passé) realized, of course, what a gold mine they had, and saw to it that she got to play every slut in the history of theatre. I swear to you, on stage she looked like something straight out of the girlie bars: that same walk, that same way of batting her eyelashes and swinging her hips. (No thanks, I still have some. Well, top it off then, since you insist. Don't forget my ice cube. Perfect.) They never gave her the part of an ingénues or a matron, but she didn't ask for them, either. Playing the Prostitute (which is, after Yerma, the most prized by any moody actress), she felt sure of herself and completely at ease. In her daily life she put on an innocent face, so skillfully made-up that when she stepped on stage and peeled off her mask, she looked for all the world like a precocious veteran. People who knew her only superficially might have mistaken that dissipated look she had for "being in character;" but the truth is that off stage she was one and the same character, Ana Silvestre. I followed her brief career every step of the way, so I can assure you that Mariana was made for cynicism rather than introspection. For her, nothing was sacred—not the Church, not the National Anthem, not Motherhood, not even Democracy. I remember that one night in the Punta Carretas house (February 3, 1958, to be exact), she got it into her head to organize a secular mass (a "grey mass," she called it), and on her knees, with utter shamelessness, she began to pray: "Lead us into temptation." I think she went too far that time. That's where she began the downhill slide that landed her where she is today. Because God—are you with me?—took her at her word: He led her into temptation. You might ask what temptation, if she already knew them all. But let me go on, I'll get to that. Olascoaga's group was rehearsing some little Uruguayan play. That was the year they subsidized the Municipal Theaters, so there was an epidemic of them. You are lucky not to have been here. Playwrights were climbing out of the woodwork all over the country. One time there were six of us at Chocho's, and five of us were Uruguayan playwrights. Can you imagine? I'm the only one that survived. Well, the play Olascoaga's group was rehearsing was not exactly one of the worst. I believe it even won Third Prize in the Festival. It had a coy sentimentality that struck a chord with the critics. I'll be honest with you and admit that I don't remember the situation, or the crisis, or much less the development. But I do remember that the main character: a woman totally given over to purity. The author, Edmundo Soria, you know who he is? Now he's a lawyer and a politician. They say he got rich chasing after Communists, a real ingenuous type. Well, this guy Soria put that lady character of his through hell. You name it, it happened to her. First her father dies, and she's still pure; then her stepfather beats her up, and she's still pure; then her boyfriend abuses her, and she stays pure. Then she loses her job, she stays pure; then she gets attacked by a damn street gang, they steal everything but her virtue. At the end she dies, probably from an overdose of virtue. It was just unbearable, and I mean really. Unbearable. Maybe I sound a little nasty, but that's because I was just disgusted at the time to see such a lousy play get such good reviews, and to hear some discerning people I know (I mean, I know these people) justify Soria with the flimsy reasoning that "once you decide to write a melodrama, you've got to go all the way." The truth is that without Mariana that play would have been a real disaster. But there's more to the story. Originally, this other actress, Alma Fuentes (real name, Natalia Klappenbach), was cast as Soria's virtuous lady—Mariana wasn't even in the running. For three whole months, Almita had been rehearsing with a passion, total commitment; she's got an incredible memory for lines. Then, three days before the opening, she came down with measles, and Olascoaga's got a problem that's not just artistic but contractual. He had leased the Colón for the only three weeks available that whole winter season; and when you pay half down on the biggest theater in Buenos Aires, cancelling isn't an option. I was there the afternoon he called the cast together for an emergency conference.

"Which one of you ladies is willing to learn the part between now and Friday, and save us from bankruptcy?" he asked, and before the other six beauties could even size each other up, Mariana had already responded:

"I already know the lines."

"You?" sputtered Olascoaga, so astonished he sounded furious. I looked at him and knew he was thinking: how can I cast the company whore role of unimpeachable saint? But I also looked at Mariana's face and saw that a transformation had begun. She had an expression, I won't say of sanctitude, but certainly of intent to clean herself up. I believe Olascoaga saw the same thing I did, because he asked her:

"Are you really up for it?"

"Yes, I am," she replied. And was she ever! From opening night on, she was nothing short of a revelation. I couldn't believe my eyes: she was a saint, an absolute saint. I swear, all she was missing was the halo. When that gang grabbed her, you wanted to shoot them, the criminals. When her boyfriend insulted her, someone even shouted from the balcony, "Drop dead, you animal!" It didn't matter that the dialogue was inane; she injected it with a conviction so moving that even I had tears in my eyes. When, at the end of the second week, Almita saw her, she had a nervous fit ("Mariana's got the part," Olascoaga told her, after promising her Phaedra). Imagine, she was so jealous that her left cheek and her right eyelid developed a twitch. Poor Almita. But the big surprise came at the end of the season (thanks to its wild success, it had been extended to six weeks). The very night of the last performance, as the curtain was still falling, Mariana announced that she was leaving the theatre. Everyone burst out laughing, except Olascoaga and me. We both knew it was true. Just to do the right thing, Olascoaga asked her why.

"I was born to play this part," she said, with a new, beatific smile on her face, "and I never want to play any other." Then she added, in a voice so low she seemed to be speaking just to herself: "In the theater or in life."

You see? As I told you before: God had taken his revenge. (Whoa, no more whiskey. Well, all right, just a little. But this is definitely the last. Don't forget the ice. Thanks.) Yes sir, God had taken his revenge. He led her into temptation. But into the temptation of virtue, the only one she hadn't tried. Since that day, she's a changed woman: no more parties, no more fooling around. She even moved out of her aunt's house. Now she reads all the time, listens to classical music, Mozart and all, even takes guitar lessons. She's become a good woman, damn it. The worst thing is I think she believes in what she's doing, so it's hopeless. A week ago I ran into her in town and invited her for a coffee (well, coffee for her, grappa for me), because I wanted to see what she'd say just like this, without her audience, face to face with someone she realizes knows her inside and out. So can you guess what she said to me?

"I'm a different person, Tito, can you believe it? Before Soria's play, I had never appreciated the good side of things; I didn't know what it felt like to be virtuous, or generous, or sincere. But when I got into Soria's character, it was like pulling a dress off the rack only to find that it fits perfectly without any alteration. I felt that it was made for me. Only it wasn't a dress, you see. It was more as if I were trying on my destiny, do you understand? Right then and there, my life changed; I was won over, or lost, call it whatever you want, but I could never again be what I had been. When I first learned the part, before Alma got sick, I did it as a joke. My plan was to parody her in one of our rehearsals. But when I saw the chance for me to say those words, for me to imagine I was like that, I had the nerver to go for it. And when I went on stage and played the part, I swear to you, Tito, it was me speaking. I swear to you I had never said things that were more me than those words someone else had written." And then, hold on tight, the revelation: "I'm engaged, did you know? Don't make that face, Tito. You might not be able to convince yourself that I'm a different person now, but I know I am, without a doubt. He's Argentinian. His parents are Dutch. He wears glasses and when he looks at you, it's like he's looking right into your soul. But I don't care, because my soul is clean. He knows nothing about my past. He only knows about the person I am now and he likes me this way. I don't want him to find out, you know why? Because I am a different person now. He is blond and has a kind face. I'm not lying to him; I'm not deceiving him, because I really am changed. He's real tall, over six feet, so he always seems to walk with a stoop. He's a dream. He has long hands and slender fingers. He came three months ago, and he's leaving again in a couple more. The main thing is, he's taking me with him, and I'm saved. There's really no need for me to tell him about what went on before, because he's not strong, and he probably couldn't take it. We are going to live in Rotterdam. And Rotterdam is a long way from Punta Carretas. Besides, God is on my side. Don't you see, Tito?"

The little fool was crying, but what's worse, it was from happiness. What a shame. She's thinner, her hair is wavier, what do I know? I didn't even get up the nerve to give her the ritual pat on the bottom, always our way of saying goodbye. To be honest, I don't know to think. The one thing I would like to know is, who's the idiot that's taking her off to Rotterdam. Tall, blond, with glasses.... Long hands, slender fingers, seems to stoop.... Hey, here's a good one—he's just like you. Don't tell me.... No, that's all we needed. Oh, Jesus, but it's your fault for making me drink four whiskies one after the other. And your name is Van Daalhoff. Clear as crystal. Well, I apologize for calling you an idiot, anyway. But what could I do? Well, there's no going back now. Poor Mariana. Admit at the very least that God was not on her side.

1961

Translated by Tim Richards

Requiem over Tea

Yes, my name's Eduardo. I can understand why you're asking me that: it's your way of starting a conversation. But you've really known me for a long time now. From a distance, the way I've known you. Since the days when you and my mother started meeting at that café on the corner of Larrañaga and Rivera or right here, in this one. I hope you don't think I was spying on you, because it wasn't that at all. If you think I was spying, then you just don't know the whole story. Unless Mama told you. I've been wanting to talk to you for some time now, but I didn't dare. So, I'm really glad you beat me to it. And you know why I've wanted us to talk? Because you strike me as a good person. Mama was good too. We never said a whole lot to each other, she and I. In fact, no one talked much at home except my father, when he came home drunk, that is, which was almost every night; and then what he mostly did was yell. All three of us were scared of him—Mama, my little sister Mirta, and me. I'm thirteen and a half now and I've learned a few things, so I know that people who yell and hit you and call you names are jerks. But at the time I was much smaller, and I didn't understand. Mirta still hasn't figured it out. But she's three years younger than me, and sometimes she wakes up crying in the middle of the night. That's because she's scared. Have you ever been scared? Mirta keeps expecting the old man to show up drunk, and take off his belt to hit her. She's still not used to the way things are now. But I've been trying to get used to it. By the time you showed up a year and a half ago, my old man had been drinking for ages and as soon as he started getting plastered, he started hitting the three of us. He'd give it to me and Mirta with his belt, and that hurts a lot, but he'd go after Mama with his fists. Just like that, for no good reason, because the soup was too hot or too cold, or because she hadn't waited up for him until three in the morning, or because her eyes were swollen from crying all the time. Then little by little, Mama stopped crying. I don't know how she did it, but when he beat her she wouldn't even bite her lip and she'd refuse to cry, and that used to make my old man even madder. She knew that, but she still wouldn't cry. By the time you met Mama she had really been through a lot and she looked it, but I can still remember how pretty she was just four years before. Besides, she was really tough. Some nights, after my old man passed out on the floor and started snoring, we'd get him up between the two of us and drag him to bed. He weighed a ton and with him so out of it and all, it was like trying to move a corpse. But it was Mama who really lifted him. Pretty much all I ever did was hold up his legs, him with his muddy pants and those brown shoes with the laces untied. You probably think my old man was always that mean. But he wasn't. He got that way after someone pulled some dirty deal on him. And that someone was a cousin of Mama's, the one who works down at City Hall. I never found out what the deal was, but Mama always felt a little guilty that it was a relative of hers who did him dirty. So to some extent, she would forgive my old man for losing his temper. They never told me what that dirty deal involved but the fact is, every time Papa got drunk he'd blame Mama like it was all her fault. Before that dirty deal came along, we had a pretty good life. I don't mean moneywise, because my sister and I were both born in the same apartment near Villa Dolores (it was practically a slum), Papa never made enough for us to live on, and it was a miracle Mama even managed to put food on the table and buy us a sweater or a cheap pair of shoes once in a while. Lots of days we went hungry (I can't describe how awful that feels), but in those days at least things were peaceful at home. My old man wasn't drinking, he didn't hit us, and sometimes he'd even take us to a matinee. Once in a while on Sunday, when we could spare the money. I don't think they ever cared all that much for each other. They were too different. Even before the dirty deal changed everything, before he started drinking, Papa lived in his own world. Sometimes he'd get up at noon and he wouldn't say a word all day, but at least he didn't hit us then or call Mama names.

Why couldn't we just have gone on like that? Of course, that's when the dirty deal came along, and he fell apart and started hanging out in bars and coming back after midnight, stinking of booze. Toward the end, things got even worse. He was drinking during the day too, so we didn't even get a breather. I know the neighbors could hear all the yelling, but of course, nobody would say a word because Papa's this great big guy, and they were scared of him. I was scared too, for me and Mirta, but especially for Mama. Sometimes I'd even skip school, not to play hooky or anything, but so I could hang around the house, in case my old man came back during the day drunker than usual and ready to beat the hell out of her. Not that I could have defended her, you can see how short and skinny I am and I wasn't even this big then, I just wanted to stick around so there would be someone to call the police. Did you know Mama and Papa both came from good families? My grandparents aren't exactly rich, but at least they live in decent places, with balconies facing the street and real bathrooms, with tubs and bidets and all. After everything happened, Mirta went to live with Grandma Juana (that's Papa's mother) and for now, I'm staying with my other grandma, Blanca. This time they almost had a fight over which one we would go to, but when my folks first got married, they were so dead set against the idea (now I think maybe they were right) that they wouldn't have anything to do with us. I say us, because Mama and Papa didn't get married until I was six months old. I heard that one day in school and I punched Beto in the nose, but then when I asked Mama, she told me it was true. Anyhow, the reason I've wanted to talk to you (and I'm not sure how you'll take this) is that you're important to me, just like you were to Mama. I really loved Mama, you know, but I don't think I ever got to tell her. We were always so scared, there was never time for anything like that. Still, sometimes when she was watching me I'd look at her and feel—I can't describe it—not exactly sorry for her, but kind of loving and resentful at the same time, because she was still young, but so hopeless, so worn down by something that wasn't her fault at all, and by all those beatings she didn't deserve. Maybe I don't have to tell you this, but my mother was real smart, a lot smarter than my father, I think, and for me that was the worst part: knowing she couldn't fool herself about that horrible life of hers, because no matter how poor, or beat up, or even hungry she got, she stayed just as sharp as ever. Not that things didn't get her down. Sometimes she had such dark rings under her eyes they were almost blue, but she'd get mad when I asked her if anything was wrong. Actually, it was more like she'd act mad. I never really saw her mad at me. Or at anyone else. But before you came along every day she seemed more depressed, more exhausted, more alone. Maybe that's why I noticed such a change. Besides, one night after she was a little late getting home (although she still got in way before Papa), there was something different about how she looked at me, so different that I knew something had to be up. It was as if she had realized for the first time that I could understand her. She gave me this big hug—almost like she was ashamed of something—and then she smiled. Do you remember her smile? Boy, do I remember.... The change in her had me so worried I even skipped work a few times (by then, I had a job delivering groceries), so I could follow her around and find out what was going on. That's when I saw the two of you together. You and her. And I was happy too. Maybe I'm some sort of freak for feeling that way, and I shouldn't have been so glad my mother was cheating on my father. I'm afraid people will think that, so I never talk about it. But with you, it's different. You loved her. And for me, that felt kind of lucky. Because she really deserved to be loved. You did love her, didn't you? I saw you together lots of times, and I'm pretty sure. Of course, I try to see things Papa's way, too. That's hard, but I try. You know, I've never been able to hate him. Probably because no matter what he did, he's still my father. Whenever he hit Mirta and me, or when he went after Mama, no matter how scared I was, I always felt sorry for him.... For him, for her, for Mirta, for me. And now I feel sorry for him too, now that he's killed Mama and who knows how long he'll be in jail. At first, he didn't want me to go there, but I've been visiting him at Miguelete for at least a month now and he hasn't stopped me. It feels funny to see him so sober—I mean, now that he isn't plastered all the time. He looks at me and mostly, he doesn't say anything. When he gets out, I bet he won't hit me anymore. Besides, by that time I'll be a man—maybe even married, with kids of my own. But I don't think I'll hit my kids, do you? Besides, I'm sure Papa never would have done what he did if he hadn't been so drunk. Or do you think he would have? Do you think he would have killed Mama anyway, that afternoon he went looking for me and caught the two of you together instead? I don't think so. Remember, he didn't lay a finger on you. It wasn't until later, when he was even drunker than usual, that he went after Mama. I think if things had been different he would have realized that Mama needed love and understanding, and all she ever got from him were beatings. Because Mama was good. I'm sure you know that as well as I do. That's why a little while ago, when you came over and asked me to join you for tea, right here in the same café where the two of you used to meet, I felt I should tell you all this. Maybe you didn't know any of it, or you didn't know the whole story; because Mama was never much of a talker, especially when it came to herself. Now that you're crying, I'm sure I did the right thing. Because with Mama dead and all, it's like some sort of prize for her, because she never ever cried.

1966

Translated by Louise Popkin

The Night of the Ugly Ones

1

We're both ugly. And not a common ugly either. She has a sunken cheekbone. From the operation she had when she was eight. My disgusting scar comes from when I was just a teenager and got a horrible burn next to my mouth.

It can't be said that we have sensitive eyes, either. Those self-justifying beacons truly ugly people can sometimes claim as approximating a kind of beauty. Certainly not. Her eyes, like mine, full of resentment, reveal only the barest acceptance of our misfortune. Perhaps that's what brought us together. Well, maybe *together* isn't the best word. I refer to the relentless hatred each of us feels for his own face.

We met by chance outside a movie theatre, waiting in line to see two run-of-the-mill beautiful people on the screen. It was there that, for the first time, we looked each other over with a kind of unsentimental but murky solidarity. It was right there, at first glance, that we took note of our respective solitudes. Everyone in that line was standing two by two, but the others were real couples: man and wife, boyfriend and girl friend, lovers, young, old, who knows what else. Everybody stood arm in arm, or hand in hand—with someone. She and I were the only ones whose hands hung tense and unattached.

We each looked at the other's ugly mark slowly, insolently, matter-of-factly. I examined the gouge in her cheekbone with the assurance that my shrunken cheek afforded me. She didn't blush. It pleased me that she was tough, and that she returned my gaze to peruse that shiny, slick, beardless patch of my old burn.

We finally got inside and sat in separate but nearby rows. She couldn't see me, but even in the dark, I could make out the back of her blond head, and her pert, shapely ear. It was the ear on her normal side.

For an hour and forty minutes we admired the respective good looks of the brash hero and the sophisticated heroine. Personally, I have always been able to admire pretty things. Loathing I reserve for my own face, and sometimes for God. Also for other ugly faces, for other frightening people. Maybe I should feel pity, but I can't. The truth is, they' seem a little like mirrors. Sometimes I wonder what the myth would be like if Narcissus had a sunken cheek, or an acid burn, or only half a nose, or stitches across his forehead.

I waited at the exit for her and walked beside her for a few yards before I spoke. She stopped to look at me, and I had the impression she was wavering. I invited her to come chat a while in some café or coffee shop. She immediately agreed.

The place was full, but just then a table opened up. As we walked past the other tables, we left looks and gestures of astonishment in our wake. My antennae are particularly adept at capturing the morbid curiosity, the unconscious sadism of people who have nondescript, miraculously symmetrical faces. But this time my well-developed intuition wasn't even necessary, since I could hear all the muttering, throat-clearings, and fake coughs. A single horrible face evidently arouses some interest, but two together constitute a great spectacle, only somewhat less synchronized. Something you should watch in the company of one of those good-looking men or women with whom one ought to share the world.

We sat down and ordered two ice creams. She had the guts (which I also liked) to take a little mirror out of her purse and fuss with her hair. Her beautiful hair.

"What are you thinking about?" I asked.

She put the mirror away and smiled. The deep pit in her cheek changed shape.

"Nothing very profound," she said. "To each his own."

We talked for a long time. After an hour and a half, we had to order two coffees to justify sitting there so long. I suddenly realized that both of us had been talking with such penetrating openness that we were in danger of crossing a line between sincerity and something like hypocrisy. I decided to go for broke.

"You feel excluded from life, don't you?"

"Yes," she said, still looking me in the eye.

"You admire all the beautiful ones, the normal ones. You'd like to have a face as smooth as that young girl's on your right, even though you're intelligent and she, judging by her laugh, is a hopeless idiot."

"Yes."

For the first time she lowered her eyes.

"I'd like that, too. But you know, there's a chance that you and I could amount to something."

"Like what?"

"Like loving each other, damn it. Or just be friends. Call it what you like, but there's a chance."

She frowned. She didn't want to think about hope.

"Promise you won't think I'm a nut."

"I promise."

"Our chance is to climb into the night. The deep of night. Total darkness. Do you follow me?"

"No."

"You've got to understand! Total darkness. Where you can't see me, and I can't see you. You have a nice body, didn't you know that?"

She blushed, and her sunken cheek turned scarlet.

"I live alone, in an apartment, and it's close by."

She looked up again, and this time her eyes were full of questions, questions about me, as she tried desperately to arrive at a diagnosis.

"Let's go," she said.

2

Not only did I turn out the light, I also drew the double curtains. She was breathing at my side, but it wasn't a heavy breathing. She wouldn't let me help her undress.

I couldn't see a thing, not a thing. But all the same, I could tell she was waiting, motionless. I stretched out a hand, cautiously, and found her breast. My touch sent me a powerful, stimulating sense

29

of her. And in this way I saw her belly, her sex. And her hands saw me.

Then suddenly, I realized that I had to yank myself (and yank her) out of that falsehood I had fabricated. Or tried to fabricate. It hit me like a bolt of lightning. This wasn't what we were about. We weren't about this.

It took all my courage, but I did it. My hand slowly ascended toward her face, it found that ditch of horror, and it slowly began a convincing and convinced caress. The truth is, my fingers (shaky at first, then gradually calmer) passed over her tears again and again.

Then, when I least expected it, her hand reached up to my face and went over the rib of the scar and the slick patch of skin, that beardless island of my sinister mark. We cried until dawn. Wretches, happy. Then I got up and opened the double curtains.

1966

translated by W. Nick Hill

The Widowers of Margaret Sullavan

One of the few real names that appear in my first stories ("Idyll," "Gloria's Saturday") is Margaret Sullavan's. And it appears for a simple reason. As adolescents we're all bound to fall in love with a movie star, and that love usually turns out to be definitive as well as formative. A movie actress is not exactly a woman; she's more of an image. And at that age, falling in love with images of Woman instead of flesh and blood women is a natural first step. Eventually, real life teaches us that a celluloid woman—who, of course, can only be seen and heard—is a poor substitute for real women, who can be smelled, touched and tasted, as well.

But the actress who first takes your breath away and keeps you awake at night also gives you a chance to try out your emotions, to put together what amounts to a first draft of love. A draft that can be revised years later with some girl—or woman—who probably looks nothing like that first dream-woman, but yet has hands you can feel, alive with the messages of life, lips you can kiss without any ceremony, eyes that you can not only admire but that admire you as well.

Celluloid affairs are important, though. They're like an advance screening. Sitting face to face with that image, that smile, those eyes, that expression, all of them so revealing, a young boy gets to test his strength, do his first emotional flipflops, and, sometimes, even hear bells. And since, after all, they're risk free (the image is generally out of reach, way off in Hollywood, or Cinecittà) he can shelve all his inhibitions and dream to his heart's content, dedicated and truthful, even if the love at the root of all his candor is a fiction.

Margaret Sullavan was all that for me. Of course, when I wrote those stories, I was certainly no adolescent. Although films from her later period were still screened from time to time in Montevideo, and, of course I never missed a single screening, my first draft had already been through numerous revisions; consequently, I could look back on it from a distance, objectively, though also with a certain warm nostalgia and a happy sense of gratitude, the way we always look back across the polished expanse of time, at the woman who, in some sense, helped us take our first steps along the path of love.

Nevertheless, it was only years later that I truly understood what a central niche the indomitable and magnificent protagonist of Little Man, What Now? and The Shop Around the Corner occupied in my life. In January, 1960, I was in New York with my wife. One afternoon we got together with four Uruguayan friends and decided to have an early dinner, then go to a theater in the Village to see José Quintero's famous production of Thornton Wilder's Our Town. The play had been running for several months, but it was still hard to get tickets just before a performance; so, while the others sat down to dinner in a noisy Italian restaurant, I ran down to the theater to see if they had six seats available.

My first surprise was a ticket salesman who didn't look the least bit like one, although if anyone had pressed me, I would have been hard put to say exactly what a ticket salesman was supposed to look like. This fellow was young and thin; he had on glasses with dark frames and thick lenses, and he looked like a student of literature, or a first clarinetist. The lobby of the theater was empty, and that got my hopes up. But the reason was very simple: the performance was completely sold out. When I asked whether there was even a remote possibility of coming up with six tickets ("only six"), the young man looked up from a dog-eared copy of the "New Yorker" and glared at me with cutting disgust: "Six tickets, now? What planet are you from?" The guy had a point. I wasn't at all sure I was on the right planet. I felt like was a country bumpkin who people laugh at because he's afraid to step on an escalator or use a public phone. Nevertheless, I didn't leave immediately. I stood there for a few minutes, looking at the photos of the cast, perhaps hoping secretly that someone would come walking in to return exactly six tickets.

That's when the phone rang. Again, the young man looked annoyed, since he had to interrupt his reading of the "New Yorker" for a second time; or maybe, he was just tired of repeating, in that nasal voice of his, that they were all sold out. Then, suddenly his expression changed. He yanked off his glasses and blurted out, almost sobbing: "Oh, no! No! That's impossible!" Then he hung up with a sudden, detached gesture, mechanical and hopeless; looking totally crushed, he pressed his thin, trembling fingers against his temples. I was the sole witness to that gesture of despair. In spite of his recent rudeness, thinking he might be ill I went up to him; I touched him lightly on the arm, so he would realize I was there, and asked if something was wrong, if he had had some bad news, if there was anything I could do, and so forth. He raised his head and looked at me without his glasses, as if through a rain-streaked window or a memory frozen in time.

"Margaret Sullavan is dead." He said the words slowly, stressing every syllable, as if to make it clear that he wasn't putting on an act, that he was feeling utterly defenseless and bereft. Then it was my turn, and in a different way and a different language, I murmured to myself: "No, it can't be." The young man didn't understand my Spanish, but he certainly realized how shocked and sad I felt. I leaned up against a wall, needing the support of something solid. We looked at each other, the ticket salesman and I: he, somewhat astonished to have unexpectedly met up with another of Margaret's widowers, right there, in the theater, within reach of his bony hand; I, only half-aware that at that very moment, the last faint glimmer of my already distant adolescence was flickering out.

Suddenly, the ticket salesman rubbed his hand over his eyes, openly wiping away his tears, and asked me in a voice still choked with emotion: "How many tickets did you say you wanted? Six?" He opened a little drawer and took out six tickets, all pinned together, and gave them to me. I paid him, without a word. A tip, under those circumstances, would have been an insult, something unthinkable between two widowers of the same dream. We even shook hands, just as if we were relatives, feeling like Jimmy Stewart might have been feeling then, as Margaret's partner in so many films.

As I headed back to the Italian restaurant, I too wiped my eyes, in my own way: not with the palm of my hand, but with my knuckles. Really, I had no idea why that irascible, nearsighted ticket salesman could be so stunned and devastated. But I certainly knew why I was: for the first time in my life, I had lost a loved one.

1974

Translated by Daniel Balderston

The Demitasse Cups

There were six: two red, two black, two green, modern, non-breakable, and imported, besides. They had been last year's birthday gift from Enriqueta to Mariana and from the day they arrived, the conventional wisdom was to mix up the colors of the cups and saucers. "Red and black are great together," was Enriqueta's aesthetic advice. But in a discreet flair of independence, Mariana had decided not to do it that way: she would pair each cup with a saucer of the same color.

"Coffee's ready. Should I serve it now?" Mariana asked. Her voice was directed at her husband but her eyes were fixed on her brother-in-law. Her brother-in-law blinked and said nothing. José Claudio answered, "Not just yet. Wait a bit. I want to smoke a cigarette first." Now she did look at José Claudio and thought, for the thousandth time, that his eyes weren't the eyes of a blind man.

José Claudio's hand began to move, feeling its way along the sofa. "What are you looking for?" she asked. "The lighter." "To your right." His hand changed direction and found it. With the characteristic tremor of a hand used to groping, his thumb flicked the little wheel several times. From an already calculated distance, his left hand tried unsuccessfully to sense heat. But the lighter had failed to light. Then Alberto came to his aid with a match. "Why don't you throw that thing away?" he asked, with a smile that like all smiles for the blind also modulated the tone of his voice. "I haven't thrown it away because I'm fond of it. It's a gift from Mariana."

She opened her mouth every so slightly and ran the tip of her tongue along her lower lip. As good a way as any to start reminiscing. It was March, 1953, when he had just turned thirty-five and still had his sight. After a lunch of rice with mussels at his parents' house in Punta Gorda, they had gone for a walk on the beach. He had put

35

his arm around her shoulders, and she had felt safe—maybe even almost happy. They went back to the apartment, and he kissed her slowly, lingeringly, as he used to kiss then. They had christened a lighter on a cigarette they shared.

Now the lighter didn't work. She didn't have much confidence in symbolism, but, after all, what did still work from those times?

"You didn't go to the doctor this month either," Alberto said.

"No."

"Can I be honest?"

"Certainly."

"I think that's really stupid of you."

"Why should I go to the doctor? To hear him say that I'm as strong as an ox, that my liver's in great shape, that my heart beats the way it should, that I've got fantastic bowels? You want me to go for that? I'm sick of being in perfect health and blind."

Even before he lost his sight, José Claudio hadn't been very good at expressing his emotions; but Mariana hadn't forgotten how his face looked before it took on this current tension, this resentment. Their marriage had had its good moments: she couldn't, and wouldn't, deny that. But when trouble hit, he had been too proud to accept her help, seeking refuge instead in a fierce, obstinate silence, a silence that persisted, even when he wrapped himself in words. José Claudio had simply stopped talking about himself.

"Anyway, you should go," Mariana agreed. "Remember what Menéndez always told you."

"How can I forget? It's Not All Over For You. Oh, and that other famous line: Science Doesn't Believe In Miracles; Neither do I."

"And why shouldn't you try to have some hope? It's only human."

"Really?" he said out of the corner of his mouth, still dragging on his cigarette.

He had hidden inside himself. But Mariana wasn't made to take care of a self-absorbed man, just to take care of him. Mariana needed something else. A little lady you had to handle with supreme tact. Although there were plenty of ways around that. She was flexible. It was a real disaster that he had gone blind, but that wasn't the worst part. The worst part was that he had done everything he could to refuse her help. He disparaged her attentions. And she would have liked to protect him—sincerely, effusively, magnanimously.

Well, that was before, not now. The change had been gradual. First, her affection for him had begun to wane. The care, attention, and support she had always lavished on him became mechanical. She was still efficient, no doubt about it, but she no longer enjoyed being solicitous. Then she started living in terror of even a routine discussion. He was always looking for a fight, always ready to say the most hurtful things, to show her just how mean he could be. He had this uncanny way of coming up with the perfect insult, the most cutting words, the most searing comment, just when she least expected it. And always from a distance, hiding behind his blindness, using it to insulate himself from the uncomfortable insensitivity of others.

Alberto got up from the sofa and went over to the window.

"What a lousy autumn," he said. "Have you noticed?" The question was for her.

"No," José Claudio replied. "Why don't you notice for me."

Alberto looked at her. They smiled at each other in that silence. On the margin of José Claudio, but still, on account of him. All of a sudden, Mariana knew she was pretty. Whenever she looked at Alberto, she became pretty. He had told her so for the first time last year, on the night of April 23rd. Exactly one year and eight days ago, after José Claudio had shouted some very ugly things at her, and she had cried and sulked despondently for hours, feeling utterly demoralized. Until she found Alberto's shoulder and then, she had felt understood and safe. She wondered where Alberto got his ability to understand people. A few words with him, or even a look, and right away she could feel him pulling her out of the doldrums. "Thanks," she had said that night. And even now that word kept coming to her lips, straight from the heart, without intervening thought, without claims. At first, her love for Alberto was sheer gratitude, but that (and she saw it clearly) didn't diminish him. For Mariana, love had always been a question of mutual gratitude, of being thankful and being thanked. In the good times, she had been

37

grateful to José Claudio—so brilliant, so lucid, so wise—for noticing someone as insignificant as her. Where she had obviously failed was in making him thankful to her in return, and under the most absurdly auspicious circumstances, at that: just when he seemed to need her most.

On the other hand, she was grateful to Alberto for the initial impulse, the generosity of that first helping hand that had saved her from her own chaos and, above all, helped her to be strong. But Alberto had a lot to thank her for, too, because he might be easygoing, respectful of his brother, and fanatically sensible, but he was also a real loner. Over the years, he and Mariana had kept up a superficially caring relationship, on terms that were spontaneously and discreetly formal, and only rarely offered glimpses of a deeper bond. Perhaps Alberto was a little envious of his brother's apparent happiness, of his good fortune of having found a woman that Alberto himself thought charming. In fact, not so long ago Mariana had gotten him to confess the reason why he was still a confirmed bachelor: the eligible women he met always came out on the losing end of certain comparisons he couldn't help making.

"And Trelles was here yesterday," José Claudio was saying," softsoaping me with one of those visits the guys from the factory pay me three times a year. They probably draw lots, and the loser gets a ribbing and then comes to see me."

"Maybe they respect you," Alberto said, "maybe they miss having you as their boss, and they really care how you're doing. People aren't always as bad as you seem to think these days."

"You don't say.... Well, you learn something new every day." His smile was accompanied by a brief snort, meant to indicate another level of irony.

When Mariana had gone to Alberto in need of advice, tenderness, and protection, she had immediately realized that by simply doing so she was giving him a gift in turn. She was sure he was as much in need of help as she, and had good reason to feel desperate too, even if he was too scrupulous (and perhaps, a little too modest) to acknowledge it. Indeed, she began to feel responsible for him. That was why he was grateful to her, she decided: she didn't insist on spelling things out, but simply let him lavish on her all the tenderness he had kept inside for so long; because now, he could take all those images of her, the images he had paraded through his gloomy, sleepless nights with never a hope of anything more, and adapt them to this unforeseen reality.

But before long, their gratitude bubbled over. As if the stage had been set for a moment of mutual revelation, as if all that stood between them and the fulfillment of their yearnings was a single look, within a few days all the important things had been said and they were seeing more and more of each other in secret. And suddenly, Mariana felt her heart swell, and there was nothing else in the world but her and Alberto.

"You can heat up the coffee now," José Claudio said; and Mariana leaned over the little table to light the warmer. For a moment, she was distracted, contemplating the cups. She had only brought three, one of each color. She enjoyed seeing them arranged like that, in a triangle.

Then she leaned back against the sofa and her neck found Alberto's warm hand, cupped and waiting to hold her as she'd hoped. What a delight, my God. His hand began to move gently, and his long, thin fingers spread through her hair. The first time Alberto worked up the courage to do that, Mariana had felt terribly edgy; her muscles knotting up in a painful spasm that kept her from enjoying the caress. Not any more. Now she was at ease and could enjoy it. It seemed to her that José Claudio's blindness was a kind of divine protection.

As he sat there facing them, José Claudio breathed normally, almost blissfully. Over time, Alberto's caresses had become a sort of ritual, so Mariana knew exactly what to expect. Just like every other afternoon, his hand stroked her neck, brushed her right ear, slowly touched her cheek and chin. Finally it paused on her half-parted lips. Then, just like every other afternoon, she silently kissed the palm of his hand, and closed her eyes for an instant. When she opened them, José Claudio's face looked exactly the same as before: detached, reserved, distant. Still, that moment always held a bit of fear for her. A groundless fear, since they had practiced their chaste, daring, insolent routine until their technique was as smooth as it was silent.

"Don't let it boil," José Claudio said.

Alberto withdrew his hand, and again Mariana leaned over the little table. She turned off the burner under the coffee and filled the cups straight from the carafe.

Every day, she switched the cups around. Today José Claudio would get the green one, Alberto the black one, she herself the red one. As she handed the green cup to her husband, she encountered his strange, tight little smile. And with it, a sentence that sounded something like: "No dear, I think I'll have the red cup today."

1959

translated by W. Nick Hill

The Attic

It's up there. I can see it from here. I always wanted an attic. When I was nine years old, and when I was twelve. I can see it from here, and it's good to know it exists. The light's on. It's a hundred-watt bulb but when I look at it from the patio all I see is a glow. I always wanted an attic, so I could run away. From who? I've never figured that out. Frankly, I'd like to know if everyone else is sure who they're running away from. Nobody knows. Maybe a mouse knows, but I don't think a mouse is what the doctor calls a typical fugitive. But I am. I wanted an attic just like Ignacio's, for instance. Ignacio had books up there, calendars, maps, postcards, stamp albums. Ignacio used to go straight from his attic out onto the roof and from there, he could see all the other rooftops nearby, with and without skylights, and with washtubs and flower pots on the ledges. Then he didn't have the eyes of a fugitive anymore, but the eyes of a king. Looking out over the rooftops is almost the same as looking into people's private lives. People hang out their underwear to dry, they pile up all their old junk, they sunbathe without putting on a show, they work out for themselves and not for the girls, like they do at the beach. A roof is like a back room in a store. Sure, some rooftops have dogs on them and that's a problem; but you can always throw stones at the dogs, or scare them away by yelling. Anyway, Ignacio and I never liked it when a dog was looking at us. A rooftop with a dog on it has no privacy and then it's no good, especially if the dog has human eyes. I don't even like dogs with dogs' eyes. Cats don't bother me: they're just like part of the furniture. I can still feel like I'm completely alone with the sky, an airplane, a kite or a cat. Even with Ignacio I used to feel almost like I was alone. Maybe that's because he didn't talk. He'd just grab the opera glasses, take a good long look at the Rissos' rooftop, and once he made sure Mecha or Sonia wasn't up there, he'd hand them to me, and I'd give the Antuñas' rooftop a thorough going over, to make sure Luisa or Marta hadn't come up. I always wanted an attic. Ignacio's attic was really great; the trouble was it wasn't mine. Oh, I know Ignacio never made me feel like a stranger, or an intruder, an enemy, a nuisance, or an outsider; but then, I always felt like one anyway, so I didn't need anyone to remind me. If you want to escape, to run away when you don't even know what you're running away from, you have to do it all alone. And when I'd run away (like that time I smashed my aunt's glasses and flushed them down the toilet and she lost her cool and got furious and screamed you goddamn little mongoloid, all because your father was such a souse—even though the doctor's not sure I'm retarded because of my old man being a drunk, may he rest in peace) and when I'd run away to Ignacio's attic to be alone, I could never be alone because obviously, Ignacio was there. And sometimes the neighbor's dog, too, and he's the kind that looks at you with human eyes. All that went on when I was 12 years old, and when I was 9, too. When I was 13, there was no more attic because I started going to that school for retards. I don't remember anything I did at that school. After all, I was only there for three days, and then that big bully of a kid beat me up and I had to stay in bed for a long time, and I couldn't open this eye that's open now and besides, I kept trying not to breathe. Because of my broken rib, of course. Finally, though, I'd have to take a breath, because I'd start turning red, first red like a tomato, then red like a beet. So then I'd start breathing again, and it really hurt. That's the end of the school for retards, my uncle said. Well, he's almost normal anyway, my aunt said. I was crouching, when I suddenly felt that cold metal key in my eye. So then I backed away from the keyhole and put on my shirt. She'll be here to teach you starting tomorrow, my aunt said, when she tucked me in and gave me a kiss on the forehead. I still didn't have my attic and I couldn't go over to Ignacio's because his father had a fight with my uncle, not with fists but with bad words. She came over every morning to teach me, and she taught me more than just lessons. Like she showed me her legs that were so hairy, I couldn't stop looking at them. I told her that I was almost normal, and she smiled. She asked me if there was anything I liked a whole lot and I said, the attic. Right away I was sorry I said that because it was like double-crossing Ignacio, but she was going to figure it out anyway because she always looked at me with her eyes wide open. I don't think she ever closed her eyes, or maybe she always blinked exactly when I did. Sometimes I'd hold back on purpose, but she'd figure out what I was up to and she'd keep from blinking too, and maybe then she'd blink exactly when I did because I never saw her close her eyes. Actually, just once I did, but that doesn't count because she was dead. All her ex-students brought her a bouquet of flowers. I was an ex-student but I didn't like her all that much. I sure liked those legs of hers because they were so hairy, but there was other parts of her too. Anyway, she only lasted a month and a half. What a shame; he was doing so much better, my aunt said. He even knew how to multiply by eight, my uncle said. I knew how to multiply by nine too, but of course I never let on because a guy has to have a few secrets, right? I don't know how anyone can live without secrets. Ignacio says that the most secret secret he has, is...but I'm not going to say it because I promised not to tell anyone. I swore on that dead dog not to tell. I don't know exactly when. I've never been able to keep my dates straight. I can just finish doing something, and it'll seem like I did it ages ago. Or sometimes something from way back feels like I did it five minutes ago. Sometimes I know when something happens, especially now that my uncle gave me my mother's watch, may she rest in peace. Pobrecito, it'll give him something to do, my aunt said. But I don't want something to do, I mean I didn't, because that was when I was 12 years old and now I'm 23. My name is Albertito Ruiz, I live at 569 Solano Antuña, my uncle is Mr. Orosmán Rivas, and my aunt is Mrs. Amelia T. de Rivas. The T stands for Tardáguila. I finally got my own attic. Just for me. I got it yesterday, the day before, or maybe five years ago. I don't care about the date. My attic is up there. I can see it from here. I always wanted my own attic. The doctor says he's not exactly retarded, my aunt sighed, and I was peeping through the keyhole so I saw exactly how she sighed, or rather, what I saw was her bosom going up and down and her little chain with the cross on it going up and down. Then I'd come down from my attic and find my uncle drinking mate and he'd ask me how I liked it up there. It's great, I'd say. My attic has a lantern with a 75-watt bulb. Officially, that is. I cheated and put in a hundred-watt bulb, but my aunt thinks it's just 75 watts. Sometimes all that light hurts my eyes. My uncle realized that it's a hundred-watt bulb even though it says 75, but I know he won't tell my aunt on me, because he has a 75-watt bulb on his night table when she only said he could have a 40-watt. Watts is another word for little bugs. If Ignacio hadn't come over a little while ago, I'd be up in my attic right now. But he came. I hadn't seen him in a long time. He said it was eleven years. I heard his family moved, and that he didn't have an attic any more. Hi, he said. Ignacio never said much, not even back when he had that attic he was so proud of. Now I've got mine. I like to go out onto the roof in the afternoon, and lucky for me, there are no dogs around here that look at you like humans. There's a real little one on the Tenreiros' rooftop, a tiny little one whose name is Goliath, but that one looks at you like a dog so it doesn't bother me that much. Hi, I said too. But I knew why he had come. I knew right away. He said we hadn't seen each other for 11 years, and he was in his third year of college. It looked like he had a mustache. I can't get mine to grow. Your uncle said I could come up and see you, he said, so I wouldn't catch on. Your uncle says that you're much better, he added, to make sure I wouldn't catch on. My uncle talks a lot of crap. He went over to the window. He looked up at the sky. The sky looked back at him. So, how is it up there? my uncle asked when I came downstairs. Great, I said. I left the light on and I can see the glow from here. Nobody's ever going to take my attic away from me. Nobody. Ever. Nobody. I didn't double-cross him, and now that big phony comes around here looking up at the sky so I won't know what he's up to. Everybody knows he lost his attic, but that's not my fault. How is it up there, my uncle asked. Great, I said. The light's still on, the hundred-watt bulb, but I'm sure it's not bothering Ignacio, because before I came downstairs, I said I was sorry and I closed his eyes.

1966

Translated by James Graham

The Stars and You

The son of a grade school teacher and a seamstress; tall, thin, with dark eyes and soft hands, he could have passed for a typical resident of Rosales, that germfree, literate and industrious little town, whose most visible destiny is tied to two factories (powerful, smoke-belching, square-shouldered) controlled by foreign capital. Oliva became Police Commissioner just as he might have become a mason or a banker—that is, not by vocation but by chance. Moreover, for many years the Police were almost superfluous in the daily life of Rosales, since there weren't any criminals. The last crime, at least twenty years old, had been a typical mercy killing: Don Estévez, the owner of the general store, had killed his wife, who was dying of an incurable cancer, simply to spare her a few final weeks of unbearable agony. Some nights two or three men would get a little drunk and crack open a bottle in the town square (which was dominated by the church and police headquarters); but the Police never intervened because those fellows were happy drunks who never did anything worse than sing old *milongas*, or recite a litany of innocent, adolescent jokes that they considered incredibly obscene.

The Commissioner frequented the local bar, where he would throw a few dice with the dentist or the druggist; sometimes, he even turned up at the Club, where he would get into friendly arguments on sports and international affairs with Arroyo, the journalist. In point of fact, Arroyo's journalistic specialty was neither sports nor international affairs, but the elusive, esoteric field of astrology; his daily horoscope column ("The Stars and You") made regular and verifiable reference to particular aspects of a future supposedly close at hand. These references covered three areas: international, national, and local. He had scored so many direct hits in each that his column in *The Rosales Thorn* (the morning paper) was fervently and respectfully read, not just by women, but by everyone in town.

It may be worth noting that the town's name wasn't—and isn't—Rosales. That name has been used here solely as a precaution. In today's Uruguay, not only individuals, political groups and trade unions have had to go underground; entire neighborhoods, small towns and suburbs are in hiding as well.

It was after the 1973 coup d'état that Police Commissioner Oliva underwent his radical transformation. The first visible sign was his appearance: whereas before he had seldom worn a uniform and could often be seen in his shirtsleeves in summer, since the coup he and his uniform had become inseparable. That lent a rigid, authoritarian quality to his face, his posture, his walk and his orders that a year before, would have been absolutely unbelievable. What's more, he had gotten rapidly and uncontrollably fat (the Rosaleros liked to say he had "porked up").

In the beginning, Arroyo regarded the change in Oliva with a certain scepticism, as if he thought the Commissioner was putting on a colossal act. But the night Oliva gave orders to arrest the three perpetual drunks for "disorderly conduct and offenses against decency," when in fact they were simply singing and carrying on like they always had—that night Arroyo realized it was for real. The next day "The Stars and You" began airing gloomy predictions for Rosales's immediate future.

The one secondary school in town staged its first student strike. As in other towns in the Interior, people of very different ages attended the school: some were almost babies, others almost grown. For that first strike, the young people protested against the coup, the closing of Parliament, the banning of trade unions, and the use of torture. Totally unaware of the change in Oliva, they paraded around the plaza with banners; and before they could make it around a second time, they were under arrest.

Even so, the police apologized (some were uncles or godfathers of the "rioters"), adding in a whisper that fluctuated between criticism and fear, that this was "all Oliva's doing." Of the sixty arrested, the Commissioner released fifty before twenty-four hours were up, but not before treating them to a long tirade, in the course of which he said, among other things, that he wasn't about to tolerate "any little snots calling me a fascist." He held the ten remaining students (the only adults in the group) incommunicado at the station house. At dawn, moans, pleas for help, and ear-splitting shrieks could be heard all over town. It took a lot to convince the fathers, and especially the mothers, that their children were being tortured at the police station. But in the end, they were convinced.

The next day, Arroyo's astrological pronouncements were even gloomier: "Someone will inflict sinister forms of repression on Rosales, in an attempt to destroy our way of life. Blood will be spilled, but he will not prevail." As there was only one practicing lawyer in the entire town, the parents went running to him to see if he'd defend the ten youths; but when Doctor Borja went looking for the judge, he discovered that the latter was a prisoner as well. Ridiculous, but true. Then, he bucked up and went down to the police station, but all it took was a few phrases like habeas corpus and the right to strike, and the Commissioner threw him out. So the lawyer decided to make a trip to Montevideo; but lest the parents get their hopes up, he warned them that Montevideo very likely supported Oliva. Of course, Dr. Borja never came back, and a few months later, the Rosaleros were sending him cigarettes at the Punta Carretas Prison. Arroyo predicted: "The hour of injustice is upon us. Hatred will take root in the hearts of the righteous."

And then came the dance hall incident, something unheard of in the entire history of the town. One of the town's two factories had built its workers and employees a Community Center, with the secret intent of neutralizing future labor disturbances; but, in fact, the Center was used by everyone in Rosales. On Saturday nights, young and old showed up there to chat and dance. Those Saturday night affairs were probably the most important social event in town. At the Community Center, the week's gossip was exchanged; future courtships were set in motion, christenings organized, wedding plans made; and the list of the ill and convalescent was updated.

Before the coup, Oliva had been a regular at those gatherings; everyone regarded him as just another neighbor, which he was. But since his transformation, he had holed up in his office (most nights he slept at the police station "in an official capacity"); and he no longer went to the local bar, or to the Club (his estrangement from Arroyo being obvious), much less to the Community Center. However, this particular Saturday he showed up, with bodyguards and without warning. The ragged little band collapsed with a wheeze of the concertina, and the couples on the dance floor stood there motionless, still holding on to each other, like a music box whose motor has suddenly broken down.

When Oliva asked, "Which of you ladies wants to dance with me?" everyone realized he was drunk. No one answered. Twice more he asked the question, and still no one answered. The silence was so thick that everyone (police, musicians, and neighbors alike) could hear the carefree chirping of a cricket. Then Oliva, followed by his goons, walked over to Claudia Oribe, who was sitting next to her husband on a bench near the big window. In the sixth month of her first pregnancy, Claudia (blond, personable, young, high-spirited) was feeling very heavy and, on her doctor's orders, moving very carefully, so as not to risk a miscarriage.

"You want to dance?" asked the Commissioner, talking to her personally for the first time, and grabbing her arm. Her husband, Aníbal, a construction worker, stood up, pale and nervous. But Claudia quickly answered:

"No, sir, I can't."

"Well, with me you can," said Oliva. Then Anibal shouted:

"Can't you see the belly she's got? Leave her alone, why don't you!"

"I'm not talking to you, " said Oliva. "I'm talking to her, and she's going to dance with me." Anibal went at him, but three of the goons held him down.

"Take him away," Oliva ordered.

And they carried him off. Then, nodding to the musicians to proceed, the Commissioner put his uniformed arm around the overflowing waist of the pregnant woman; the whiny little band took up where it had left off; and Oliva dragged Claudia out onto the dance floor. Everyone could see that the girl was short of breath, but no one dared intervene, one powerful reason for this being that the guards had pulled out their guns. The couple danced three tangos, two boleros and a rumba, without stopping. At the end of the rumba, with Claudia about to pass out, Oliva led her back to the bench, saying, "See, you can dance just fine," and off he went. That very night, Claudia Oribe lost the baby.

Her husband was held incommunicado for several months. Oliva had a good time with him, taking personal charge of the interrogation. Taking advantage of the fact that the Oribes' doctor was the first cousin of an Undersecretary, a group of prominent citizens headed by the doctor went to the capital to ask him to intervene. But all he would offer by way of advice was: "I think it's better to leave well enough alone. Oliva has the confidence of the government. If you insist on reparations or try to get him fired, he'll just want revenge. These are times to lie low and wait. Look at what I'm doing myself. I'm waiting, right?"

But back in Rosales, Arroyo wasn't content to wait. From the day after the incident at the dance hall, his campaign was systematic. That Monday, his column predicted: "It will soon be time for someone to pay for his actions." Wednesday's column added, "A grim future awaits the strong man who oppresses the weak." On Thursday: "The strong man deserves to lose out, and he will." And on Friday: "The stars say that the demise of the apprentice, the tyrant's apprentice, is close at hand."

On Saturday, the Commissioner showed up at the editorial offices of The Rosales Thorn. Since Arroyo wasn't there, Oliva decided to go looking for him at his house. On the way over, he dismissed his guards:

"I'll handle this one personally. That faggot-son-of-a-bitch is no match for me." When Arroyo opened the door, Oliva shoved him aside and walked in, without a word. Arroyo didn't lose his balance; nor did he look surprised. Keeping a certain distance from the Commissioner, he simply walked from the foyer into the adjacent room that served as his study. Oliva was right behind him.

Pale and tight-lipped, the journalist positioned himself behind his desk. He didn't sit down.

"So, the stars are saying it's all over for me?"

"That's right," said Arroyo. "I have nothing to do with it. It's what's the stars say."

"You know something? Besides being a son-of-a-bitch, you're a liar."

"I disagree, Commissioner."

"You know something else? You're going to sit down right this minute, and you're going to write tomorrow's column."

"Tomorrow's Sunday. There's no paper."

"Okay, then Monday's column. And you're going to write that the stars say the tyrant's apprentice will live for many years to come. In happiness and good health."

"But the stars don't say that, Commissioner."

"Fuck the stars! You're going to write it anyway. This minute!"

Arroyo moved too quickly for the Commissioner to dodge or defend himself. It took just one shot, point blank. As Oliva collapsed, wide-eyed and speechless, Arroyo added calmly:

"The stars never lie, Commissioner."

1974

Translated by James Graham

Sic Transit Gloria

Even before I woke up, I realized it was raining. At first I thought it must be a quarter past six in the morning, time to go to the office, but I'd left my overshoes at my mother's house so I'd have to line my regular shoes with newspaper; otherwise, the dampness of a day like this would drive me nuts, freezing my feet and ankles off. Then I thought it was Sunday, and I could lie there for a while under all those blankets. Knowing I have the day off always makes me feel like a kid with a new toy. Knowing I can do anything I want, as if I were my own man, and I didn't have to run those two blocks, four mornings out of six, to punch in on time at work. Knowing I can even get philosophical if I feel like it, and think about really important things—like life and death, and soccer, and war. The rest of the week, I have no time. When I get to the office, there are always fifty or sixty transactions waiting to be entered into the books, stamped with the date, and initialed in green ink. By noon, I'm done with about half of that, and I run four blocks to try and squeeze onto the bus. If I don't make a run for it, I end up hanging onto the outside, and scraping up against all those streetcars really makes me sick to my stomach. Well, not exactly sick. More like scared; scared out of my mind.

It's not that I'm afraid of getting killed; what gets to me is imagining myself lying there with my head smashed in, or my guts hanging out, and two hundred supposedly worried curiosity-seekers leaning over me, all trying to get a better view, so they can tell the family about it over lunch the next day, while they sit there enjoying their dessert. A family lunch, just like the one I have to put away all by myself in just twenty-five minutes. Gloria has to be at the store half an hour earlier, so she leaves everything ready for me in four pans on the stove, over a low flame. All I have to do is wash my hands; wolf down my soup, macaroni, omelet and applesauce, glance at the newspaper, and rush out again to catch the bus. When I get back to the office at two, I take care of the twenty or thirty transactions still left over from the morning. At about five, notebook in hand, I answer the V. P.'s buzzer so he can dictate to me the customary half-dozen letters which I have to deliver, translated into English or German, before seven o'clock.

Twice a week Gloria comes by the office to get me, and we go out together to some movie, where she cries her eyes out while I fiddle with my hat or chew on the program. The other days, she goes to see her mother, and I do the books for two bakeries, whose owners—two Galicians and a Majorcan—make pretty good money peddling buns made with rotten eggs, and even better money renting out rooms by the hour in the seediest hotels in town. So by the time I get home, Gloria's usually asleep. Or when we come home together, we eat dinner and fall right into bed like two exhausted animals. We hardly ever have any energy left over for lovemaking. Instead, without reading a single book, without even a word about all the arguments between the guys I work with or that loudmouthed Boss of hers, who claims he's such a pushover while he pushes everybody else around. Sometimes, without even saying goodnight, we fall asleep with the light on—because she wanted to take a look at the crime reports and I wanted to read the sports page.

Our conversations have to wait for Saturdays like this one (because, as it turned out, it was Saturday afternoon, and I was waking up from my siesta). I get up at three-thirty to make us some tea, and bring it back to bed. Then she wakes up, checks to see that her chores are done, makes sure all my socks are darned, and gets out of bed at a quarter to five, to listen to the bolero hour. But this Saturday there wouldn't have been much conversation; because last night after the movies I got carried away talking about how great Margaret Sullavan is, and Gloria started pinching me. And when I still wouldn't stop, she came back at me with something much sneakier and crueler: how much she liked this guy at work. And that's cheating, because Margaret Sullavan is just a film actress, but that guy's a genuine flesh and blood jerk. Because of that silly argument, we weren't on speaking terms at bedtime—although we each waited half an hour with the lights off to see if the other one would start kissing and making up. I wouldn't have minded going first, like I have so many times, but we fell asleep before we could stop pretending we were mad, so the kissing and making up got put off till whatever was left of today's siesta time.

That's why I was so glad it was raining. The bad weather meant we were pretty much stuck with each other, and neither of us would be dumb enough to spend a whole Saturday afternoon sitting around with a long face and refusing to talk in a two-room apartment where there's no such thing as privacy, so you're practically face-to-face all day long with whoever else is there. When Gloria woke up moaning and groaning, I didn't pay much attention, because she always moans and groans when she has to get up.

But once she was wide awake and I looked at her face, I could tell she was really sick from the dark circles under her eyes. I forgot that we still weren't on speaking terms and asked her what was wrong. She had a pain in her side. It hurt a lot, and she was scared.

I told her I was going downstairs to call the doctor, and she said yeah, I should call her right away. She tried to smile; but her eyes were so dark and sunken that I wasn't sure whether I should leave her to go make that phone call. I finally decided I'd scare her even more if I didn't go, so I ran down to the corner and called the doctor.

The guy that answered the phone said the doctor wasn't at home. For some reason I didn't believe him; so I said that wasn't true, because I had just seen her walking into the house. Then he told me to hang on, and five minutes late he came back and said you're in luck, the doctor just walked in. I said well, isn't that nice, then had him write down the address, and how urgent it was.

When I got back, Gloria was dizzy, and the pain in her side was much worse. I didn't know what to do. I gave her a hot water bottle, and then an ice pack. Nothing calmed her down, so I gave her some aspirin. At six, the doctor still wasn't there, and I was much too nervous to be able to keep anybody's spirits up. I told her three or four stories I thought were funny, but her smile was such a grimace that I hated myself, because I could see she was just trying not to upset me. I felt so queasy that all I could manage to get down was a glass of milk. At six-thirty, the doctor finally showed up. She's this huge cow of a woman, way too big for our apartment. After a couple of giggles that were supposed to be encouraging, she leaned over and started pressing down on Gloria's stomach. She would dig her fingers in, then suddenly let go. Gloria would bite her lips and say, yes, it hurt here, and a little worse there, and even worse in that other spot. Wherever the doctor pressed, it hurt worse.

The cow kept digging her fingers in and suddenly letting go. When she finally stood up, she looked scared too, and she asked for some alcohol to clean her hands. Out in the hallway, she said it was peritonitis, and they'd have to operate at once. I told her we had insurance, and she promised to call the surgeon. I saw her out, called a taxi and Gloria's mother, then walked back upstairs to the apartment, because someone on the sixth floor had left the elevator door open. By then, Gloria was all doubled up; her eyes were dry, but I could tell she had been crying. I wrapped her in my overcoat and muffler; and that reminded me of one Sunday when she dressed up in my pants and a windbreaker, and we laughed ourselves silly over those unmanly hips of hers, and the way her butt stuck out.

But this Gloria was a parody of the other one, and we had to get her out of there in a hurry; there was no time to think. Just as we were leaving, in walked her mother saying, "You poor thing," and "For God's sake, put on something warmer." That's when Gloria seemed to resign herself to it. On the way to the hospital, she cracked a few jokes: now, they'd have to give her some time off at the store; and what would I do for clean socks on Monday; and—as by this time her mother was practically a fountain—what did she think this was, anyway, a soap opera? I knew the pain was getting worse and worse all the time; and she knew I knew, and she snuggled up against me.

By the time we got to the hospital, all she could do was moan. We brought her to this tiny room, and a little while later the surgeon walked in. He was a tall guy, with a kind, absentminded look about him; his white coat was unbuttoned and dirty. He sent us out and closed the door. Gloria's mother sat down, crying harder and harder. I just stared out at the street. The rain had stopped. I couldn't even comfort myself with a cigarette; by high school, I was already the only one in a class of thirty-eight who had never smoked. That was when I met Gloria, back in high school. She had black pigtails, and she was having trouble passing biology. There were two ways to get to know her: teach her biology, or learn it together. The second option was better and naturally, we both learned.

Then the doctor came out and asked me if I was her brother or her husband. I said I was her husband, and he coughed like an asthmatic.

"It's not peritonitis," he said. "That doctor is an idiot."

"Oh."

"It's something else. We'll know more tomorrow."

Tomorrow, I thought. That means....

"That is, we'll know more, if she makes it through the night. If we operate now, she's had it. It's very serious, but if she makes it past today, I think she'll live."

I thanked him—I don't know what for—and he added, "It's against the rules, but you can stay with her tonight."

First, a nurse came by with my overcoat and muffler. Then they wheeled Gloria by on a stretcher, with her eyes closed, unconscious.

At eight, they let me into the private room where they had put her. It had a bed, a chair and a table. I sat down straddling the chair and leaned my elbows on the back. I had a nervous around my eyes, as if I were straining to keep them open. I couldn't stop looking at Gloria. She was so pale that her face looked like an extension of the sheet, and her forehead was all shiny, like wax. It was bliss just to hear her breathe, even lying there like that, with her eyes closed. I pretended the only reason we weren't talking right now was that I'd said I liked Margaret Sullavan, and she'd said that guy at the store was so nice. Deep down I knew the truth, and I was totally up in the air, as if my forced insomnia was just a horrible nightmare, and I would come down any minute from the suspension I was in.

After what seemed like an eternity, I heard a clock strike somewhere off in the distance; about an hour had passed. Once I got up and went out into the corridor to stretch my legs. A fellow came up to me, chewing on his cigarette, looking nervous but radiant:

"Are you waiting, too?" he asked.

I said, yes, I was waiting too.

"It's our first," he added. "Apparently, she's having a hard time."

I started feeling weak in the knees, so I went back into the room and straddled my chair again. I started counting the tiles and playing these superstitious games, trying to kid myself about what was happening: I'd estimate how many tiles there were in a row, then tell myself she wouldn't die if there was an uneven number. And I'd count, and there would be an uneven number. Or I'd decide that she'd live if the clock struck before I counted to ten. And the clock would strike when I got to five or six. Suddenly I found myself thinking, "If she makes it past today...." and I got panicky.

I had to invent us a future, come up with one at all costs. I simply had to, so I could snatch Gloria away from that budding death. So I started thinking about how we'd spend next summer in La Floresta, and how next Sunday (for we needed an immediate future, too) we'd have dinner with my brother and his wife, and we'd laugh over the way my mother-in-law had carried on. And how I'd announce publicly that I was through with Margaret Sullavan. And how Gloria and I would have a kid together, two kids, even four; and every time I'd be out there pacing in the corridor....

Then a nurse came in and made me leave, while she gave Gloria a shot. Afterwards, I came back in and went right back to work on that effortless, transparent future. But she shook her head, muttered something, and that was that. My whole present was her struggle to survive, just Gloria, and me, and the threat of death; just me, hanging onto the blessed air moving in and out of her nostrils; just this tiny room, and the sound of that clock.

Then I pulled out my notepad and started writing this, so I could read it to her when we got back home, so I could read it to myself when we got back home. Back home. How good that sounded! And yet it seemed so far away…as far as a first lover, when you're only eleven years old; or arthritis, when you're only twenty; or death, when it was only yesterday. Suddenly my mind wandered, and I thought about today's soccer game, and whether they'd suspend it because of the rain, and about the British referee, who was supposed to be at the Stadium for his first game today, and about the transactions I had processed this morning. But then she caught my eye again, with her forehead all shiny like wax, and her parched mouth chewing on her fever; and I felt very out of place in that Saturday I could have had.

It was eleven-thirty and I remembered God, and how I used to hope there might really be one. I refused to pray; that would have been dishonest. You can only pray to a God you really believe in. And I can't believe in God; I only hope He exists. Then I realized the only reason I wasn't praying, was to see if God would be moved by my honesty. So I went ahead and prayed. One hell of a prayer, exhausting, full of doubts (so that it would be clear I didn't want to and couldn't flatter Him), a hand-to-hand combat of a prayer. As I listened to my own silent stammering, all I could hear was Gloria's hard, labored breathing. Another eternity went by, and the clock struck twelve. If she makes it past today…. And she had. She had definitely made it, and she was still breathing, and I dozed off, and I dreamed of nothing.

Someone shook my arm, and it was ten past four. She wasn't there. Then, the doctor came in and asked the nurse if she had told me. And I shouted, yes, she had told me (although that wasn't true); and I told him he was an animal, an even bigger idiot than the other doctor, because he had promised that if she made it past today, and now, look…. I shouted at him frantically, I think I even spit in his face; and he just stood there with those kind eyes of his, and that despicable understanding look.... And I knew I was wrong...because I was the guilty one, for falling asleep, for taking my eyes off her when they were the only eyes around, for taking away the future I imagined for her, and my mortified, excruciating prayer.

And then, driven by a pointless curiosity, I asked them where I could see her. I wanted to see her disappear, taking with her all my children, all my days off, all my tenuous connections to God.

1950

Translated by Darwin J. Flakoll

The Price of Rage

Though the man's leg barely moved, Fido, under the table, was deeply gratified by that gentle caressing of his muzzle. It was almost as nice as eating pieces of roast meat straight from his master's hand. Though he was unsuited to this way of life by both temperament and build (solid, chunky paws, thick shoulders, pointed ears), for two years now Fido had been an apartment dog, a role better suited, it seemed, to the effeminate, hysterical, leaky pooches whose presence lowered the tone of the second floor.

Fido was no purebred, but he was a disciplined, conscientious animal, usually able to postpone his physical necessities till noon, when he was taken down to the sidewalk to do his tree survey. He had also learned how to stand on his hind legs on command, carry the newspaper in his mouth each morning, give a good, baritone bark when the bell rang, and double as his lord and master's doormat, when the latter came home from work. Fido spent most of the day lying in a corner of the dining room or on the bathroom tiles, sleeping or just gazing at the hypnotic green of the bathtub.

On the whole he was no trouble. He felt no special affection for the woman; but as she was the one who took care of his food and filled his water bowl, Fido would hypocritically lick her hands once or twice a day, to ensure those vital services. His favorite was the man, of course, and when after lunch, the latter would stroke the woman's neck or waist or breasts, the dog would get upset and retreat to the darkest corner of the dining room, feeling jealous and mistrustful.

For Fido, the highlights of the day were his two meals, his diuretic outing to the sidewalk, and especially, this moment of calm right after dinner, when the man and woman would chat about this and that while he enjoyed the affectionate caress of those flannel trousers.

But tonight Fido was strangely uneasy. His tail-wagging was not, as it usually was after dinner, a sign of grateful affection, an old dog's pact with life. Tonight, Fido was feeling the burden of the immediate past. A series of fairly recent images had piled up behind his rheumy, knowledgeable old eyes. In the first place, the Other Man. Yes, one afternoon when he was alone in the apartment, dozing beside the bathtub, the woman had come home with the Other Man. Fido had barked fearlessly and portentously, like a prophet. The fellow had called him repeatedly in an affectionate falsetto, but Fido had not liked his sharply creased black pants, or the man's unpleasant smell. Two or three times he fought back his distaste and came close for a sniff, but in the end he had retreated to his corner of the dining room, where the smell of the fruit bowl was stronger than that of the intruder.

That time the woman had only *talked* to the Other Man, though she had laughed much more than usual. But on another occasion when she and Fido were alone and the man arrived, they held hands and ended up kissing. After that his round face, black mustache and bug eyes began appearing more and more often. They never went into the bedroom, but they did things on the sofa that made Fido violently nostalgic for the little bitches out on the farm where he had spent his puppyhood.

One afternoon, for some unknown reason, they noticed him again. From the start Fido had realized that he shouldn't approach them, that he'd better not repeat those prophetic barks of the first day. For his own good, to ensure those vital services and his longed-for trip to the sidewalk. So, while he didn't lick anyone's hand, he didn't interfere in any way either. And yet they noticed his presence. Actually it was the woman, which was natural, because Fido had nothing in common with the guy. Perhaps she suddenly realized that the dog existed, that he was there with them, a witness, the only witness. Fido had nothing to reproach her for, or rather, if he did, he didn't know it; still, there he was in the bathroom or the dining room, watching. And at the sight of those moist, bleary eyes, the woman began to feel uneasy. Before long, she was filled with violent, unbearable hatred.

Naturally, little of this had reached Fido. But one thing did get through to him: the resentment with which she treated him, the unaccustomed anger with which she tolerated his imposition.

Right now, while he was receiving his daily quota of affection, while he felt that gentle caress on his muzzle, and the smell he preferred above all others, he felt protected and secure. But later on? His problem was a certain memory, his most recent one. Yesterday, or two days ago, or three (a dog doesn't keep track of time) the fellow had had to leave in a hurry (why?), and had left something pretty, hard, and golden—his cigarette case—on the little table in the living room.

The woman had hidden it away, also in a hurry (why?), behind the pantry curtain. And as soon as he was on his own, Fido went over to give it a sniff. It had the fellow's unpleasant smell, but it was hard, metallic, shiny, all of which made it easy to lick, push around and clink against the floorboards.

The man's leg stopped moving. Fido realized that the party was over for today. He stretched his legs lazily and got up. He gave one last lick to a little piece of ankle that was showing between the worn-out sock and the trouser leg. Then he trotted off without growling or barking, his pace slow and arthritic, to his quiet corner.

But then something unexpected happened. The woman went into the bedroom and came right out again. She and the man talked, relatively calmly at first, then shouting at each other. Suddenly the woman stopped talking, took her coat off the hanger, stuffed her arms into it, and—without the man's making any effort to stop her—stormed out the door, slamming it so violently that the dog couldn't help barking.

The man was nervous, intense. Fido decided that the time had come. It wasn't vengeance; he really didn't know what it was. But instinct told him this was the right time.

The man was so deep in his thoughts that at first he didn't notice the dog pulling at his pant leg. Fido had to give three short barks. His intention was clear, and after hesitating for a moment, the man reluctantly followed him. Not far. Just into the pantry. When the dog pulled the curtain aside, the man drew back and looked for a moment, then bent down and picked up the cigarette case.

Fido was not really expecting anything. His find had no great importance for him. So when the man pounded the wall in that bizarre way, and began yelling, and crying like one of the pooches on the second floor, he drew back too, startled by the commotion he had caused. He stayed quiet, close to the doorway, and watched the man shouting and moaning and grinding his teeth. Then he decided to go and lick him tenderly, as was his duty.

The man lifted his head and saw that wagging tail, that nuisance coming to pity him, that witness. Fido panted with satisfaction, his dark, wet tongue hanging out. Suddenly it was all over. He was old, he was faithful, he was trusting. Three poor reasons why he felt no fear when that kick smashed his muzzle.

1956

Translated by Rachel Belash

Jules and Jim

The first call came on a Saturday afternoon, waking him from his siesta. Still half asleep, he had reached for the phone and a man's voice, neither shrill nor especially deep, had uttered the threatening words he would hear so often from then on: "Hi there, Agustín, we're going to kill you, we don't know if it'll be this week or next but either way, you're going to die, bye for now, Agustín." That day he was too flustered to say hello or who is it, but the next time, on another Saturday afternoon, he managed to ask why, and the voice answered, "You know damn well, so don't play dumb."

That had been the end of Agustín's Saturday siestas. He thought his way through his political activities, his business affairs, his love life, searching for an explanation. But none of those offered even the slightest clue. He had campaigned for the Frente Amplio in 1971, but only locally and not very intensely at that. While he shared the concerns and values of all those vital, committed young people, he couldn't stand their constant heated arguments that lasted until midnight, so he would duck out as soon as he got a chance. And though he had contributed regularly, helped out whenever he could, he had never considered himself a true activist. After the coup, he had simply made himself scarce.

In his business dealings, he inspired neither envy nor animosity. He employed just a few people at the small hardware store he had inherited from his dad, none of whom had ever given him problems. Two of his employees lived near him in Pocitos and more than once, he had run into them at neighborhood political meetings. Except they would always stay until the discussions were over and the next day at work, he could never bring himself to ask them what had been decided—simply because he had never approved of mixing business and politics.

Where women were concerned, his forty-or-so years of what looked increasingly like confirmed bachelorhood had not precluded a fairly stable relationship with an old friend of his sister's (the one who married a dentist and settled in Maldonado), whose mature attractiveness Agustín had rediscovered during a trip to Buenos Aires some six years earlier. Once involved in that pleasant, fulfilling liaison with Marta, he had renounced the short-lived and often risky affairs of his youth. Therefore, that private sector was no more likely than the others to be a breeding ground for grudges or blackmail.

His family life was similarly devoid of conflict. What few relatives he had were scattered around cities and towns in the Interior: his aunts and uncles in Paysandú, his mother in Sarandí del Yi, both sisters and a niece in Maldonado. They rarely made it into Montevideo and for his part, he was only dimly aware of having seen less and less of them.

At first he didn't take his new situation seriously. He told himself that times had changed since 1972 or '73, those nightmare years when what was now an anomaly could have had any number of plausible explanations. It might conceivably be a joke, but which of his few friends would be mean enough to keep such a dubious prank going for so many weeks? Blackmail? Maybe, but what enemy would be sadistic enough to harass him in such a shameless and sinister way? Besides, everyone had to know that the store earned him just enough to live on and no more.

The fact is, he had decided not to leave his apartment on Saturday afternoons. As the recipient of those sadistic threats, he was determined to respond with his own personal brand of masochism. But there was a certain logic to his obstinacy as well: if he disappeared on Saturdays, the probable reaction of his phantom assailant would be simply to shift the threatening phone calls to Tuesdays or Fridays.

So it was that Agustín came to view his life in a new light and live it at a different pace. When he went to work in the morning, he no longer used his car. Although he knew from the outset that if somebody was determined to do away with him there was nothing he could do to prevent it, he had nevertheless taken a few obvious and elementary precautions. Like taking the bus. He would walk a block and a half to catch the #121, which was rarely full, so he could ride comfortably; at the same time, there were always enough other passengers around to make whoever his enemy was think twice before shooting. But who had said anything about shooting? He was just as likely to be attacked in some elevator—let's say, the one in his building—between the second and third floors, or maybe vice versa; and as he couldn't rule that out either, he stopped taking the elevator unless he could share it with several of his neighbors. But what if his anonymous caller turned out to be just that—a neighbor? For a week, he walked down all eight flights of stairs; then, realizing that at certain hours when hardly anyone was around, they could just as easily jump him in a stairwell, he went back to taking the elevator.

Carmen, the woman who came over three times a week to cook and clean, had been with him since 1970; and he considered her completely reliable. Even so, he asked a few discreet questions about her ex-husband (I haven't heard a thing from him in over a year, Don Agustín) and her brother (he's gone to Australia, what choice did the poor guy have, a skilled worker like him, just sitting around doing nothing?). As part of their long-standing arrangement, Carmen only worked on weekdays; so she had never taken one of those calls. Agustín hadn't warned her either, maybe for fear she would panic and leave him high and dry.

As for Marta, she never came to Agustín's apartment. Agustín had always preferred getting together downtown at her place, and when she asked him why he had started showing up without his car, he just mumbled something about the price of gas going up. After all, what was the use of passing his anxiety on to her? Still, in as stable and ongoing a relationship as that quasi-couple enjoyed, each partner's body grows so sensitive to the slightest sign of stress or tension in the other, that words and gestures become superfluous. And tension was precisely what Marta's lovely body sensed. Agustín mentioned work, the state of the economy, his debts, the mini-devaluation's, you know how it is. But three days later and for the first time in five years, he was a failure in bed; and while Marta drew upon her richest reserves of tenderness and understanding, he didn't dare tell her how far his thoughts often strayed from her breasts and pubis, as alluring as ever.

So he went back and forth. Watching and feeling watched. Sometimes he'd go to a movie, but he couldn't concentrate unless it was full of threats and assaults, heists and kidnappings. And if it was, he would leave before it was over, preferring not to know whether the victim died or got away.

At the store, they only got one suspicious call. And it was Luis, the cashier, who happened to take it. It was a man's voice, he asked for you, Don Agustín, I told him you were waiting on a customer, and what he said was it didn't matter, he'd call you at home as usual, on Saturday afternoon, but he refused to leave his name, I thought it was kind of strange. Agustín told Luis not to worry, he was sure he knew who it was, and on Saturday at three thirty there was that same voice again repeating the same words, "Hi there, Agustín, we're going to kill you, we don't know if it'll be this week or next but either way, you're going to die, bye for now, Agustín." He would never hang up on the voice, he'd let it finish talking, but he wouldn't ask any questions either, he didn't want the other guy clobbering him again with that other line of his, "You know damn well, so don't play dumb."

In his pre-telephone days (as he came to regard them, with a certain strange nostalgia), if he didn't go over to Marta's in the afternoon, he would come back to his apartment, take a shower, pour himself a drink, and turn on the stereo. He preferred two kinds of music when he needed to relax: solo guitar and Latin American protest songs. Until 1972 he had listened almost every day to Viglietti, Los Olimareños, Zitarrosa, Soledad Bravo, Alicia Maguiña, Mercedes Sosa. Since the political situation had gotten so complicated, he had done less of that—and always with headphones. He didn't want certain new neighbors (the ones from Buenos Aires on the seventh floor, or those well-to-do snobs up on the ninth) drawing conclusions about his politics based on his musical tastes. Then once the calls started, he hadn't felt like listening at all—to guitars, protest songs, or anything else. He still liked his shower, and his whiskey as well; but instead of Narciso Yepes or Victor Jara, he would have a second drink, and sometimes a third.

Until he ran into Alfredo Sánchez at closing time that Tuesday afternoon, he hadn't mentioned his problem to anyone. He hadn't heard from Sánchez in ten years, but in the excitement of seeing him again and of finding him just as pleased about their meeting, Agustín threw caution to the winds. They sat down in a café, chatted for hours, got caught up on each other's lives. They had been classmates back in high school, where Agustín was a brilliant student and the apple of every teacher's eye (especially the women), while Sánchez barely managed to get himself promoted; each spring he would end up with a failing grade, and each summer—reluctantly— he would have to spend his whole vacation studying like a madman, in order to pass all his courses. Agustín had always felt that Sánchez was secretly envious of him—although maybe what he took to be envy or resentment was really just shyness, reticence, reserve. Agustín would offer to help; he'd invite Sánchez over to study, suggest reviewing things together. But Sánchez, proud and somewhat sullen, would always turn him down. Once Agustín got interested in chemistry and Sánchez in law, they had seen considerably less of one another, which might explain why their relationship had evened out. Years later—Agustín couldn't recall if there had been any particular reason—they had gone their separate ways.

Now, as they went back in minute detail over the different paths they had taken, Agustín was aware of a curious contradiction, which he was quick to point out to his long-lost schoolmate: he, the once brilliant Agustín, was nothing but a modest shopkeeper who had never even finished high school (when his dad died, he had to take charge of the store and at that point, either he had found it impossible to go on studying, or he had simply gotten lazy once his finances returned to normal); on the other hand, Sánchez, the seemingly mediocre student who had always barely muddled through, was now a highly successful attorney, who shared his practice with two first-rate partners and acted as advisor to important domestic and foreign firms. What's more, Sánchez was married, with three children, two girls and a boy, he showed Agustín their photos, a pretty wife, adorable kids; whereas Agustín was a confirmed bachelor (there was no point in mentioning Marta), with nothing to look forward to but loneliness, inexorable, ready to pounce and willing to wait (oh, well, those are the breaks, I guess). It was after they had talked and talked and reminisced about old teachers and classmates ("Did you know Casenave died? And Sharkey, that kid from Math class, he's a bigshot somewhere in the States now.... And that fat Moreno girl, who ever dreamed she'd end up marrying a soccer referee?").... It was after they had reclaimed all those years of friendship, that Agustín decided to open the floodgates and share his agonizing secret. Sánchez listened attentively, for which Agustín was deeply grateful. His final confession, "At this point, I don't know what to do anymore, I'm so confused and besides, to be honest with you, I'm really scared," was met with a forthright, encouraging smile from the new Alfredo.

"You can't go on like this, that's for sure," Sánchez remarked, and for a moment he sat there lost in thought, staring at the wall.

"Look, if it's been seven weeks now and they're still calling you and you're still O.K., it's probably all a joke or someone just trying to bug you. When something like that happens, it's reasonable to be scared, but part of it—and this is understandable—is that your imagination takes over and blows things up even more. Since you've always been a music buff, do you remember that Eladia Blásquez tango that talks about our imaginary fears? 'What we all have in common/ are those imaginary fears.' Well, I don't agree. To me, those imaginary fears are the most dangerous of all. They're the ones you have to get rid of, and right away, because it's those imaginary fears that can drive you nuts. Agustín, it's a good thing I ran into you, or you ran into me because I'm going to get you out of the rut you're in. This Saturday you're coming with me. I always spend the weekend with my family at this lovely little cottage I have outside of town, almost in the country. I'm not very big on the beach, you know how it is, the crowds, all the noise. Besides, a guy like me prefers grass to sand. And it just so happens that this Saturday, my family can't go. I don't want to spend it by myself, so you're coming along and that's that. You can read there, listen to music, play cards, watch TV, whatever you want. What you need is a whole weekend with nothing to worry about."

So it was all arranged. That Saturday a little after twelve, just as Agustín got through closing the store, Sánchez came by for him in his brand new Mercedes. They had lunch in a cozy little restaurant tucked away in the old part of the city.

"Nobody has heard of this place," said Sánchez in an almost conspiratorial voice, "but the food is terrific."

Agustín didn't find it all that terrific, but he thought Sánchez's invitation was a nice gesture. For the first time in several weeks, he felt good. As far as he was concerned, telling Sánchez the whole bizarre story had been almost like leaving it behind. He felt freer, almost calm.

"Hey, is it a good thing I ran into you when I did; I don't know if I would have landed in the emergency ward, the loony bin or the morgue, but I sure was ready for one of the three."

"Don't be an idiot," said Sánchez, and Agustín had to laugh.

The traffic was ghastly—the usual Saturday afternoon mess—but that didn't faze Sánchez.

"What kind of music do you go for these days? Classical?"

"Yeah, especially guitar."

"How about singers?"

"From Argentina and Uruguay, I guess, and the rest of Latin America."

"Oh. Viglietti? Chico Buarque? Los Olimareños? Silvio Rodríguez and Pablo Milanés?"

"Mm-hmm, I like all of those."

"Tell me, Agustín, you were always a bit subversive when it came to music..."

"Come on, not really; besides, it's hard to find those recordings now."

"Sure it is, but I can get them; I have my ways, how about that?"

The cottage wasn't a cottage at all but a magnificent house with a yard, surrounded by a high wooden fence.

"That's to keep the dogs from getting out," Sánchez explained.

Those dogs were definitely not to be messed with. As soon as they spotted a stranger, they came charging over with their prodigious fangs bared, but Sánchez quieted them down: "Jules! Jim!"

"You've got to have a couple of these critters around, there's no alternative, with all the break-ins and muggings in this area, besides, we're just too isolated out here, it's better not to take any chances. My cousin, the Chief of Police, he trained them personally. Now, don't get the wrong idea; it's a better guarantee than all the guns and burglar alarms in the world. There's this old man who comes over every afternoon to feed them—he lives about half a mile away, but he claims the walk does him good—except on weekends, because we're around then."

As Agustín walked none too calmly between Jules and Jim (it's my modest tribute to Truffaut, you remember the film, I loved it), he marveled at their size.

"Are they always loose like this?"

"Of course, what good would they be tied up? Besides, when we're here—the family, I mean—they're tame and they do as they're told. I do tie them up, though, just in case, when the kids want to play in the yard."

The inside of the "cottage" was very comfortable. Sánchez showed Agustín to his room and offered him a T-shirt and a pair of shorts to change into.

"Its no big deal, I think we wear the same size, if it gets chilly later on we'll light a fire."

Then, while Sánchez made them drinks, Chivas no less, Agustín checked out the books, the records, the tapes. There was something there for every taste. Who ever would have thought that moody kid who was such a dud at arithmetic and a budding hypochondriac to boot, would grow up to be this friendly, knowledgeable, understanding guy, who knew how to enjoy life and had even begun to cure him of his imaginary fear.

"You know, Agustín, threats are a lot like watchdogs. If you act scared of them, they'll go after you; but if you face up to them calmly, they'll keep their distance."

71

When the phone rang, Agustín almost dropped his glass. Sánchez noticed how jumpy he was, "Take it easy, pal, no one's going to call you here, even if it is Saturday."

He took the call himself, listened with a look of surprise, then:

"Calm down, I'm on my way; you call the doctor to save time." He seemed more annoyed than worried.

"What's wrong?"

"It's really nothing; last night my youngest kid had a slight fever and now it's suddenly shot up to almost 104. He's a little frail, you see; so each time he gets sick, my wife is a nervous wreck. Damn, what a shame.... I have to go."

"I'll go with you," said Agustín.

"You will not, you're staying right where you are, and you're going to relax, take it easy, get your strength back, read anything you want, listen to guitar music (I've got Segovia, Julian Bream, Carlevaro, Yepes, Williams, Parkening, so there's lots to choose from), or do whatever else appeals to you. Nobody knows you're here, so nobody's going to call you. Help yourself to what you want from the refrigerator, there's enough meat, salad, fruit and drinks there for you to eat like a king for a week. But in any case, I'll be back for you tomorrow afternoon, at the latest. The one thing you'd better not do is go out into the yard. On account of the dogs, you know, they'd come right after you; that's why there are bars on the windows, here inside you'll be safe. All you need is a little rest. And some peace and quiet. So have a ball."

With that Sánchez grabbed his bag, his beret, and the keys he had dropped on the coffee table as they came in. Before leaving, he slapped Agustín on the back.

"I hope whatever's wrong with your kid isn't serious," said Agustín.

"Don't worry, he'll be fine. I've learned to roll with the punches; my wife's nerves are worse than the kid's fever. But I do have to go."

Then, as he headed out the door, "You said you liked Los Olimareños, didn't you? Well, their latest tape is right over there on that shelf. 'Where the Home Fires Burn.' Friends sent it to me from Barcelona. It's really terrific, especially the second side where they sing 'My Heart Weeps,' so help me, that song would wring tears out of a stone. Besides, it was smuggled in, so you're one of the chosen few.... Be sure to listen to it."

Sánchez closed the door with a thud. Agustín heard the two hounds barking "Jules! Jim! Quiet! That's enough!" and then the sound of the Mercedes taking off. The unexpected change in plans had him a little unnerved. Still, he got ready to enjoy himself as much as possible. Poor Sánchez, as determined as he was to help a friend bounce back.... Agustín sat there polishing off his second Chivas and looking over the pictures, one by one. They were just prints, Miró, Torres García, Pollock, Chagall, but really good ones. It was time to sort things out. Suddenly he made a decision. If he managed to overcome his imaginary fear and, needless to say, his reasonable fear as well, he would marry Marta.

A noise at the window startled him, and behind the bars he spotted the enormous heads of Jules and Jim. They weren't barking, just staring at Agustín, as if they were defining their target. Since those huge dogs were hardly the embodiment of hospitality, he directed his attention to the records and tapes. How stupid of him; he hadn't asked Sánchez for his number, so he could call him later in the city and ask about the kid. Still, albeit a little apprehensively, he went over to the phone and picked up the receiver. There was no dial tone. The line must have gone dead after that last call. So much the better, that way I'm sure my Saturday caller can't reach me. And it was back to the tapes. He chose one by Segovia, and the Olimareños tape Sánchez had recommended. He loaded the first one into the tape deck and pressed the play button.

With the empty case in one hand and his glass in the other, he kept track of what he was hearing: Fantasia, Suite, "Hommage pour le tombeau de Débussy," Variations on a Theme by Mozart. The guitar sounded warm and welcoming in that room, so spotless and tidy it seemed no one had ever lived there. Making the most of the peace and quiet (total, except for the presence of Jules and Jim at the window), Agustín pondered the turmoil of his last several Saturdays and the several before. When Sánchez comes for him tomorrow, he'll declare himself free of Those Imaginary Fears.

Thanks to Sánchez, all that's left now is his Reasonable Fear, and even it has begun to look less threatening, more manageable. The guitar music ends on a grave and melancholy note and the tape deck stops automatically. He removes the Segovia tape and inserts the other one (making sure side B is facing up). But before pressing the play button to listen to Los Olimareños, he pours himself another Chivas and takes a good long swallow.

"Ha ha, what a swell, comfy little place his friend Sánchez has, his best buddy, Alfredo Sánchez. Well, I'll be damned, I think I'm drunk," he says as the outlines of the huge bookcases lose their sharpness and their colors begin to merge. "Let's see what that song 'My Heart Weeps' sounds like."

When he finally presses the button, he hears a long humming silence, then that marvelous stereo system saying "Hi there, Agustín, we're going to kill you, we don't know if it'll be this week or next but either way, you're going to die, bye for now, Agustín."

1983

Translated by Louise Popkin

Fable with Pope

I turned the corner and the Pope was there, alone and yawning, with his white vestments, leaning against the brick wall. I always knew I was going to meet him, but I didn't think it would be so soon. His eyes were closed, or perhaps squinting, like those of a nearsighted man bothered by the sun. But he was clouded over.

"Hello, Holiness," I said tentatively.

He raised one hand lazily in a sign of greeting. He was tired and without charisma. I felt a little ashamed for having surprised him in such a private solitude. But after all we were in the street, which is to say a communal space.

"What do you want? Benediction?"

"No, Holiness."

He made an effort and opened his eyes completely. He seemed a little disconcerted. One second before, in an almost automatic gesture, he had started to extend his hand for the ritual kiss, but he restrained himself, and pulled back his hand. After hesitating a little, he passed his fingers over his forehead.

"Does your head hurt?"

"Yes, a little. Many people, too many. I ask them for silence and they keep yelling. They don't let me speak. Sometimes I think they cheer the opposite of what I've said."

"Would you like an aspirin?"

"No, thank you."

The street was deserted, but in the distance could be heard an imposing choral murmur, with salutes, cheers, howls, ovations.

"How did you get away, your holiness?"

"An old man's tricks."

He smiled almost imperceptibly, as if it were the smile of another person.

"But you like that they applaud you, you like all this success. I can see it."

"That could be, but it's not for myself. Who they applaud and love is the Vicar of Christ, the Successor of Peter, the Bishop of Rome..."

"Et cetera."

"I am simply a pastor."

"You know, all this reminds me of the cult of personality. All a ritual. In its moment it was very cultivated by Stalin and De Gaulle."

The Pope gritted his teeth and stared at me with incredible sternness. If this had not been the Holy Father, I would have said that the stare had a little bit of hatred, but surely it was from strength of principles or something like that. Or maybe he didn't like it that I compared him with De Gaulle.

"Holiness, sometimes you unnerve me."

"Why?"

"All that about abortion."

"The death of an innocent can never be justified."

"There are lots of cases."

"He who denies the defense of the weakest and most innocent person, the human being already conceived, although not yet born, commits the gravest violation of the moral order."

I noted that he had begun to use his celebrated declamatory tone.

"I have the impression that you concern yourself more with the children not yet born than with those who are already born."

"Oh, no. About the already born I have said that they should receive religious education."

"Does your holiness know that already this year more than a million children have died in Latin America?"

"I read something like that in a footnote of *L'Osservatore Romano*."

"So?"

"I will respond with the words of the apostle: 'Do nothing from a spirit of rivalry or vanity.'"

"They are dying of hunger, Holiness."

"The family is the only community wherein man is loved for himself, for what he is and not for what he has."

"These children are not loved for what they have, because they have nothing, and less for what they are, because they are needy."

"The family..."

"The family is also dying of hunger."

The Pope passed his fingers across his forehead again.

"Give me that aspirin, son."

"Help yourself, Holiness."

He swallowed it dry and made a gesture of disgust, not like the Vicar of Christ that he is, but like the obscure parish priest that he could have been.

"As the apostle said: 'I delight myself in the law of God, following the interior man, but I feel another law in my members that disgusts the law of my mind.'"

"Holiness."

"What is it?"

"Why are you so conservative? Sometimes you seem preconciliar."

"Me preconciliar?"

"Yes, but of Nicea."

"Which Nicea? Year 325 or year 787?"

"Let's say 787."

"That's not so bad."

The Pope yawned again.

"Am I boring you?"

"No, son."

"Then tell me. You have beatified Angela Guerrero, an Andaluz who wore cloth shoes. How will she feel later in the Vatican, surrounded by so much pomp, so much wealth?"

"Pomp and wealth?"

"Yes. *Totus tuus?*"

"That's ridiculous. All the property belong to God and He distributes it among some as his administrators. I already told you."

"Yes, but when you said it you added: ...so that they can distribute it among the poor."

"I said that?"

"Yes, Holiness."

"I must have referred to other properties. Probably those of the spirit."

The Pope raised his two arms slowly, as when he salutes the multitudes.

"There's nobody here, Holiness."

He lowered his arms and began to squint again.

"May I be frank?"

"Frankness does not figure among the theological virtues."

"I understand."

"Not even among the cardinals."

"I understand. But may I be frank?"

He inclined his head in a neoecclesiastical sign of affirmation.

"Forgive me, Holiness, but I liked Pope John the thirteenth better. John the thirteenth is, after Christ, the figure of Christianity that I like the most."

He moved his lips slowly, as if he were praying. But he was not praying. Perhaps he was saying something in Polish.

"I only seek to be a good pastor."

"And also a good actor, no?"

"I was in Krakow, a long time ago."

"And still."

"It is convenient to continue purifying the memory of the past."

Now I am the one who needs an aspirin, but I feel incapable of swallowing it dry like he did. My head hurts. And my neck. The Bishop of Rome looks without happiness at the old flagstones he stands on.

"I listen to many, I speak with few, I decide alone."

"And because you decide alone you are infallible?"

"Naturally. Papal infallibility exists for a hundred and twelve years now, since the Vatican council approved it by 451 votes against 88."

"How nice."

"Infallibility?"

"No. How nice these 88. I confess that I have always been anti-infalliblist."

"Ah. Like Döllinger, Darboy, Ketteler?"

"If you say so."

"Like Hefele and Dupanloup?"

"I don't know who those people are."

"I do know."

He examined his white clothing and noticed that he had stained himself by leaning against the brick wall. He tried to clean the cloth with his smooth hands, but he only succeeded in spreading the spot. He looked up (it was still cloudy) and shrugged his shoulders.

By this point I believed that I was going to wake up and probably would be in front of a television set where, without my being able to refute him, the Pope would be telling me: "Because the Church, happily respecting the spheres outside its domain..." But no. I did not wake up. I continued to sleep soundly. So soundly that I could see how the Pope moved away down the empty street, in the direction of the far-off multitude and its cheers. His tired step was that of a veteran actor who, after a brief exit, returned to the stage ready to recite the role of Lear, or that of Titus Andronicus, or that of Coriolanus, or that of Karol Josef Wojtyla.

1982

translated by Gareth Price

Miss Amnesia

When the girl opened her eyes, her confusion was overwhelming. She remembered nothing. Not her name, not her age, not her address. She saw she had on a brown skirt and a beige blouse. She didn't have a purse. Her wristwatch said a quarter past four. Her tongue felt pasty, and her temples were throbbing. She looked down at her hands and noticed she had on clear nail polish. She was sitting on a bench, in some square with trees and an old fountain in the center; the fountain had cherubs on it, and what looked like three dishes stacked one on top of the other. She thought it was ugly. From her bench she could see stores, and big signs. The signs said Nogaró, Cine Club, Porley Furniture, Marcha, Partido Nacional. Next to her left foot she spotted a broken piece of mirror, shaped like a triangle. She picked it up. She felt a sort of morbid curiosity as she came face to face with her own reflection. It was as if she were seeing it for the first time. It didn't trigger any memories. She tried to figure out how old she was. I must be sixteen or seventeen, she thought. Oddly enough, she remembered the names of certain objects (she knew this was a bench; that, a column; that over there, a fountain; that other thing, a sign), but she couldn't get her bearings in time and space. Again she thought, "Yes, I must be sixteen or seventeen;" this time she spoke the words, to see if they sounded like Spanish. She wondered if she spoke any other languages. Nothing. She remembered nothing. And yet she felt relieved somehow, at peace, almost innocent. She was startled, of course, but that wasn't unpleasant. She had the vague impression that this was better than anything else, that she had turned her back on something ghastly and degrading. Overhead, the treetops were a mosaic of greens, and she could hardly see the sky. The pigeons flocked around her, but flew off at once, disappointed. She really had nothing to give them. Throngs of people walked right by the bench, paying no attention to her. Except for the young men who paused now and then to look her over. She was willing, even eager, to talk to them; but after a moment's hesitation, those erratic onlookers would continue on their way. Then, somebody stepped out from the crowd. He was fiftyish, well-dressed, with slicked-back hair, a tiepin, and a black briefcase. She sensed he was about to say something. Maybe he recognizes me, she thought. And she was afraid he would thrust her back into her past. She was so happy in this comfortable oblivion. But the man simply walked up to her and asked, "Is something wrong, Señorita?"

She studied him for a long time. Something about his face made her trust him. In fact, she was inclined to trust everything. "A little while ago I opened my eyes right here on this square; and I can't remember anything from before that." She sensed she had said enough. She realized she was smiling when she saw the man smile back.

The man held out his hand. He said, "My name is Roldán. Félix Roldán."

"I don't know my name," she said, but she shook his hand.

"It doesn't matter. You can't stay here. Do you want to come with me?" Of course, she did. As she stood up, she looked down at the pigeons that were flocking around her again, and thought: Great, I'm tall. The man named Roldán took her gently by the elbow and led her away.

"It isn't far," he said. What wasn't? It didn't matter. The girl felt like a tourist. Everything seemed so familiar; yet she couldn't place a single detail. Spontaneously, her weak arm took hold of his strong one. His suit was soft, made of combed wool, undoubtedly expensive. She looked up (the man was very tall) and smiled at him. He smiled back, this time with his lips slightly parted. The girl glimpsed a gold tooth. She didn't ask what city she was in. It was he who told her, "Montevideo." That word fell into a deep void. It meant nothing. Absolutely nothing. Now they were on a narrow cobblestone street, where there was lots of construction going on.

81

The buses were passing very close to the curb, splashing everything with muddy water. She rubbed a few drops of mud off her legs and realized she wasn't wearing stockings. She remembered the word stockings. She looked up and saw some old balconies, with clothes hung out to dry and a man in pajamas. She decided she liked this city.

"Here we are," said the man named Roldán stopping at a double door. She went in first. In the elevator, the man pressed the button marked five. He didn't say a word; but when he looked at her, his eyes were restless. As she looked back at him, hers eyes were full of trust. When he took out the key to open the apartment door, the girl noticed a wedding band on his right hand, and another ring with a red stone. She couldn't remember what those red stones were called. There was nobody in the apartment. When the door opened, she felt a rush of stale, stuffy air. The man named Roldán opened a window and offered her one of the armchairs. Then he brought some glasses, ice, and whiskey. She remembered the words for ice and glass. But not for whiskey. The first swallow made her choke, but it felt good. The girl looked around at the furniture, the walls, the paintings. Overall, she didn't find the place particularly attractive; but she was in a good mood, so that didn't bother her. She looked at the man again, and she felt comfortable, secure. I hope I never remember anything from before, she thought. Then the man let out a guffaw that startled her.

"O.K., Little Miss Innocent. Now that we're alone, you can tell me who you are."

She choked again and opened her eyes very wide. "I already told you, I don't remember."

Suddenly, she could see the man changing before her eyes; he was looking less and less like a gentleman, more and more like a swine, as if a horrible, murky brutishness had suddenly started seeping out from under his tiepin or his combed wool suit.

"Miss Amnesia? Is that it?"

And what did that mean? She understood nothing, but she was beginning to be afraid, almost as afraid of this absurd present as she was of her enigmatic past.

"Come off it, Miss Amnesia," the man guffawed again. "You're pretty original, you know that? So help me, I've never seen anything like this before. Are you new wave, or what?"

The hand of the man named Roldán came closer. This hand was part of the same strong arm she had grabbed onto spontaneously on the square. Yet it wasn't the same hand at all. This hand was chunky, hairy, impatient. Too frightened to move a finger, she realized she was at his mercy. Now the hand was on her neck, trying to force its way into her blouse. But there were four buttons there, which made that difficult. So it yanked at her neckline and three of the buttons went flying. She heard one of them roll all the way across the floor and hit the baseboard. Until it stopped rolling, neither of them moved. The girl made the most of that brief, inadvertent pause and jumped to her feet, the glass still in her hand. The man named Roldán lunged at her. She felt him pushing her toward a big green sofa. All he would say was: "Little Miss Innocent, Little Miss Innocent." She could feel his foul breath, first on her neck, then on her ear, then on her lips. She could feel those powerful, disgusting hands trying to get her clothes off. She was sure she couldn't take much more; she was about to suffocate. Then, she noticed her fingers still clutching the empty whiskey glass. It took another superhuman effort, but she managed to sit up and ram that glass straight into Roldán's face, without letting go. He staggered backwards, then slipped and fell next to the green sofa. The girl knew only that she had to get out of there. Jumping over the man's body, finally letting go of the glass (which landed in one piece on a throw rug), she made a run for the door, opened it, dashed out into the hallway, and still in a panic, bolted down the stairs to the street.

On the street she was able to put herself back together, thanks to that one surviving button. She started walking very fast, almost running. Terrified, miserable, sad, and with just one thought in her mind: I've got to forget this, I've got to forget this. She recognized the square, and the bench where she had been sitting. It was empty now. So she sat down. One of the pigeons seemed to look her over, but she wasn't in any shape to respond. She was obsessed with a single thought: I've got to forget; oh, God, make me forget this shameful thing too. As she leaned her head back, she could feel herself blacking out.

When the girl opened her eyes, her confusion was overwhelming. She remembered nothing. Not her name, not her age, not her address. She saw she had on a brown skirt and a beige blouse. She didn't have a purse. Her wristwatch said twenty-five after seven. She was sitting on a bench, in some square with trees, and an old fountain in the center; the fountain had cherubs on it, and what looked like three dishes stacked one over the other. She thought it was ugly. From her bench she could see stores, and big signs. The signs said Nogaró, Cine Club, Porley Furniture, Marcha, Partido Nacional. She remembered nothing. And yet, she felt relieved somehow, at peace, almost innocent. She had the vague impression that this was better than anything else, that she had turned her back on something ghastly, degrading. People were walking by, with their children, their briefcases, their umbrellas. Then, someone stepped out of that endless procession. He was fiftyish, well-dressed, with slicked-back hair, a briefcase, a tiepin, and a little white patch over one eye. Maybe he knows me, she thought. And she was afraid he would thrust her back into her past. She was so happy in this comfortable oblivion. But the man simply walked up to her and asked, "Is something wrong, Señorita?" She studied him for a long time. Something about his face made her trust him. In fact, she was inclined to trust everything. She saw the man hold out his hand, and heard him say: "My name is Roldán. Félix Roldán." But after all, who cared what his name was.... So she stood up and spontaneously, her weak arm took his strong arm.

1964

translated by Flaurie S. Imberman

Perhaps Beyond Repair

When the loudspeakers announced that Central American Airlines was delaying its Flight #914 for twenty-four hours, Sergio Rivera's face registered his annoyance. Of course, he was familiar with the standard argument in such cases: better a prudent delay than a defective plane ("perhaps beyond repair") that's already airborne. Anyway, this particular delay was throwing a monkey wrench into his plans for the next stop, where he had already scheduled appointments for tomorrow noon.

He made up his mind to accept his lot. The velvety female voice coming over the loudspeaker was saying that the Airline would issue vouchers to its passengers for dinner, an overnight stay, and breakfast at the International Hotel near the airport. He had never been in this Slavic country before and wouldn't have minded seeing it; but he wasn't about to change any dollars for just one night (even though the airport Bank was open for passengers in transit). So he went over to the LCA counter, got into line for his voucher, and decided not to order any extras at dinner.

It was snowing when the bus dropped them off in front of the hotel. He realized this was only the second time he had seen snow. The first had been three years ago in New York, on another last-minute business trip he had made at his Company's expense. The pain of eighteen degrees below zero clamped onto his ears, then sent a shudder through his whole body, making him wish he hadn't forgotten his blue muffler on the plane. Luckily, the glass doors slid open before he could even touch them, and immediately he felt a welcome rush of warm air. He thought about how much he would have liked to have his wife Clara with him just then, and Eduardo, his five-year-old son. After all, he was a family man.

In the restaurant, he saw that there were tables for two, four and six. He picked a table for two, secretly hoping to eat by himself and read quietly. But just then, another passenger asked: "May I?" and sat down in the free chair before he could answer.

The intruder was an Argentinian with an uncontrollable fear of planes. "Some people carry good luck charms," he said; "I've got one friend who won't board a plane without a certain keyring that has a turquoise on it. And I know of someone else who always travels with an old copy of Martín Fierro. Personally, I carry two little Japanese coins—look, here they are—that I bought, don't laugh now, in Chinatown, in San Francisco. But they have yet to invent a good luck charm that can really calm me down."

Rivera answered in grunts and monosyllables, but within ten minutes he had given up trying to read and began talking about his own good luck charms. "My own superstitions have just suffered a mortal blow. I've always taken this Schaeffer pen on plane trips, without any ink in it. For two reasons: on the one hand, there's no chance it'll stain my suit that way; and on the other, I've always assumed nothing could happen to me, as long as it was empty. But for this trip, I forgot to pour out the ink; yet here I am, alive and kicking."

The other man didn't seem too convinced by what he was hearing, and Rivera felt obliged to add: "As a matter of fact, I'm quite a fatalist. When your time comes, what difference does it make if it's a Boeing or the proverbial flowerpot falling on your head from the seventh floor?"

"Okay," the other man said, "but I'll still take the flowerpot. It might turn you into a zombie, but at least you'd be alive."

The Argentinian didn't finish his dessert ("Who ever said they knew how to make chocolate mousse in Europe?") and went up to his room. Rivera was no longer in a reading mood. He lit up a cigarette and waited for his Turkish coffee to settle. He stayed on in the dining room for a while; but when he noticed the tables beginning to empty, he quickly got up, so as not to be the last one out, and went to his room on the second floor. His pajamas were in his suitcase, back on the plane, so he got into bed in his shorts. He read for some time, but Agatha Christie let the cat out of the bag long before he felt sleepy. He was using a picture of his son as a bookmark. From on top of a sand dune far off in El Pinar, with a little pail in his hand and his belly button showing, Eduardo smiled his infectious smile, and Rivera smiled back. Then he turned off the night lamp and switched on the radio. But that emphatic voice was speaking a language he couldn't make head or tails of, so he turned it off too.

When the phone rang, he had to grope around for the receiver. A voice said good morning in English, adding that it was now eight o'clock, and passengers on LCA Flight #914 would be picked up at the hotel entrance at 9:30, since "theoretically," the flight was scheduled to leave at 11:30. So there was time to bathe and have breakfast. He didn't much like taking a shower, then getting back into the same underwear he had worn since leaving Montevideo. As he shaved, he wondered how he would be able to squeeze the interviews he had missed into what was left of the week. "Today's Tuesday the 5th," he thought. He decided the best he could do was to draw up a list of priorities, so he did just that. He recalled the final instructions he had gotten from the Chairman of the Board: "Don't forget, Rivera, that your next promotion will depend on how your talk with Sapex goes." And he decided to skip several minor interviews, in order to devote all his time on Wednesday afternoon to those nice people at Sapex. Maybe that evening, they would take him to the nightclub where the striptease act had made such a big impression on Pereyra two years back.

He had breakfast alone, and at 9:30 sharp, the bus pulled up in front of the hotel. The snow was coming down even harder than the day before, and the cold outside was almost more than he could take. At the airport, he went over to one of the big glass windows and watched, almost resentfully, as the LCA plane was serviced by an entire crew of men in gray overalls. It was 12:15 when the loudspeaker announced that LCA Flight #914 was being delayed again, more than likely for three hours, and that the Airline would issue vouchers to its passengers for lunch at the airport restaurant.

Rivera felt a wave of scepticism flow through him. As usually happened when he got nervous, he belched twice in a row and noticed a strange pressure in his jaws. Then he went over to the

LCA counter and got in line. At 3:30 the inauspicious voice said, sounding admirably unruffled, that "because of technical difficulties, LCA had decided to delay its Flight #914 until 12:30 tomorrow." For the first time, a somewhat aggressive murmur was heard. Rivera's trained ears picked up statements like, "This is intolerable!"; "They ought to be ashamed!"; "How inconsiderate!" Several children started wailing, and one wailing voice was abruptly silenced with a hysterical slap. The Argentinian looked at Rivera from a distance, shook his head and moved his lips as if to say: "What do you make of this?" A woman to his left commented hopelessly: "They could at least let us have our luggage."

Rivera felt a surge of anger in his throat when the loudspeaker announced that personnel at the LCA counter were issuing vouchers for dinner, hotel room, and breakfast, all courtesy of the Airline. The poor girl who was handing them out had to carry on the same useless, idiotic discussion with each passenger. Rivera figured it was better just to take the voucher with an ironic, condescending smile. He assumed the look the girl flashed him was her way of thanking him for keeping his reprisal so low-keyed.

This time Rivera decided his rotten mood could stand some company, so at dinner he sat down at a table for four.

"They ought to be shot," said a woman in a mousy wig that was somewhat askew, as she chomped away on her food. The man sitting across from Rivera slowly unfolded his handkerchief to blow his nose, then picked up his napkin and wiped his moustache.

"I should think they could shift us to another airline," the woman insisted.

"There are too many of us," said the man with the handkerchief and the napkin.

Rivera ventured a minority opinion: "That's the trouble with flying in winter," and immediately realized he had departed from the group's working hypothesis.

Naturally, the woman's mouth watered at the prospect of an argument: "As far as I know, the Airline has said nothing about the weather. Don't you think it's something to do with engine failure?"

Now the voice of the fourth man at the table was heard for the first time; it was guttural, with a strong German accent: "One of the hostesses told me there's something wrong with the plane's radio system."

"Well," Rivera said, "in that case, there's a good reason for the delay, isn't there?"

Over at the other end of the restaurant, the Argentinian was making wild gestures, which Rivera interpreted as more and more insulting to the Airline. After coffee, he went to sit across from the elevators. There must have been a dance party going on in the seventh floor ballroom, because crowds of people kept coming in from the street. After leaving piles of overcoats, hats and mufflers in the checkroom, young men in elegant, dark suits, and svelte, attractive young women waited for the elevator. Other couples came walking down the stairs, talking and laughing, and Rivera would have liked to know what they found so funny. Suddenly he felt idiotically alone; he wished one of those young couples would ask him for a light, or kid him, or ask some silly question in that impossible language of theirs that apparently allowed for humor, though he would never have guessed. But no one even so much as glanced at him. They were all too busy with their cryptic language, and their own particular way of having fun.

Depressed and irritated at himself, Rivera went up to his room. This time it was on the eighth floor. He undressed, slipped into bed and got out a piece of paper to redo his schedule of interviews. He put down three names: Kornfeld, Brunell, Fried. He tried to write down a fourth and couldn't. He had completely forgotten it. He could only remember that it began with the letter E. This sudden lapse upset him so much that he turned out the light and tried to sleep. For a while it looked as if it was going to be one of those dreadful, sleepless nights that had plagued him some years back. The worst part was, this time he had nothing to read. A second Agatha Christie book had stayed behind on the plane. For a while he lay there thinking about his son, and suddenly he realized with a shock that he hadn't thought of his wife for at least twenty-four hours. He closed his eyes, determined to get to sleep. He could have sworn only three minutes had gone by when the phone rang six hours later and a voice announced in English as usual, that the bus to the airport would pick them up at 12:15. The thought of wearing the same dirty underwear made him so furious that he decided to skip his bath. Even brushing his teeth was an effort. On the other hand, he was in a very cheery mood at breakfast. He felt an odd and totally unfamiliar pleasure as he took the LCA voucher out of his pocket and left it under the flowered sugar bowl.

At the airport he had lunch at LCA's expense, then sat down on a big sofa that was unoccupied, perhaps because it was just opposite the rest rooms. Suddenly he realized that a little girl—five years old, blonde, freckled, with a doll—was standing right next to the sofa, staring at him.

"What's your name?" she asked in charmingly simple German.

Rivera decided a name like Sergio would mean nothing to her, so he extemporized: "Karl."

"Oh," she said, "mine's Gertrud."

Rivera responded in kind: "What's your doll's name?"

"Her name is Lotte," Gertrud said.

Another little girl—also blonde, about four years old, with a doll—had come walking over. She asked the German girl in French:

"Does your doll close her eyes?"

Rivera translated the question into German, and then the corresponding answer into French. Yes, Lotte could close her eyes. The French kid's name turned out to be Madeleine, and her doll's, Yvette. Rivera had to explain most carefully to Gertrud that Yvette could close her eyes and say "Mama," too. The conversation touched on subjects as diverse as candybars, clowns and their respective mummies and daddies. Rivera spent a whole fifteen minutes interpreting for them, but the two little blondes hardly looked at him. A mental comparison between them and his son led him to conclude objectively that Eduardo wasn't all that bad. He took a deep, contented breath.

Suddenly, Madeleine held out her hand to Gertrud, whose first impulse was to pull away. Then she seemed to reconsider, and held out her hand in return. Her blue eyes glowed, and Madeleine let out a squeal of satisfaction. There would clearly be no need for an interpreter from now on. The owners of Lotte and Yvette walked off, hand in hand, without even a goodbye for the man who had done so much for them.

"LCA wishes to inform you," said the voice on the loudspeaker, a little strained, but still capable of provoking an expectant silence, "that it has been unable to clear up certain technical difficulties, and has therefore decided to cancel Flight #914 until tomorrow morning, at a time still to be determined."

To his surprise, Rivera found himself rushing over to the counter where they would be issuing the vouchers for dinner, room and breakfast, to get a good place in line. But he had to be resign himself to being eighth. When the Airline clerk handed him that familiar slip of paper, Rivera took it with a feeling of accomplishment...a little like getting a promotion at work, or passing an exam, or simply knowing he had a roof over his head, safety, and security.

He was just getting through dinner at the usual hotel, a meal consisting of a fabulous cream of asparagus soup, Weinerschnitzel, and strawberries and cream, along with the best beer he could ever remember having, when he realized there was no rational explanation for his happy mood. Another twenty-four hour delay meant the loss of several interviews and consequently, of just as many contracts. He chatted for a while with the Argentinian he had met the first night, but he couldn't get him to talk about anything besides the Peronista threat. Rivera had no strong feelings on that subject, so he claimed to be unaccountably exhausted, and retired to his room, which was now on the fifth floor.

When he tried to reorganize his list of interviews, he discovered he could only remember two names, Fried and Brunell. He found this new lapse of memory so funny, that he let out a guffaw loud enough to shake the bed, then wondered why no one in the next room asked him to be quiet. He relaxed when he remembered that somewhere in his suitcase on the plane, there was a small notebook with all those names, addresses and telephone numbers. He settled in under the strange, quilted sheets with buttons on them, feeling much the way he remembered feeling as a child, when he curled up under his cozy blankets at the end of a winter's day. As he was falling asleep, his eyes took in the image of Eduardo, still standing there with his pail in the photo on the dunes, but he was too drowsy to notice he hadn't even thought of Clara.

The next morning, he looked almost fondly at his underwear, which was absolutely grimy, at least at the seams of the shorts and the armholes of his undershirt. He splashed water on his face half-heartedly, and made the bold decision not to brush his teeth. He crawled back into bed, and stayed there until the phone sounded it's daily alert. Then, while he was getting dressed, he took five minutes out to acknowledge how good it was of the Airline to finance its passengers' accidental delay so generously. "I'll always travel with LCA," he muttered, and his eyes filled with tears. So he closed them for a second and when he opened them again, the first thing that caught his attention was a calendar he hadn't noticed before. Instead of Thursday the 7th, it said Wednesday the 11th. He counted the days on his fingers, and decided that page was probably from another month, or another year. That gave him a very dim view of bureaucratic routine in the Socialist Bloc. Then he finished dressing, had his breakfast and caught the bus.

This time, there was a big stir at the airport. Two married couples, one Chilean and the other Spanish, were protesting loudly about the continued delays. Since they were traveling with two infants, they argued, a boy and a girl respectively, the very least the Airline could do was supply the diapers they needed, or else get their suitcases off the plane. The clerk at the LCA counter merely repeated, in a predominantly defensive monotone, that the Airline authorities would do their best to iron out any special problems caused by the involuntary delay.

Involuntary delay. 'Delay,' and 'involuntary'. Sergio heard those two words and felt like a new man. Perhaps that was what he had been looking for all his life (which had been just the opposite: involuntary urgency; deliberate haste; hurrying, always hurrying). His eyes scanned the airport signs in a variety of languages: Sortie,

Arrivals, Ausgang, Douane, Departures, Cambio, Herren, Change, Ladies, Verboten, Transit, Snack Bar. This felt like home now.

Every now and then a voice, always female, announced an airplane's arrival, another's departure. But of course, never that of LCA Flight #914, whose plane, paralyzed but in one piece, was still sitting there on the runway, surrounded by more and more mechanics in overalls, by long hoses, by jeeps that came and went, carrying even more workmen, more tools, more orders.

"Sabotage, that's what it is, sabotage," said a huge Italian who was traveling in first class, as he passed by. Rivera, who was on his toes, stayed close to the LCA counter. That way, he would be first in line to pick up his voucher for dinner, room and breakfast.

Gertrud and Madeleine walked right past him, holding hands and no longer carrying dolls. He wondered if they were the same kids he remembered, or others just like them (those little European blondes all look alike). In any case, they seemed just as pleased as he was with the involuntary delay. It occurred to Rivera that there would be no interviews at all, not even with the people from...what was that name again? He tried to remember even one name, just to see if he could, and got more excited than ever when he couldn't.

Again he spotted a calendar; but the date on it, Monday the 7th, was so crazy that he decided to disregard it. Just then, all the passengers from a flight that had just landed entered the huge terminal. When he caught sight of the boy, he felt a flood of affection wash over him. An old, familiar affection. But the teenager walked right past, without even a glance. He was busy talking to a girl in green corduroy pants and dainty black boots. He walked over to the counter and came back with two bottles of orange juice. As if in a trance, Rivera sat down on a sofa near them.

"My brother says we'll be here for about an hour," the girl said.

The boy wiped his lips with his handkerchief. "I can't wait to get there."

"Me either," she said.

"I hope you'll write. Who knows, maybe we'll see each other sometime. After all, it's not very far."

"Let's exchange addresses right now," she said.

The boy took out a ballpoint pen, and she opened a small red notebook. Just six feet away from the couple, Sergio sat absolutely still, lips pressed tightly together.

"Write it down," the girl said. "María Elena Suárez, Koenigstrasse 21, Nüremberg. And yours?"

"Eduardo Rivera, Lagergrasse 9, Vienna III."

"How long will you be there?"

"As of now, one year," he said.

"Hey, that's great. Doesn't your old man mind?"

The boy started to say something. From where he was, Sergio couldn't make out his words because just then, the loudspeaker (the same female voice as always but now, oddly hoarse) was announcing: "LCA informs you that due to technical difficulties, it has decided to cancel Flight #914 until tomorrow, at a time still to be determined."

It was only when the announcement ended that Sergio could make out the boy's words again: "And besides, he's not my old man; he's my stepfather. You see, my father died years ago, in a plane crash."

1967

Translated by Hardie St. Martin

Five Years of Life

He sneaked a look at his watch, and his worst fears were confirmed. It was five past midnight. If he didn't start saying his goodbyes immediately, he'd miss the last metro. That always happened to him. Somebody would finally feel moved by alcohol, by nostalgia—their own or someone else's—or by a frustrated desire to be an actor, to start spilling their secrets; or one of the women would suddenly seem prettier, or more accessible, or more affectionate, or more interesting; or one of the older folks, usually some diehard anarchist, would launch into a graphic eyewitness account of door-to-door combat in Civil War Madrid. In other words, the conversation would just barely have crept past the stage of stale jokes and routine gossip; and right then, he'd be a wet blanket, stand up with an awkward smile, announce that his time had come, kiss the girls goodbye, clap the men on the shoulder, and deny his arm the sure comfort of a soft, qualified, womanly hand—all so he wouldn't miss the last metro. Everybody else could stay later, simply because they lived nearby or, in a few cases, had cars; but Raúl couldn't afford the luxury of a taxi, and—although he had actually done it on two occasions—he really didn't enjoy walking all the way from Corentin Celton to Bonne Nouvelle, a minor feat that involved crossing half of Paris.

So, having made his decision, he took those delicate fingers of Claudia Freire's, which for the last hour had been resting on his right knee, kissed each one by way of compensation, and deposited them on the green corduroy back of the sofa. Then as usual, he announced: "Well, my time has come," and put up valiantly with all the catcalls and Agustín's proclamation: "Hear! Hear! A moment of silence for Cinderella, who is forced to retire to her distant abode! Now, don't forget your size 42 slipper." Before the customary laughter died down, Raúl managed to give María Inés, Nathalie (the only French girl there), Claudia and Raquel a peck on the cheek (Raquel's being unusually cool, and the others' flushed); utter an audible "So long, folks!"; say a ritual "Thanks for inviting me" to his very Bolivian hosts, and leave.

It was a lot colder than four hours ago, so he pulled up the collar of his raincoat. He headed down Rue Renan at a fast clip, partly because he was cold, and partly because it was now a quarter past twelve. As a reward for his diligence, he managed to catch the last metro to Porte de la Chapelle, had the rare pleasure of being the only passenger in the end car, and settled into his seat, prepared to watch sixteen empty stations roll by before changing trains at Saint Lazare. Somewhere around Falguière, he started thinking about the difficulties a non-French writer like himself ("non-French" striking him, in this instance, as a more applicable category than "Uruguayan") was bound to face if he wanted to write about these people, this subway system, life in this city. As a matter of fact, he realized, the last metro was one possible topic. For example: what if, due to unforeseen circumstances, some guy were to find himself locked up in a metro station for a whole night (alone; or better yet, with company; or best of all, with excellent company)? Once you figured out a good way to get him in there, the situation had all the makings of a terrific story! At least for others, of course; never for Raúl. He could never find the details, the essence, the mechanism of a story like that. And if he tried to write it without those specifics, he was sure to make a fool of himself. Just how did they go about closing down a metro station? Did they leave the lights on? Was there a watchman? Did anyone check the platforms, to make sure they were all empty? He compared his ignorance of these details to the command he would have of the material if his hypothetical story were to be set on a bus in Montevideo—say, the #173, on its last run from Plaza Independencia to Avenida Italia and Peñón. While he didn't know all there was to know in that case either, he was fairly conversant with the basics, and he knew how to work in minor details.

He was still mulling that over when his train stopped at Saint Lazare and he had to make another dash for the last connection to Porte de Lilas. This time, seven other people ran with him, but they fanned out into all five cars. He chose the last car again, so he'd be nearer his exit when he got off at Bonne Nouvelle. But this time he wasn't alone. A girl entered and stood at the other end of the car, even though all the seats were empty. Raúl gave her a good long look; but she seemed totally engrossed in a sign warning French citizens who were planning to travel outside the country for their vacations to get their passports in order in plenty of time. Whenever he looked at a woman, especially if she was as pretty as this one, Raúl got out his mental checklist just in case. He immediately noticed that she was just as cold as he was (even though she had on a thin coat and a woolen muffler), and just as sleepy, and just as anxious to get home. In short, a kindred soul. He was always meaning to get involved in a more or less stable relationship with a French girl, as the ultimate way to get a good grip on the language. But, in fact, all his friends, male or female, were part of the Latin American crowd. Sometimes that was more of a nuisance than an advantage, but they all stuck together, so they could talk about Cuernavaca or Antofagasta or Paysandú or Barranquilla and, while they were at it, gripe about how hard it was to adjust to life in France—as if they had ever really tried to understand anything more complicated than the editorials in "Le Monde" or the menus at the self-service.

Bonne Nouvelle, at last! He and the girl left the train by different doors. Ten other passengers got off too, but they all headed for the exit to Rue du Faubourg Poissonière, while he and the girl started walking in the opposite direction, toward Rue Mazagran. The heels of her shoes echoed strangely as they clicked on the floor; his rubber heels, on the other hand, followed silently at a safe distance. But their trek through the station took an absurd turn, when they got to the exit and found the metal grate locked shut. Raúl heard the girl say: "¡Dios mio!" just like that, in Spanish; then she turned to him, looking terrified. Outside, they could hear a *clochard* snoring sumptuously away, ensconced in greasy comfort near the grate.

"Don't worry," said Raúl. "The other door has to be open." While she didn't acknowledge the fact that he had responded in Spanish, she did look relieved.

"We'd better run for it," he said, taking off in the direction they had just come from. The platform was deserted now, and the lights were dimmed. From across the tracks, a man in overalls yelled at them to hurry, because they were about to close the other exit. As they retraced their steps, Raúl remembered his recent doubts. Now I can write that story, he thought. He had the details. The girl looked like she was about to burst into tears; but she didn't slow down. For a moment he considered running on ahead to see if the Poissonière exit was still open, but he figured it wouldn't be very nice to leave her alone in those dark, deserted corridors. So they got there at the same time. The grate was locked. She grabbed hold of the bars with both hands and shouted, "Monsieur! Monsieur!" But there wasn't even a clochard around, much less a monsieur. The street was completely deserted.

"We're stuck," said Raúl. Come to think of it, he didn't dislike the idea of spending the night there with that girl. What a shame she isn't French, he thought, just for the sake of argument. What a nice long practice session that could have been.

"What about the man on the other platform?" she asked.

"You're right. Let's go look for him," he said, none too enthusiastically; then he added, "Would you rather wait here while I try to find him?"

"No, please," she begged, scared out of her wits; "I'll go with you." So back they went to all those corridors and stairs. The girl wasn't running anymore; she seemed almost resigned to the idea of spending the night there. Naturally, there was no one to be seen on the other platform. They yelled anyway, but not even an echo answered.

"We may as well get used to the idea," insisted Raúl, playing his trump card. "Let's make ourselves as comfortable as possible; after all, if that clochard can manage to get some sleep out there, why can't we do the same in here?"

"Sleep?" she exclaimed, as if he had just propositioned her. "You sleep if you want to; I couldn't."

"Oh, no! If you're going to stay up all night, so am I. We can talk."

One light was still on at the far end of the platform. They walked toward it. He took off his raincoat and offered it to her.

"Absolutely not," she said. "What about you?"

"I'm not cold," he lied. He put his raincoat down next to her, but she made no move to pick it up. They sat down on the long wooden bench. When he looked at her, she looked so frightened and suspicious that he couldn't help smiling.

"Is this really going to cause problems for you?" he asked, just to break the silence.

"What do you think?" For the next several minutes, neither of them said a word. The situation was beginning to look truly absurd. It would take some getting used to.

"How about introducing ourselves?"

"Mirta Cisneros," she said, without offering her hand.

"Raúl Morales," he replied, adding: "I'm Uruguayan. Are you from Argentina?"

"Yes, from Mendoza."

"What brings you to Paris? Are you here on a scholarship?"

"No. I paint. I mean, I used to paint, but I'm not here on a scholarship."

"You don't paint anymore?"

"I worked my butt off to scrape together enough money to get here, and now I have to work so hard just to survive that I've stopped painting. A real failure. I don't even have enough money to buy a one-way ticket back; not to mention the fact that going home would be giving in."

He had no comment; he simply said, "I write." Then, before she could ask, he added, "Stories."

"Oh. Have you published any books?"

"No. Just in magazines."

"And you've been able to write over here?"

99

"Yes."

"Are you here on a scholarship?"

"No. I came here two years ago, after I won a newspaper contest, and then I stayed on. I do some translating, type manuscripts, whatever I can. I can't afford to fly home either. And I don't like admitting defeat any more than you do." She shivered, and that seemed to convince her to put his raincoat over her shoulders.

By two AM, they had been over the state of their respective finances, the adjustment problems they had had, all the devious ways the French find to pinch pennies, and the defects and virtues of both their far-off countries. At a quarter past two, he suggested they consider themselves friends. She hesitated for a moment, then accepted.

"Since we don't have a chessboard," he said, "or a deck of cards, or dishonorable intentions, I propose we tell each other the story of our lives. What do you say?"

"Mine's pretty boring."

"So's mine. All the interesting stories either happened a long time ago, or someone made them up recently."

She was about to say something, when a sneeze interrupted her train of thought.

"Look, just to show you what a flexible, understanding guy I am, I'll go first. If you're still awake when I'm through, then it'll be your turn. And if you fall asleep, I promise I won't be insulted. Deal?" He could see this last ploy of his had won her over.

"Deal," she answered, with a big smile; this time, she did offer to shake hands.

"First piece of information: I was born on December 15th, in the middle of the night, and, the way my old man tells it, in the middle of a storm. Still, you can see there's nothing particularly stormy about me. Year? 1935. Place? I don't know if you know, but one generation back in Uruguay, there was an almost infallible law: anyone who lived in Montevideo had to be from the Interior. Nowadays, though, we're all born in Montevideo. My family lives on a street called Solano García. You wouldn't know it. It's in Punta Carretas. That still means nothing to you? O.K., just think of it as near the water. I was a disgrace as a boy. I was an only child, and sick all the time too. Always sick. I had the measles three times—that should tell you everything. And scarlet fever, whooping cough, German measles. And the mumps. If I wasn't coming down with something, I was getting over something else. Even when people said I looked fine, I was always blowing my nose."

He talked a little more about his childhood, (school days, a cute teacher, teasing cousins, a doting aunt, a bellyache from eating merengues that smelled like mothballs, never understanding how grownups functioned, etc...), but when he tried to go on to the next stage, he realized for the first time that all the halfway interesting things in his life had happened to him as a kid. He decided to go for broke and be straight with her, so he told her just that.

Mirta responded in kind: "You're not going to believe this, but I don't have any stories to tell. It's almost like I have no memories. Because my wicked stepmother and those classic beatings of hers hardly qualify as memories (to be honest, they really weren't that bad); neither do the two or three boring friends I made in the neighborhood, my spotty record at school (where I was never good at anything, and never tried to be), or the time I spent behind a counter in Buenos Aires, on Corrientes, selling pens and pencils. In fact, the best time of my life has probably been right here in Paris, even though I get frustrated and lonely sometimes, and I never have any money."

As she spoke, her eyes were focused on the opposite platform. In spite of the dim light, Raúl could see they were full of tears. And spontaneously—so spontaneously that when he tried to stop, it was too late—, he reached out and stroked her cheek. Oddly enough, she didn't seem surprised. In fact, for a few seconds there, he thought he felt her press her cheek against the palm of his hand. It was as if these unusual circumstances had changed all the old rules. He withdrew his hand and they just sat there for a moment, without a word. An occasional rattle, or rumble, or thud from the far-off amorphous street over their heads reminded them it was still there.

Suddenly he said, "I have a fiance in Montevideo. She's a nice girl, but I haven't seen her in two years now; and I'm not sure how to put this, but her image keeps getting vaguer, less and less coherent. Like I can picture her eyes, but not her ears, or her lips. If I go by what my eyes remember, I'm sure her lips are thin; but if I go by what my fingers tell me, they were thick. What a mess, huh?"

She didn't answer. He got a little more direct: "Do you have a boyfriend, or a husband, or guys you go out with?"

"No."

"Not here, not in Mendoza, and not in Buenos Aires either?"

"Nowhere."

He looked down and saw a one franc coin laying on the floor. He bent over, picked it up and gave it to Mirta. "Keep it as a souvenir of this Stille Nacht." She put it in the pocket of his raincoat, forgetting it wasn't hers. He rubbed his face with both hands.

"Actually, why should I lie to you. She's not my fiance; she's my wife. But all the rest is true. I'm fed up with that relationship, but I don't have the guts to break it off. Whenever I write her a letter hinting that I'd like to, she answers with these long, hysterical tirades saying she'll kill herself if I leave her; that's blackmail of course, but what if she does it? I guess I'm more of a coward than I seem. Or do I look like one too?"

"No. Down here I'd say you look pretty brave. Especially compared to me; I'm the one who's trembling."

The next time he looked at his watch, it was four twenty. For the last half hour, they had hardly said a word; but he had stretched out on that great big bench, and his head was resting on Mirta's soft black purse. Once in a while, she'd run her fingers through his hair: "It's so unruly," she'd say. Nothing else. Raúl couldn't get over how wonderfully wacky the whole situation was turning out to be. He knew things were fine as they were, but he also knew that if he tried to take them any further and turn this unique and unexpected meeting into a trivial one night stand, it would fall apart. At a quarter to five, he got up and walked around a little, to stretch his legs. Then he looked at her, and that was something like a revelation. If he had been working on one of those tidy, doggedly unsentimental stories of his, he would never have dared write anything as corny as "He and Mirta were meant for one another." But, luckily, he wasn't writing, and he had absolutely no problem thinking that he and Mirta were meant for one another. Then he sighed, a sigh that sounded like a beginning.

What came next was more than a state of mind; it was an organic exaltation that exploded through his whole body, ears, throat, lungs, heart, stomach, sex and knees.

He felt so moved, so exhilarated, that he broke the silence. "You know something? I'd give five years of my life if I could start all over, right here and now. I mean, if I were divorced from my wife, and she hadn't killed herself; and I had a good job in Paris; and when they opened the station again, we could walk out of here as what we really are: a couple."

From where she was sitting on the bench, she made a vague gesture, as if she were trying to shoo away a ghost, and said, "I'd give five years, too." Then she added, "Don't worry, we'll manage somehow."

The first sign that the station was coming back to life was a cold draft. They both sneezed. Then the lights came on. Raúl held the mirror while she made herself presentable. He ran a comb through his hair too. On their way up the stairs, they bumped into the first stampede of early risers. He was thinking that he hadn't even kissed her, and wondering if he hadn't been too discreet. Outside, it wasn't as cold as the night before.

With no prior discussion, they both headed down Boulevard Bonne Nouvelle toward the Post Office. "Now what?" asked Mirta. Raúl felt as though she had taken the words right out of his mouth; but he didn't get a chance to answer. A girl in black pants and a green sweater was waving at them from across the street. Raúl thought it might be a friend of Mirta's. Mirta thought it might be an acquaintance of Raúl's. When she finally managed to cross the street, the girl ran up to them, saying energetically, with a Mexican accent: "It's about time, you idiots! I've been calling the apartment all night. Where were you? Raúl, I need to borrow your Appleton. Or is it yours, Mirta?"

They just stood there in silence. But the girl insisted: "Come on! Don't be mean. I need a good dictionary; I have a translation to do. What do you say? Look, don't just stand there like two bumps on a log; or should I say two morons? Are you on your way home? Come on; I'll go with you." And she started walking down Mazagran toward Rue de L'Echiquier, swinging her hips in rhythm with her footsteps. Raúl and Mirta followed her without a word or a touch, each in their own world. The new girl turned the corner and stopped in front of number eight. All three of them climbed the stairs (no elevator) to the fourth floor. At the door to apartment seven, the girl asked:

"Well, are you going to let us in or not?"

Carefully, Raúl took his old key ring off his belt loop and noticed that the usual three keys were still there. He tried the first; it didn't work. He tried the second, and the door opened. The girl rushed over to the bookcase near the window and whisked the Appleton out of it. She kissed Raúl, then Mirta, on both cheeks, and said:

"I hope that by tonight you two have gotten your tongues back. Don't forget, we all promised to be at Emilia's. Bring records!" And out she shot, slamming the door.

Mirta collapsed into the wicker chair. Raúl inspected the apartment with a worried frown, in silence. In the bookcase he found his own books, dog-eared and marked up in his handwriting; but also some new ones with still-uncut pages. He saw his favorite Miró poster hanging on the back wall, but also the Klee he'd always wanted. There were three photos on the table: one of his parents; one of a man who looked suspiciously like Mirta; and one of him and Mirta, rolling around in the snow in each others' arms and, apparently, having a great time.

Since that girl had showed up looking for the Appleton, he hadn't dared look Mirta in the eyes. But now he did; the gaze that met his own was cloudless—a little tired, perhaps, but calm. However, that didn't do her much good, since just then it dawned on Raúl; not only that he should never have divorced the wife he left in Montevideo (hysterical but smart, moody but well-stacked), but also that his second marriage was starting to come apart. It wasn't that he didn't love the slender, thin-blooded, almost helpless woman looking up at him from the wicker chair. But it was clear now that little remained of the naive, prodigious, explosion of feelings from that incredible night five years ago—now just a fading memory—when he first met Mirta, after fate played a trick on them and locked them up together in the Bonne Nouvelle station.

1967

Translated by Maya Gross

The Other Side

1

I'm not sure why, but when my folks showed up at Carrasco to see me off, and especially when I looked back on my way to the plane and saw them waving to me from up there on the observation deck, together but apart, my old lady with her knuckles on her glasses, most likely going after a big teardrop, and me too, dammit, rubbing one eye with my free hand; anyhow, when I saw them there, two people with absolutely nothing in common—except me, that is, and probably I'm the only reason they stayed together—something hit me from out of the blue, something that happened so long ago that at first I wasn't sure it happened at all. But yes it did, because later, on the plane—which is to say, right now, sitting here in row nine (next to the emergency exit, where there's more room for these long legs God gave me)—I start rounding out that little piece of my past, firming it up with details, till now I've gotten most of it back, and I realize what a good beginning it will make for this notebook that maybe no one will ever read; or maybe someone will. And this is how it went: my family was having lunch, or rather the grownups were, my old man, my old lady (who weren't quite as old, back then), my grandfather, my uncle, and maybe somebody else; I must have been four or five at the time, and I was tearing around on a brand new tricycle, back and forth between the house and the yard, making a sound with my mouth that was supposed to be the horn on the intercity bus, and my father was signaling to me not to make such a racket, but I was just ignoring him. So suddenly here he comes, and right in the middle of one of my best blasts, he grabs me by one ear, and it hurt so much, I can remember seeing all the way to Orion (though at the time, I didn't know the constellations by name). It wasn't like me to want to get even—it's still not—but for some reason, because of whatever I was feeling, or maybe just for the heck of it, I very casually left my tricycle by the front door, pulled up a chair, sat down next to my uncle, and clobbered my old man with the following surprise announcement: "Last night I peeked under the table, and your legs and Clarita's were touching." I'll never forget the look on my mother's face; her eyes were this big. My father just sat there, tight-lipped, with a look of terrible resignation. Almost like he was the Antichrist, commanding, "Forbid the little children to come unto me," or, who knows, maybe what was going through his mind was, "You rotten little shit." In any case, the two of them didn't say a word to each other for about three months after that. Mama would talk to me, instead: "Tell your father to give you money for milk." And Papa used the same tactic: "Tell your mother I won't be home for supper tonight." Of course, Clarita never set foot in our home–sweet–home again, and today I'm inclined to think my father really liked her; she was maybe ten years younger than he was, and five years younger than Mama, thin, blond, with calm, greenish eyes and a dreamy face—but good dreams, not nightmares—and these smooth, slender hands with little bluish veins that were almost invisible, but everyone noticed them anyway, even a stupid five-year-old like yours truly (or was I six?). Because you really have to be stupid to mess up your old man's life with a dumb remark like that. Especially when Clarita seemed to like my old man, too. She probably just felt intimidated by my mother, who couldn't stand her from day one. And it wasn't just jealousy or suspicion on Mama's part; it was this out and out hatred she had cultivated slowly and deliberately.

By the time the stewardess shows up with the usual tray of Cokes, I'm deep into *mea culpas*. I can't get it out of my skull that by butting into my old man's business like that I had screwed up his life for good. Because, even before Clarita, he and Mama didn't get along very well. I'd almost say they didn't get along at all. I've never seen two people with so little in common, so made "not for each other." My old man was always a warm, sensitive guy (though a little too shy for my taste), and about as cultured as a quasi-engineer can be (which isn't saying much, but it's more than you can say for a real engineer). He's always been a big reader; likes painting and music; and, luckily, unlike some of his quasi–colleagues, he doesn't think life is a logarithm. Mama, on the other hand, is pretty stubborn (objectively speaking, which is something devoted sons aren't allowed to do, I'd have to say she's stubborn as a mule); bone dry when it comes to feelings (she only cares about her own problems, never anyone else's); proud of her encyclopedic ignorance; allergic to books and anything to do with the arts; good with her hands; basically not such a bad person (though in her case, getting down to basics takes a lot of digging); more inclined to criticize than accept; in short: a tough nut to crack. I think two things stood between my father and true liberation (also known as second childhood): a) my under–the–table investigation, which doomed a promising relationship from the start; and b) my progenitor's incorrigible Catholicism, thanks to which the divorce that could have saved and redeemed him was never even a remote possibility. Judging by my vague recollections, Clarita was cheerful, pretty, and so charming she even had me on her side. It's occurred to me more than once, now that I'm past my seventeenth birthday (which, as a matter of fact, I spent honorably, in jail), that I wouldn't mind meeting, not Clarita, of course, since by now, if she's still alive she must be an old lady of thirty–eight, but a pretty little woman just like Clarita used to be, back in the days when she rubbed those gorgeous legs of hers against my old man's trousers under the table.

2

What's happened these past several months must be one of the few things that ever brought my parents together. To make a long story short, I was in prison. That's why they got so emotional at the airport, once they finally managed to send me off to Buenos Aires. I know that's a load off their minds. Mine, too. I hope I never see a prison again, not even in the movies. As far as I'm concerned, from now on there are just two kinds of movies: with prisons and without—and I have no intention of seeing the first kind. Just thirty-four days, and I've had it with prisons. I've exhausted the subject, you might say. But lest any of you (who are you, anyway?) be inclined to stick any fancy labels on me, I want to make it perfectly clear that I didn't get arrested for my political beliefs, but just because I'm an idiot. I hate like hell to admit it, but that's the goddamn truth: I got arrested because I'm a dope. In fact, I had never done anything political in my life. Some of my classmates stayed away from politics because they really liked studying, and politics takes up a lot of time. But I don't like to study. You can say anything about me, except that I'm a grind. That made me the only surviving example in my class of a species on the verge of extinction: a student who doesn't like studying or politics. I should also make it clear that I wasn't a hopeless case; I never had to repeat a grade. I just never studied any more than I absolutely had to. To be more accurate, mostly I got by just listening to the teachers spout off. Luckily for me, facts, dates, formulas and names all seem to stick in my head. Don't assume, either, that I just don't give a damn when it comes to politics. It's not that. If I'm against math, how could I not be against fascism? I don't like anyone pushing me around, much less with a machine gun. That should be obvious. What I don't appreciate about political activists are the endless discussions where nothing ever comes to a vote till the next morning; and especially that awful self-criticism that reminds me too much of my distant and anguished attempts at confession, which I was never fond of either. And not because I've ever had anything to hide. I just never had anything big enough for confession, or for one of those self-criticism sessions. Maybe that's why I don't like them. Maybe I envy those guys who enjoy telling some flabbergasted priest about their mortal sins, or displaying their nasty *petit bourgeois* tendencies at a student meeting. Anyway, I didn't get arrested (I repeat) for any good reason, but for being an idiot. It so happens that Thursday the 22nd was the one-year anniversary of Merceditas Pombo's death. You may have seen that name in the newspapers (not in Montevideo, but in Baires); she was this really great kid who died on them while she was being tortured. The story is, they gave her the dry submarine, and she had asthma, and asthma and a plastic bag over your head don't go too well together, so.... Anyway, we had this idea (originally, it was

Eduardo's), and little by little it gathered momentum until finally we worked out a scenario: that Thursday we were each supposed to show up with one red rose to leave on the teacher's desk. The whole thing was planned in secret. Since I never did anything political, they left me for last. But I agreed to do it just the same. I'll go along with anything if you spare me those endless meetings, and the early morning votes, and the self–criticism. Besides, I liked the idea of bringing a red rose. It was—how can I put it—a poetic act, really inspired. So, I brought the rose, which of course, I swiped from a nearby garden belonging to an R. L., which stands for Retired Lieutenant (clarification for ignoramuses). Everyone brought their roses and put them on the teacher's desk. Not one of us backed down. So then, they took all of us out of the classrooms, and made us stand at attention in the central courtyard, against the wall. Was it our fault they had no feeling for poetry? Next, the goon squad arrived with the foreseeable question: whose idea was it? We all knew it was Eduardo's, but nobody said a word. What a beautiful silence that was! So then they started calling us into the custodian's office, in groups of five, for questioning. And that's where I slipped up like an idiot. In my group, I was the first one to be questioned. The guy asked me if I knew whose idea it was to bring the roses. And I told him my rose was my idea, but I didn't know whose idea the other roses were. I thought answering like that was a real smart move. But I was wrong. Because the next guy said the same thing: his rose was his idea, and he didn't know whose idea the other roses were. And so did the other three. And I don't know how word got out to the courtyard so fast, but when the next five kids got their turn, they gave the same answer, and so did all the rest. After a while we got really tired and started letting our guard down; I could see some of the others waving to me, giving me the thumbs up, even applauding. Now, mind you, I'm no hero; but I must admit, I was pretty pleased with myself. It had been so easy. I don't know where I got the idea, but it worked! Except now the goons had my number: since I was the first one to answer that way, they must have figured I was a ringleader or something. They called me back in. "So you're the intellectual author," says this guy with a thin moustache and a really gross rash under one eye. I start to tell him I only meant to bring the teacher a rose, because she was so nice, and so good at her subject, which happened to be math, no less. That's what you'd call a white lie, because I really never understood a thing the old bag said and besides, I hated her, not for anything she did to me, just for teaching math. Then this character with the moustache, who obviously doesn't find my brilliant explanation the least bit convincing, hauls off and belts me on the right cheek, which immediately blows up like a balloon. To be sure, that little detail would have puffed up my prestige out in the courtyard, and with it my pride; but before word could get out, two of the interrogators grabbed me by the arms and dragged me out of the custodian's office. And from there to the paddywagon, and straight down to Headquarters. From the outset, I made it clear that I was a minor and therefore...(punch in the stomach)...what they were doing was illegal...(kick in the ankle). Ergo: I quit reminding them how old I was. They put me in this revolting little cell; the smell of shit just about knocked me flat. During the month I spent there, they took me out several times, just to work me over. They almost never asked me any questions; all they did was beat the shit out of me. No electric prod, no submarine; just kicks and punches. What you'd call the red carpet treatment. I think they were trying to soften me up. And I was pretty scared. Who wouldn't be? The ones they put through the "machine" weren't minors like me, but they weren't that much older either. Except for one guy. I don't know if he had white hair or not, because he always had a hood on, but you could tell who was over thirty–four by their flabby asses. And that old guy was one tough bird! The younger ones didn't talk—didn't admit to anything, or give any information—but they screamed like hell when they got tortured. The old guy, though, he wasn't about to give them that satisfaction. I don't even know what kind of voice he had, because he'd just clench his fists, and that was that. He never passed out either; at the end of those sessions—and sometimes they lasted for hours—he'd actually walk out on his own. One of the others passed out, and apparently never came to. That makes them furious. The worst thing a prisoner can do is die on them. They get the doctor right in there to revive him. And that S.O.B. (the same one who tells them how far they can go, before a prisoner croaks) does whatever he can, but sometimes the dead guy is stubborn, and nobody can get him to start breathing again. Then those monsters cuss out the doctor, who doesn't say boo, because of course he knows he might be next. In the meantime, they're dumping buckets of water on the dead guy's head, and slapping him around to see if he'll react; it's the only time they seem to come down on the side of life. But some prisoners really screw them by dying. That's when the goons all start blaming each other. One day, two of them got into a fist fight; I swear I thought they'd use the cattle prod on each other, but of course everything has its limits. For the most part they kept me hooded; they only took off my hood when there was something they wanted me to see. A few times I vomited, once all over an interrogator's pants. I didn't do it on purpose, but it wasn't a bad move. I had to pay for it, of course. That was the night they really gave it to me; I thought I'd end up in the machine for sure, but I didn't. They must've had instructions: only punches and kicks for minors. A few times, I was able to talk to two guys in the next cell. I was alone in mine, and it was tiny and stank of shit, but theirs was bigger, so the shit smell was even worse. I think there were, maybe, three of them in there: a student, a bank clerk, and a worker. As soon as they felt a little better and started breathing normally again, they'd get into another political argument: about the party, the struggle, *petit bourgeois* distortions and deviations, revisionism, and on, and on, and on. Just like at those school meetings. Sometimes their arguments got so violent, you could hear them shouting all over the place. I never understood shit about what they were saying; I still don't. But when it came to the machine, all three of them got pretty much the same deal. As far as the pigs were concerned, they were all the same—*pueblo*. The pigs don't discriminate, that's for sure.

I was there for a whole month. No visitors. Just one change of clothes. No books. At one point, I was afraid they'd bring me a math book, just to torture me a little more. But they didn't even give me that. Between one kick and the next, one punch and the next, I was bored sick. Of course, boredom was definitely preferable to a pain in my liver or aching balls. One afternoon I was sure they had broken my leg, but the swelling went down in a week. At first, they asked me a few questions, but after that they just knocked me around. Still, there's something else I have to admit to: just like I got arrested for being a moron, I think they let me go for being a moron. I was consistent: I always stuck with my original story, and my poetic reason for bringing that rose. I don't think they believed it. What they must have thought is that I was either a total mongoloid, or at least a borderline retard. Or maybe what did the trick was that chat my old man had with an R. C. (Retired Colonel, for ignoramuses) he knew from back home in Paysandú. Though not necessarily, mostly because that colonel's in jail now, so he couldn't have had too much pull. Or maybe he's even a subversive himself. Since I heard how they nabbed Father Barrientos after they found a hideout in the vestry, nothing surprises me anymore. No wonder that guy liked the "Song of Songs" so much. You can be sure he didn't get busted for being an idiot. Anyway, one morning they took off my hood; they made two wisecracks that naturally had me a little worried, and returned my ballpoint pen, a package of condoms, my billfold and my belt, all of which they had confiscated the first day. On the other hand, nobody mentioned the gold watch my grandfather gave me. I was almost dumb enough to ask about it, but a quick look around kept me from fucking up again: there it was, all bright and shiny, on the wrist of the muscle-bound jerk who was letting me out.

3

To be honest, I really like Buenos Aires. And it's not that I'm comparing it to being in prison; anything would be better than that. But I'm not sure I'd like it as much if I were here as a tourist. Wow! It's got plazas! Wow! It's got trees! Wow! It's got big stores! (I dedicate the *Wow* to my old lady.) It may be a little too high-pressured for my taste, but I still think it's cool. Wow! It's got posters! Wow! It's even got a subway! And wow! Does it have girls! I've never seen such well–dressed women. But come to think of it, this is my first time out of the "silver cup of the River Plate." Now, there's a name for Montevideo; I wonder what sentimental slob dreamed that one up. Silver cup, my ass! These days, it's more like a tin spittoon; but hell, I guess there's no reason to walk around shouting about it. Wow! Baires has buses! It doesn't have beaches, though. That's really a bummer. Still, I like this city. The only thing that makes me uncomfortable is when they "exchange fire;" as soon as I hear that rata–tat–tat, I run into a mall and check out the shops. Around here, you're never too far from a mall. Pretty lucky, right? Yesterday, I saw La Presidenta passing by. She was sitting up very straight, just like a dummy in a store window. Why is it that whenever I think of dummies, I remember my old man's stories about the ones at Casa Spera. That was a men's tailor shop back in Monte, on Sarandí, right across from the Cathedral. It seems they had these positively ancient mannequins; and the way my old man tells it, even when their faces were painted to make them look young, you could still tell they dated all the way back to the days when Viera was President, and El Negro Gradín was racking up goal after goal, and the Plus Ultra flew all the way from Madrid to Monte, and the Oxford Carnival troupe was just getting started. Besides, he said, no matter what clothes they put on those dummies, they never looked right; the fat one always had on a small jacket, and vice versa. Anyway, La Presidenta looked just like a mannequin, but from Christian Dior, not (God forbid!) Casa Spera.

I'm spending most of my time these days checking out the streets. They're all new to me. Sometimes, I get on the subway and pick a station to get off at. Like maybe I decide I'll go as far as the first station that starts with a V; but then I get stuck, because I get all the way to the end of the line at Lacroze, and it turns out there was no station that started with a V. And around Lacroze there's not much to see, either. So then I catch on, and the next time I decide I'll get off at the first stop that starts with a C, because that's an easier letter; and I get on another line and get off at Congreso, which turns out to be a stroke of genius, because I emerge from the depths and I'm right downtown, where there's lots of action and a million stores and all these people, just the way I like it. And I walk home by way of Callao looking in store windows and checking out all the babes, but without making the most of the experience, because to do that you need dough; and I'm pretty broke, which is to say all I have are the few pesos my folks gave me at Carrasco the day I left. But that's O.K. with me, because my old man hadn't gotten his salary (be advised that engineers get fees, but quasi–engineers only get salaries), and my old lady had to ask Uncle Felipe for a loan before she could even pay for my plane ticket. And besides, it took me a few days to find out where the cheap food is, because sometimes you can get pretty lost around here, and just when you're feeling down and out, you spot this little restaurant that looks like a real dive, and you think, O.K., but it's not, because every once in a while some big cheese like Palito Ortega or Leonardo Favio drops by, so they soak all the other customers and rightly so, because nobody goes there for the food, they're all just after autographs, or the latest gossip, so what are they bitching about? Anyhow, I make my way calmly along Callao, among other reasons because by walking and walking, then turning right and then left, I found this pizza parlor that looks crappy and (lucky for me) really is, which means nobody famous ever goes there, just the usual plain folks: saleswomen in orange uniforms with little brown collars, and an assortment of office workers who shuffle papers while they eat. And of course, the pizza is nothing like what you get in Capri (at least, in all those Hollywood movies set in Capri), and maybe that's why I'm still burping it up the next morning. It can't even begin to compare with the pizza we used to get at Tasende's, back in Monte, where the whole gang always went after class, hoofing it the whole thirty blocks together to save on the trolley.

But I never make it to the pizza parlor because just as I'm crossing Cangallo on the red light (after all, I have my principles), I hear my name pronounced by this hoarse female voice which turns out to belong to Señora Acuña, once a close friend of my mother's, and still a friend, albeit not close, who's here in this "gorgeous city" on a shopping spree, taking advantage of the favorable exchange rate, as she puts it, "before those thieves wise up again and devaluate." She's here with her husband and the girls, her *nenas*, one of them my age and the other her own. And the one who's my age is a Libra, like me; and she's the stupid exception that confirms the intelligent rule. As for Señor Acuña, he looks so exhausted it's almost contagious; and he's being very sure to let out a little snort every so often, so his legal wife will realize what a huge sacrifice he's making. I say "legal wife," because I know who his mistress is, and he knows I know: I once saw the two of them getting out of a taxi at a drive-through hotel on Rivera, and his mistress wasn't so bad, the old guy's no idiot, so obviously that *nena* of his doesn't take after him. Anyhow, when Señora Acuña said I'd have to have dinner with them, so I could tell them all about those prisons I was in (I don't know why she made that plural), and they weren't about to let me off the hook, I said sure, because since Señor Acuña knows that I know, I figured he wasn't about to be tight when it came to ordering. The daughter who's not my age, but her own, and whose name I caught as being Sonia, refuses to quit smiling at me; and I hate it when people smile at me because I turn red and that's never good. So I start staring stubbornly at the one who's my age, and who's stupid, and whose name is Dorita; because since she makes me so nauseous I could puke, I figure I'll turn as white as a corpse, and that'll compensate for the beet red color I must be right now, because Sonia won't stop smiling. And since I'm looking back and forth from one *nena* to the other, my cheeks, my nose and my forehead eventually get back their natural color, which, as I just explained, I've carefully manufactured. Señora Acuña is still going on about the "prisons" I was in; so with all due modesty, I make it clear that there was only one, and I have no intention of making it plural. Señor Acuña, who knows I know, laughs as hard as if that line had come straight out of "Hupumorpo," just so he can stay in good with me and cover his ass. He obviously doesn't realize I might be a blackmailer, but I'm no demagogue, so I'm not about to borrow material from a TV show. Still, when Sonia asks me in a shaky voice if I got tortured, I really go into detail about what they did to me, nonchalantly, of course, since there's no better way to make something sound important. So then, Dorita puts her hand on my arm (nausea, cold sweat, etc.), and the fingers of Sonia's right hand start moving; but unfortunately, she's too far away to touch me. So as to overcome the tension I'm feeling, I dive into my melon and prosciutto, steak and fries, and caramel ice cream (two scoops), all washed down with two huge pints of foamy beer. To make a long story short, Señor Acuña very wisely picked up the tab, thus making our tacit agreement official.

4

Good God! My pension has bedbugs and cockroaches, and the walls sweat. So do I. And there's only one bathroom for all seven rooms, which really amounts to one for six, because the seventh room is being used by this young French couple who aren't exactly shower fiends. He has a mane that smells like beef stew, and she has open sandals that give public opinion a full frontal view of her jet black toenails. But even without the Frenchies, the bathroom problem is pretty serious. Because there may be only six rooms competing for the shower, but when it comes to defecatory needs, we're back up to seven. Those Frogs may not take baths, but they sure empty their bowels with European regularity. To put it another way, my room's not affiliated with the Hilton or the Sheraton chain, but (get ready to laugh) with the Toilet chain! Too bad I didn't think that one up while I was with Señor Acuña and his holy family. Him being so sharp and all, I'm sure he would have laughed his head off because of what he knows I know. Anyway, as I was saying, there's lots of action at this pensión (appropriately named *Hirondelle*, since the owner says her guests are migratory birds). Let's be clear about this: when I say action, what I mean is it's nuts. The guy in room 3, for instance, is a petty thief. He demands to be called "Pickpocket," since he belongs to the British school of petty thievery, but that's too long for a nickname, so everyone calls him Pick, or even Picky; and that makes him mad, because he claims Picky's a dog's name, but he's stuck with it anyway, because by now, it's part of what my history prof used to call "oral tradition." In room 4 there's a young couple, with whose repertoire of amorous noises I'm intimately acquainted through no choice of my own (I live in room 5); in her particular case, they're nothing short of stereophonic, so I end up picturing her with no clothes on far more often than I'd like. Her husband, or whatever he is, is fully aware of that intolerable situation. But instead of feeling sorry for me, he keeps pulling my leg by bringing it up whenever I run into him in the hall: "Che, you look even more dazed today than yesterday; what's up?" I swear at him silently, out of respect for his sonorous ladyfriend, while he cackles like Woody Woodpecker.

The Frenchies live in room 6. Their aroma sometimes filters through the cracks in the wall; but I've got to admit, they never make venereal noises. Other kinds, yes, since he's been known to play the guitar while both of them sing protest songs, in a version of Spanish that comes straight from their tonsils. Those two mind their own business. If they smelled a little better, I might even like them.

In room 7 there are two kids, hell, two girls, who never seem to do anything but pound a typewriter. Sometimes I wake up so early, that all I can hear are shrieking sirens and that machine of theirs. What on earth can they be writing?

Rooms 1 and 2 don't count, because the owner of the *pensión* uses them as her private quarters. Her name is Rosa, Doña Rosa. What we know about her (and really can't help knowing, since she discusses it in detail two or three times a week) is that she's a widow, and her husband was a Peronista from back in Evita's days. Once when she figured she could trust me, she lowered her voice and revealed, in a secretive tone: "If he were alive today, he'd be something else, you get me?"

5

I really need a job, because I'm almost out of scratch, and I can't rely on what my folks send me, which will never amount to much, anyway. I've already checked out two or three stores around Plaza Once that ran want ads in *Clarín*. But as soon as they find out I'm not a resident, I get this very touching thumbs down. I'm even skimping on cigarettes, but I think that's a senseless sacrifice. Besides, sometimes when I get an uncontrollable urge to smoke, I don't have any. Thank goodness, yesterday I ran into little Diego; I spent the whole damn night bumming cigarettes off him. He had to hightail it out of the country too. Of course, he had a much worse time than I did, because he got arrested for more prestigious reasons, not for being stupid like me. They picked him up twice (the first time spray-painting anti-military slogans on the walls of the Buceo Cemetery, and the second with a flier on him that wasn't exactly pro-government). Both times they really worked him over, electric prod and all; both times he didn't make a peep, and they finally let him go. But then he thought: "Once more, and I've had it," and beat it across the river.

I hardly knew him, because he was about four years older than I was, and he was always involved in something political. "So you blew it too," he said, such a sweet guy.... "I'd never have guessed from the way you always took care of yourself." It's hard to explain to a guy like that, who's been burned more times than the Phoenix, why I never wanted anything to do with politics. I tried, but he just didn't get it: "Excuses, kiddo, nothing but excuses." It really burns me up to hear some little turd, who's barely four years older than I am, call me "kiddo" in that condescending tone of voice. "O.K., O.K. But what do you intend to do about it now?" I ask him what he thinks I can do, in the middle of all this chaos. I don't know what made me say "chaos." "There's always something you can do," he says. I tell him what I have do first is find a job. "Sure, you're right. I've started working. If you want me to, I'll help you." Of course I want him to. I copy down a name and address. I'm to go there tomorrow. "Now come with me." We walk about twenty blocks. I would have taken a bus, but he says when you're leading a sedentary life, walking is good for the circulation. My uncle Felipe, who's a naturist, is always coming out with the same old lines. Finally we stop in front of a tall building. We go up to the fifteenth floor. A guy with long hair and beads lets us in. There are about fifteen people there, all young. They're arguing about something, but I can't figure out what. The jargon goes right over my head; I can't make out a single word. In a corner, there's this girl who's hardly saying anything. She looks bored, but she's the one who says to me: "Are you getting tired of this?" I shrug my shoulders, and maybe that looks like a yes, because she says: "Come with me," and takes off down a hallway. I follow her and we go up a carpeted staircase. This is no ordinary apartment; it's a penthouse. The staircase leads into another hallway, and the hallway into a garden. Yes, a garden, with trees and all, on the fifteenth floor! It also has chairs, tables, and what must be a hot-weather couch. "Come on," she says again and sits down on the hot-weather couch. I do too, and for the first time, I take a good look at her; then, just in case, I smile. She's got darkish skin, dark hair and beautiful dark eyes. She's probably my age, or maybe a little older. Her top has a plunging neckline. Not bad. "Do you like me?" she asks, matter-of-factly. By now, my smile might be looking a little depraved. There's something motherly about her face, and I've always had a soft spot for mothers. "As a matter of fact I do, especially if this is just the beginning." She lets out a guffaw, then without even unbuttoning her jacket, since there's enough room, puts a hand down her blouse and pulls out this naked little tit. I feel like I'm entitled to help her, but she stops me short. "Now, don't go getting any ideas. Anyway, today we can't. I'm having a visitor, get it?" And since she can see I'm disappointed, she adds: "Sorry. I only did it because you were looking so bored." Then she tucks her little tit away.

6

The address Diego gave me is a publishing house, presumably leftist. This time they hire me, in spite of my official tourist status. "We'll find a way to deal with that," says the manager. "The main thing is that you start working, because I assume you've got to eat, or am I wrong?" I tell him of course he's right, and he offers me a pretty good salary, especially considering I'm here under somewhat unusual circumstances. I thank him, and he says the least Argentinians can do, after so many of them have been in exile in

Uruguay, is offer us their solidarity now that we're in hot water. "When I was a kid, my old man spent about two years in Montevideo, peddling the *empanadas* he made, and people were always helping him out." You can't imagine how overjoyed I was to hear that my fellow Uruguayans gave his *porteño* father a hand. Besides which, I got the wildest craving for *empanadas*. Actually, that happens to me fairly often: somebody mentions something to eat—say, a dessert, or a flavor of ice cream—and I want it so badly my stomach starts churning. At those times, I'd give anything to get hold of the food in question, but since I almost never have any dough, the craving is as far as I get. And really, that's not such a catastrophe; since it's one of the things that comes with being a have-not, it's teaching me about class struggle.

For the time being, what I'm doing at the publishing house is correcting proofs. I once did that as a stand-in for someone back in Monte. But I got fired unjustly for letting a typo slip through that the author considered gross, degrading and inappropriate: venereal for *venerable*. I don't think it was such a big deal. I guess intellectuals are hypersensitive, by definition. Let's hope they're not that squeamish around here.

Since I've already started my new job, I wrote to Mama to tell her they can relax: I'm not about to starve to death. On the other hand, I can't swear I won't get killed by a car, trying to make it across the umpteen lanes of traffic on Libertador, or by a stray bullet from one of those shootouts that make this metropolis such a delightful place. Actually, I threw all that in to give them a few extra things to worry about, since their relationship only seems to improve when they're anxious about something.

I often run into neighbors from across the river. Although maybe I shouldn't call them that. I find it a little scary that for us Uruguayans, people from Baires are "neighbors," but the *porteños* never refer to us that way. Especially to the sports commentators on the radio, we're always "the other side." Here in Baires, they never use the phrase "beyond the River Plate" either, so I guess no *porteño* could write about sports for the Montevideo papers.

Almost all the Uruguayans I've run into and/or met in Baires have jobs, though very few have more or less permanent housing, and I know at least one who doesn't have a passport or a national I.D. card. I was too tactful to ask him how he got into the country. He could have lost them, of course. A friend walks me past the Uruguayan consulate, and just to play it safe, I cross over to the other side of the street. In that neighborhood, there are an awful lot of faces I recognize from back in Monte; but I'd much rather point my ravishing eyes in some other cardinal direction, since most of them belong to the informers we used to spot in the downtown cafés. Good old Diego, who's on the ball as usual, warns me to stay out of the cafés and pizza parlors on Corrientes, especially between the Obelisk and Callao; it seems there are so many Uruguayan plainclothesmen running around loose in those places, they've even started spying on each other. That's too bad; because I really like Corrientes, especially at night.

Since I know I'll be getting a salary, I loosen up a little on my budget and buy a pack of cigarettes. Mama's always telling me if I keep on smoking like this, I'll die of lung cancer just like my grandfather; but considering he kicked the bucket at age 81, I figure I've got another 64 years to go, so why get nervous now, a little caution is fine, but let's not overdo it. Besides, what if they kidnap me or shoot me full of holes next week (knock wood!), and I end up in Purgatory, before I've even had a chance to enjoy this pack? So, in the next half hour, I go through more cigarettes than three bats put together. I threw in the line about the bats, just to keep things nice and colloquial: I've never even seen one bat smoke, much less three. What I really should have said is "more than three monkeys put together," since whether they're in the dictionary of idioms or not, there definitely are monkeys who smoke; I can vouch for that personally, since I happen to know of one at the Villa Dolores Zoo back in Monte, and another one here in Palermo, and this second one would even use his mate's hand as an ashtray, masochistic little monkey that she was.

When Doña Rosa hears I finally have a job, she's so excited that she gives me a chaste, sweaty kiss on each cheek. Since the sonorous lady is hogging the bathroom, I have to wait a whole thirty-eight minutes to wash my face. Of course, Doña Rosa didn't do it on purpose but still, it's a pain in the ass. At least she's a good person, though in my opinion, when she gets worked up about something, she goes a little overboard. Personally, I don't find much to get worked up about these days. Even the soccer games are pathetic. I have a feeling the reason we and the *porteños* are so crazy about each other lately, is that misery loves company, and it's a tossup as to whose teams are playing worse. But Doña Rosa turns out to be a Vélez fan, and that's really the limit. She can't even root for a heavy duty team like Boca or River! She'll listen to a whole game on the radio, then at night, she'll watch all the goals again on TV; and that's even weirder, considering those goals are mostly scored by the other team, against Vélez! Masochist number two. That's why I let her give me all those chaste, sweaty kisses on the cheeks, so she'll have another outlet for her enthusiasm. Anyway, when the sonorous lady finally gets out of the bathroom, I go in and wash off the gunk.

7

I'm enjoying my job quite a bit, at least this first week. To date, nobody's complained. True, by the end of the afternoon my skull feels like some kind of rattle. Brain burnout...who would have dreamed that I'd ever stoop so low? I, who certainly never taxed my brain as a student? Me, with brain burnout, like a regular bookworm? To make matters worse, on my way out one day, I bump into Leonor and her daughter, Laura. I've always liked that family, but today I'm a basket case by the time they get through with me. Leonor's husband is a prisoner at Libertad. She saw him right before she came over; and she says he aged ten years in four months. They've made a total wreck of him. He was the one who insisted Leonor and Laura leave the country. Leonor didn't want to, but it seems he was so upset, she finally promised she would. Now they don't know what to do. Laura keeps looking at me, expecting me to come up with some brilliant idea. But I knock my brains out, and I

123

still can't think of a thing. And Leonor just sits there crying to herself (not to Laura or me, since not a sound's coming out of her). I ask Laura about her brother Enrique, who used to share a desk with me in grade school. "We haven't heard anything for a whole year. He's just gone poof. Every day we buy the Montevideo papers, to see if his name's on some list; or, I should say, terrified we'll find him on one." I just stand there like a moron; I don't know what to say or do. I tell them I'm working for a publishing house, and I'll let them know if I hear of anything for Laura. They give me a friend's phone number. Then they leave, holding onto one another for dear life. I can't eat a thing. The shame of it!. That night, when I go to bed, I suddenly get this weird, shaky feeling I can't explain, and then I cry for fifteen minutes straight. All that, and it's not even my problem. Or is it?

8

I had only seen Celso Dacosta twice in my life, in the Prado, back in the days when both of us hung out at the Club Atahualpa. But when he spots me on the corner of Viamonte and Pueyrredón, he shouts and comes sprinting across the street between all the buses. He gives me this big hug, asks if I'm living here, hugs me again and says he can't stop because he's in a rush, but let's get together. For now he wants to know if I'm free Saturday night for a little party some friends of his are having at their place. "They're filthy rich," he says, "but they're on our side. The well–dressed people will never be defeated." And he insists: "So don't give it a second thought. Here's the address; just show up after ten." I say O.K.

And I go. It's one hell of a place, this time on Libertador. I show up at ten–thirty, but Celso isn't there yet. I feel pretty lost. There are about sixty people. And they're all famous, I've seen those faces in *Gente*, or in *Siete Dias*. I'm introduced to three or four of them, but as soon as I can I wander off by myself, glass in hand, and pretend to admire some awful painting. Luckily, they forget about me. So then I get to take a look at everybody else. I'm wearing my best clothes, but anybody can tell I flock with birds of a different feather.

They all have on sports clothes, and wow, are they sporty! The women all laugh quietly to themselves, so their makeup won't get smeared; their giggles sound like they're coming from inside a cave. And the men keep on telling them jokes, to bug them of course, till they finally make one of the women laugh out loud, and she messes up all her carefully pressed-out wrinkles.

When Celso finally gets there, he catches me sneaking a look at a quiet, darkish woman who's been standing around drinking orange juice the whole time. Do I know who she is, he asks, and do I want him to introduce me? Then, before I can answer, we've been introduced. And he leaves us standing there together, her with her juice, and me with my whiskey. She lets out a little snort, as if to say what a drag (Celso, that is). And just to be doing something, I start frowning. I tell her I've seen her in *Sueñorreal* and I think she's got what it takes to do much better than that. "That movie's a piece of garbage," she says. As soon as she opens her mouth, even to say something as insipid as that, she looks five or ten times prettier. When she's quiet, there's something hard, almost aggressive, about her; but once she starts talking, she softens up and comes across as being warmer. I tell her that. "So I guess you're pretty observant." No, usually I'm not. I've just enjoyed watching her. "Why?" Well, she's very beautiful (she laughs; I snicker); but besides, there's something mysterious about her (she raises her eyebrows), not very mysterious, just a little. She guffaws, not a bit concerned about her makeup. "So, I'm a little mysterious, am I? Why only a little?"

Because the mystery could clear up, disappear, at any time. "And may I know just who this mystery has to do with?" Up to now, I've managed to avoid addressing her as u*sted* or *vos*; but now I have to take a stand. I decide against formality: "*Con vos*, with you," I reply. My use of that familiar form surprises her (she's at least twenty-six, maybe older); she didn't see it coming, and she was even less prepared for what it implied. She takes a gulp of her juice to stall for time. There's a gleam in her dark eyes. "What kind of work do you do?" I tell her. "Why don't you come by for me tomorrow after rehearsal?" I like her, and I don't. I like her body, especially her face; also her hands and legs. And I like that mystery I dreamed up for

125

her. But there are three things I don't like: she's an actress; she's famous; and she's too old. Can you see me with a twenty-six-year-old woman? But the temptation is enormous. "Are you afraid? Look, I'm not going to eat you up. It's just so we can chat. And you know why? I like what you said just now. I think you're right: there is something a little mysterious about me, and it has to do with me. Maybe you can help me figure it out." Now I'm the one gulping my drink to stall for time.

9

Let's just call her Isabel. Of course, that's not her real name. But I don't want to give away any secrets. Although tomorrow or the day after, they may very well announce in *Antena* or *Radiolandia* that the beautiful leading lady of *Sueñorreal* (not a real title, either) was seen in the company of a certain lanky young man. Anyway, let's call her Isabel. That lanky young man spends a number of hours thinking he'll go get her after rehearsal. The problem is what to wear. But there's an easy solution. Seeing as how I can't compete with that crowd, I figure I'll just dress like a bum. And not feel guilty about it. As if I were actually proud of that pullover my mother knitted me.

I get there so exactly on time it's embarrassing, so I walk around the block three times before stationing myself at the theater entrance. I might just as well have gone around seventeen times, because she's one hour, twenty minutes, and twenty seconds late. I engage in a bloody skirmish (as Radio Carve would say) with my self-respect, which keeps insisting I should bail out and dump this V.I.P. actress. Nevertheless, I stay. I don't know why, but I stay. I'm sick of waiting, but I stay. Finally, she comes prancing out of the elevator with a whole army in tow. I'm the only one waiting, so there's no way she can possibly miss me. But she walks right by me, giggling and waving her hands around (she looks very ordinary to me, just then); throws me the kind of passing glance you might give a cornice, a hinge, or a cockroach; and goes on laughing and gesticulating with her peers. I'm odd man out. They climb into three cars and take off with a huge racket. Conclusion: a certain lanky young man won't be making it into R*adiolandia* or *Antena* after all. Suddenly I realize I'm in a sweat. That pullover my old lady knitted me must be too heavy.

10

I have a cigarette, and that makes me feel better. Come to think of it, what does their world have to offer me, anyway? After all, being an actor's not the same here as in Monte, where you can bump into Candeau on the trolley, or Estela Medina at the bakery. I don't know if that's better or worse, but it's different. Back home, nobody makes big bucks in the theater, and they don't make movies. Here they do, and in the movies there are millions to be made. On TV too, and even in the theater. They're always talking about how this or that contract is worth so many thousands. And what a P.R. apparatus they've got, gossip and all! Why wouldn't those hot shots think they're the center of the universe?

By this time of night, the subway isn't running, and there are hardly any buses. Sure, there are cabs, but I'm broke. So I walk all the way back to my *pensión*. It must be at least a hundred and twenty blocks. Maybe even three hundred and fifteen. But the walk does me good. At first, I'm feeling pretty disappointed; but then I get mad, and eventually, I more or less calm down. Does that mean I'm growing up? No way! I solemnly swear I'll never grow up. Like Heraclitus once said, the ripest fruit rots first. Well, I don't know if Heraclitus really said that or not, but it never hurts to quote a first-class source. Maybe no one ever said it, and I can put my own name on it. When the alternatives are Grow Up or Die, then naturally, I'd rather die. If I had said that to Isabel the night before last, maybe she would have remembered who I am. A few smooth words never hurt. Words can get you things. Women, too.

Not all cities are nice to walk around in at night, especially when you're down in the dumps. But I even like Baires under these stormy conditions. There's always a stray dog or two ready to keep a lone, lanky young man company; and sometimes, like tonight, there are as many as four. They come crowding around me, fan back out, close ranks again, escort me across each intersection, but only after they've looked left and right (I bet whoever decided the right was right was no leftie) and waited for that long tanker truck to go roaring by. Then they join up with me again, and they're so busy watching out for my hide, they don't even bother sniffing the garbage cans or fornicating (to use Biblical lingo)—all of which goes to show you that to them, this nocturnal parade is no mere hedonistic display; it's their solemn duty. So on we go, all five of us, at a nervous pace, no time for dawdling. And there's a whole day's worth of litter swirling around us in the wind, and only a few yards away, this big-nosed lug delivers two prudent punches to the head of a hefty whore (he must be trying not to break her eardrum); and she doesn't even bat an eyelash, just comes back at him with a terrific kick to the femoral condylus (see how well I know my anatomy?). Still further away—luckily, well beyond my immediate surroundings—we can hear the familiar shriek of sirens. And though they're nowhere near us, the four dogs stop and give me this anxious look, as if they're expecting me to size up the situation, warn them of any danger, tell them what to do. But I just keep walking. So then the four of them look at each other and decide they'd better make sure I'm O.K. Ten blocks later, these two goons spot our little group of five from a distance and decide to check us out. But all together we must be a pretty formidable sight, because on second thought, they let us walk right by them.

11

At the publishing house, I correct proofs till they're coming out of my ears. For the past two weeks now, I've had my hands full with a journal on economics. First came this seventy-page essay on the stages of economic development in pre-industrial England. I found fifteen typos under sheepraising, twenty under theft of communal lands, and twelve under Church holdings. The subject isn't exactly a barrel of laughs. At night, I dream about vestiges of feudalism and the rationalization of production. Today's article is on the applicability of the Laws of Economics. This time I find nine typos under unintended consequences of natural laws; eighteen under inevitability of social production, and just four under collaborative actions by workers. So tonight I can expect to dream about scientifically-based technocratic norms and socially-determined mean time. And I thought math was boring! As I work my way through the text, I decide not to pay attention to content for two reasons: first of all, even when I do, I can't make head or tails of it; and second, if I'm concentrating on the subject, I miss the typos. Once I backed up a little after my mind wandered, and was that a lucky move (backing up, that is, not letting my mind wander), because I had missed things as obvious as "set" and "links."

I know it's idiotic, but I keep thinking if I blink, I'll miss the one typo that's lurking among all those Laws of Economics. So sometimes I read and read without blinking, till I end up absolutely bug-eyed. When that happens, I put my fingernail (which, by the way, could use a cleaning) on whatever piece of gibberish I've gotten to, look sideways, blink till my eyes quit feeling so dry and uncomfortable, and go back to the galleys. Only then do I take my fingernail off the page, but first I scrape the grime out from under it with the corner of a card.

12

I run into Dionisio—a twenty-two-year-old chemistry student from my old neighborhood—on the corner of Cordoba and Canning. I saw him just six months ago, but he looks like he's aged ten years. I can't explain it, but somehow he's not his old cheerful, energetic, mischievous self. Still, he's not hysterical like most of the other Uruguayans I meet up with; he's quiet instead. I don't know which is worse. Because behind that quietness of his, he's incredibly sad. At first, I'm not sure what to say, what to ask him. He was always more sensible, smarter, more self-assured than the rest of us. So who am I to be giving him advice, commiserating with him, trying to boost his morale? Besides, what could we have to commiserate about? I ask him if he wants to go for a beer. And he says yes.

When the waiter puts those two pints in front of us, Dionisio smiles for the first time, but it's a dull, gray, burned-out smile. "Remember how sure I used to be of everything?" Of course I do. I can't wait another minute, so I ask him. Naturally, he'd been in prison; who hadn't? Just four months. They nabbed him and five others, including Ruben, during a meeting at Vicky's place. "You remember Vicky, don't you?" Sure. How could I forget her? I almost say so, but I hold back, maybe because he looks like he's about to burst into tears, and I have a feeling she's the main reason. Vicky was his girl friend. And it sure looked like the real thing. You'd see them everywhere together: in the park, at student meetings, on the bus, at the movies, at the University. "They ran her in with the rest of us. At first, they pretty much went by the book. One of them tried the 'good guy' routine. But when they couldn't get anything out of us that way, they handed us over to a 'bad guy,' who didn't even bother beating us up. He just went straight to the machine. You can't imagine what that's like. What they do to everyone else feels just as horrible as what they do to you. They never worked over two of us at once. They'd give it to one at a time, and the rest of us would have to sit there with our hoods on, imagining the worst. It gets so bad that when your turn comes, you try to scream as little as possible (there's no way to keep from screaming at all) to make it easier for the ones who can hear but not see. They kept at it for two weeks." Suddenly his face crumples, and he covers it with both hands. Then, I can hear his voice cracking through his wet, clenched fingers. "The only time they took my hood off was when they raped her, right in front of me. They had me naked, with my hands and feet tied. Her too, and she was strapped down by her wrists and ankles to this big wooden board on the floor, just a few feet away from me. There must have been ten of them. And she knew I was there, helpless. At first she screamed her head off; then she fainted, but they just went on and on. I kept trying to close my eyes, but each time the bastards caught me, they would force me to look. They had to put her in the Military Hospital; she almost died on them. A month later they let all of us go, except Ruben." I don't know what to do. I put my hand on his arm. Everyone in the place can hear him sobbing and carrying on. The waiter comes over to ask "what's wrong with my friend," and I have to make up a story about "bad news from his family." He mutters "poor guy," and walks away with an order of Cinzano and olives for another table. Little by little, Dionisio calms down, and I ask him where Vicky is now, and how she's doing. "She's alive, but it's like she's not there. She's never gotten over it. She hasn't said a word since that day. I saw her. I talked to her. She doesn't answer. She doesn't recognize anybody. Her old man is loaded, and he wants to take her to Europe, to see if they can do something for her over there. The doctors didn't think I should see her again, at least for now; they said it would be counterproductive. Besides, the military showed up twice at my house, looking for me. Finally, I had to leave; I still don't know how I did it. I crossed into Brazil by way of Rivera, into Argentina by way of Uruguayana, then I hitched all the way to Baires. It took me twenty days." I can't get Vicky out of my mind; she was so beautiful, so talented, such a great athlete, such a good student. Dionisio, dry-eyed by now, raises his head and mumbles, staring at the toe of one shoe: "And I still haven't told you the worst part." I have to lean across the table to hear him: "She's pregnant." What a soap opera this friggin' life can be!

13

I hear machine-gun fire nearby, so I hightail it into one of the *galerías* on Santa Fe. To kill time, I start looking in the shop windows. There's a whole crowd in there with me. The owners of those boutiques must do very well with all the gun rattling. Because when people take cover in their shops, the superstitious ones, at least, always end up buying something—as a way of thanking their lucky stars they were near a safe place when the shooting started. It's one thing if a "shootout" (as the TV calls them) catches you on the corner of Santa Fe and Talcahuano; it's another if you're crossing 9 de Julio, where except for the blacktop, you might as well be in the middle of a huge open field. I can't even think of buying anything, because I'm flat broke, so I check out the window with the cassettes, then the one that's full of clothes for playboys, then the one with all the beads for hippies (at the end of the row), then the one with the pottery (back this way), and the one with all the colored candles, and the one with the tape decks, and the one with the cameras. By now, I've looked at everything except women's clothes; so I stop in front of a window full of women's clothes, not looking at anything in particular, mostly trying to decide what to do next. Suddenly, I see someone waving at me from inside the boutique. She has to wave again, because at first, I think she's waving at someone else who's stranded in there, waiting for the shooting to stop. It's only when she smiles, that I realize it's Let's–Call–Her–Isabel. I wave back none too enthusiastically, and she signals for me to wait. The reason I didn't recognize her is that her hairdo's different; so's the color of her skin (which is kind of a copper tone); and especially, so are her clothes: instead of that skimpy little sports dress she had on the night I met her, or the long coat she showed up in when she stood me up twenty days ago, she's wearing one of those outfits with a tight jacket and wide pants. I seem to remember my mother calling them "palazzo pants," but to me, they're just fancy pajamas.

She finally comes out, loaded down with packages; and this time, she looks at me like I'm a lanky young man, not a cockroach or a cornice. She even gives me a peck on the cheek. Her perfume really works. I don't know if you read me (who are you, anyway?): it's subtle, but what a knockout! All of a sudden, the whole gallery starts smelling like her. Subtle. But a real knockout.

She's in a cheery mood today. Not sullen and bored like the night of the party, or loud and cocky like the night she stood me up. Just cheery. And she doesn't mention that incident, so neither do I. Talking about it would be too humiliating. I'm in shirtsleeves today. Hey, maybe she really didn't recognize me in the pullover my old lady knitted me. But in that case, she'd probably be scolding me for standing her up. Or maybe that would feel too humiliating to her. "What brings you here? Are you shopping?" I explain that I ran into the *galería* when all the shooting started. "So did I, but it's turning out to be expensive. Look at all the stuff I've bought." I help her with her packages. "Come with me. Or do you have other plans?" No, I've got no other plans. "My car's half a block away. And they've stopped shooting. At least, for today." She's right. Little by little, everyone's moving out into the street. Santa Fe is getting back its characteristic craziness. People are shouting, laughing, calling to each other. Two convertibles, each piloted by a crew of flamboyant queens, weave in and out between the buses and cabs, trying to make the next intersection before the light changes. You'd never know that this year alone, nine hundred people have died for political reasons.

Before we get to the parking lot, it starts drizzling. Even so, she signs two autographs—one for a girl with a squeaky voice, and the other for a respectable-looking matron. She seems to be enjoying all the fuss. Other people aren't asking her for autographs, but they're pointing her out. Now the drizzle turns to rain. I'm feeling as free as a bird; nobody's noticing me, hallelujah. She arranges the packages on the back seat. "Che, I'm freezing. Come, let's go to my place for a drink. After all that shooting and all that shopping, we need one, right? Besides, running into each other like this calls for a celebration."

Her one-room apartment isn't exactly the Taj Mahal, but it's still pretty classy. I flop down on this weird piece of furniture that's too small to be a bed, and too big to be a sofa. I could lie there for hours. From the depths of that *whatcha-ma-callit,* I start looking the place over. I decide that whenever I settle down, my greatest ambition in life will be to have an apartment just like this one. Not now, because I'm still a nomad. Besides, I've noticed that when people settle down, they're always old. Or at least, more or less mature like Let's–Call–Her–Isabel. I ask her if she considers herself settled. "What's that?" she inquires, sounding a little drippy, since she's in the bathroom brushing her teeth. I explain that people are settled when they stop moving from house to house, meadow to meadow, and country to country; the ones who are always on the move are called nomads. If my history teacher could hear me, she'd be very proud. But she's not proud; she's in jail. "Then I guess I'm settled. I hate meadows, and I hate moving." Just like I thought. That's probably because she's got so many things to move. Me, on the other hand, I'm all the luggage I've got. "That's so beautiful; it sounds just like Antonio Machado. Did you know I got my start doing a Machado recital?" No, I didn't. Evidently she's so full of herself, she thinks we're all up on her biography. But so she'll realize I know who Antonio Machado is, I recite: "Your eyes are ablaze with a mysterious fire, oh, virgin (pause), my shy companion (pause). Is it hatred or is it love, the feverish flame (pause) of your black fuchsia flower?" With that, her head pops out the bathroom door. Well, not really her head; Let's–Call–Her–Isabel does. "How very literate of you, young man. You get an A+, by unanimous vote." Now she's got on blue jeans and a blue T-shirt. She changed in two seconds flat. So? Actresses do that. "Do you take your whiskey straight or on the rocks?" On the rocks, of course. She comes in with two glasses and flops down on the rug, Buddha-style, with her legs crossed. "Don't sit there on that cot. Come on down and join the *pueblo*." I'm sorry to leave that weird piece of furniture. Besides, I don't like sitting on the floor, even with a soft, fluffy rug between me and it; my legs are so long, I never know where to put them, and when I'm on the floor I feel like I've got legs on all sides. Still, looking at her from that cot, as she called it, wasn't especially comfortable; and sitting on the rug's not so bad when what you've got on all sides isn't just legs, but Let's–Call–Her–Isabel too, in a one–room apartment where there's no one to get on your case.

"The other night you said there was something a little mysterious about me. And it had to do with me." I don't think I'm feeling resentful anymore. In the last few minutes, I've started treating her better. But little by little, little by little. Some punks will fall all over actresses like her. Not me. I like them, or I don't. But I never fall all over them. This one, for example, I like. Anyway, she's not completely relaxed either. And I'm sure she's an old hand at dealing with lanky young men like me.

"You know what that little mystery that has to do with me is?" Between two sips of booze, my head says no. Good thing she doesn't know I only said what I did the other night to make small talk. She must think I'm a fortune teller, or a mind reader or something. "It's that I'm leading a false existence." Oh. "What you said kept churning around in my noggin. It wasn't easy to admit it, you know." Aha! "That's why last time, on my way out of that rehearsal, I pretended not to see you." I'm figuring I should say aha-a-a-a, but I sneeze, so I don't have to. I also blow my nose discreetly. "Did you catch cold out there in the rain just now? Anyway, that's why I walked right by you, giggling like an idiot. Because I wasn't sure." Sure of what? "Well...that I really wanted to talk to you about all this. You may not know it, but we actors are very superstitious. So, I decided I'd leave it all to chance: if I run into him, I'll tell him; and if I don't, that's that." Well, she ran into me.

By now, it's like Let's–Call–Her–Isabel is transfigured. I don't know what's happening to her. She seems to sparkle. Like glass. Holy shit, can I be falling in love? Whew, that sparkle just disappeared. What a relief! But I'd best be careful. "Yes, I'm leading a false existence. But that wasn't always the case; I used to be much better than this. I come from a real working-class family. You'd never guess, would you? Until three years ago, my old man was still working at the factory, and my mother used to sew for the rich ladies in the neighborhood. Not now, because I make very good money, so I bought them a little house and I give them a hand. Besides, my old man's retired. My brother helps out, too. He's a simultaneous translator, and that pays really well. But why did I start telling you this? Oh, yes. I was saying I'm from a working-class family. And no born actress (which I am) from a working-class family should be doing garbage like Sueñorreal." (Remember, that's not the real title). "I always wanted to be an actress, but mainly because I wanted to do something useful—help people understand things, not confuse them, the way I am now. I'm really confusing myself, too."

Let's–Call–Her–Isabel seems a little reticent. She looks especially pretty when she gets that way. She pauses, and takes another slug, but that's the last one. "I know someday I'll have to make a choice.

A serious choice. Because I either go right on confusing myself and other people, or I break away from all this crap. It's not easy. Maybe it's easy for you, because you're at square one. Like you said before, you're all the luggage you've got. But I've been tempting myself with creature comforts, and giving in to them, for a long time now. Remember how hard it was for you to get off that contraption after just fifteen minutes, when I asked you to come down and sit on the rug? Well, everything's like that. All this stuff I've accumulated is pretty cushy, and it keeps getting cushier. It soothes you, pacifies you, and eventually, it cripples you. And if you accomplish anything in spite of that, it's so you can earn more money to buy yourself more stuff. I bought that huge thing so I'd have a comfortable place to read. But I have to confess: all I've ever done on it is take naps. Which is all it's fit for, because it's not even good for making love."

I'm wondering what she's getting at, but Let's–Call–Her–Isabel doesn't seem to be dropping any hints. Or may be she is, and I don't realize it. God, why do I have to be so damn adolescent? For the moment, she pours me another whiskey, since she's left the bottle right next to the rug, where she can reach it. Was she trying to tell me that contraption's no good, but the rug is? I decide to look at Let's–Call–Her–Isabel, but suddenly I realize I'm not dropping any hints either. The subject is probably too serious. I ask her what makes her feel so bad about her work. "Oh, maybe it's all the distance between what I am and what I could be." And why doesn't she try being what she could be, dammit? "Reason number one: I'm scared. Scared of a whole lot of things. Like obviously, what if they set off a bomb, or kidnap me, or threaten me, or kill me? As long as I'm doing these inane parts, I'm safe, because—and I'm fully aware of this—indirectly, I'm collaborating with them, so I'm useful to them. 'Kitsch as a source of alienation'—that's the title a sociologist friend of mine gave to one of his papers—and the cynic dedicated it to me. But there's something else I'm afraid of too, and that's giving up my standard of living, this apartment, all the creature comforts, that contraption, this rug, the scotch. And I swear, I don't know which of those fears is the bigger one—which one is holding me back and doing me in at the same time. Because I could always aim for some middle ground, you know, something that's at least honest. I don't think I've got the nerve to do political theater or poetry; these days, that can cost you your skin. But I could refuse to do plays, or movies, or recitals unless they've got good, decent texts. Seeing as how I don't have the guts to fight for justice, much less the revolution, that way I'd at least be doing something for culture." So? "But you don't get rich that way. I know this filthy business. I'm up to my ears in it. I know what makes for success. And I can assure you, it stinks."

All this time I'm listening to her; but for a while now, I've been in a fog, paying less and less attention to what she's saying. She's lying there face up on the rug, just a few inches from my hand, staring at a little piece of the ceiling. Her T-shirt is hiked up a little, and I can see a thin strip of suntanned skin. I reach out in that direction, and I feel her skin shudder like a horse trying to get rid of flies. But that doesn't get rid of me. Besides, Let's–Call–Her–Isabel's suntanned skin is very soft. She stops right in the middle of a sentence. Maybe I've taken her by surprise. She doesn't say a word, just leaves things up to me. As usual, there's a metal zipper that gets stuck, so she gives me a hand with it. She proceeds very calmly, as if what was coming was a foregone conclusion. What's surprising is, her body looks so young, as if she were fifteen instead of twenty–six. I take my time undressing too, trying to seem casual. What the hell, she's not the only one who can act. I even have the presence of mind to stretch out next to her (the truth is, I'm a bit cold), as she lies there face–up, looking at the ceiling. With one hand I turn her head toward me, so I can see her eyes. She's crying. I wasn't expecting that, and I can't help feeling moved. I run my fingers across her cheek. She says: "There's less of a difference between you and me this way. It doesn't matter if my clothes are exclusive models, and yours are as cheap as the clothes I used to wear back in grade school. It doesn't matter; they're all lying there in a heap, where they can't make any difference. And when you make love to me (you will, won't you?), it won't matter that you don't have a penny to your name and I have a big fat bank account. You see, bodies don't have pockets in them. It doesn't matter either, that you're running away from those Uruguayan goons of yours, and I'm running away from myself. Hey, look, your pubic hair and mine are almost the same color." I bring mine closer, so Let's–Call–Her–Isabel and I can compare. She's right; they are almost the same color. When they're matted together, you don't see any difference. You really can't tell mine from hers.

14

Dionisio needs to understand why he and his country have taken such a clobbering. "Do I have a right to feel undone just because they made a cactus out of Vicky, and a raging, shame-filled witness out of me? Weren't we inexcusably naive to count on winning, and never even consider we might lose?" I can't think of a thing to say. The truth is, I, personally, never counted on anything—winning or losing. Could that be because I hate math? I didn't even count on the beatings I got in prison. "That just proves we were a bunch of kids. We thought the enemy was conservative, but civilized, and he turned out to be a murderous beast. Can you tell me what to do now with all this rage? I can assure you it's not the least bit constructive. Besides, it's blind: I don't know who they are, because whenever they took my hood off, they put theirs on. Sure, I remember their voices; I'll never forget them. But how do you put a name and a face on a voice? Because what really sucks, politically speaking, is that right now I don't give a damn about winning; all I care about is finding the monsters who made basket cases out of Vicky and me, so I can blow their fuckin' brains out. It's not right, but I can't help feeling that way."

By the time he's through, I feel almost like he does, or I think I do. It's hard to get inside somebody else's skin. And it's probably a lot harder for me, because I've never loved a girl the way Dionisio loves Vicky, and so I can't even begin to imagine what it must be like to watch a bunch of goons take turns humping the girl that means everything to you. Or almost everything, which is quite enough. Let's see, how would I feel if I had to sit there, tied up and helpless, watching a dozen of those apes give it to Let's–Call–Her–Isabel? Of course, I'm not in love with Let's–call–Her–Isabel. Still, having to watch something like that has got to be the pits; it must be hard enough even if you don't know the woman. At least I don't think I'm in love with Let's–Call–Her–Isabel. I had a really great time at that jam-session the other afternoon, and she's got fantastic skin, and a fabulous body, but I'm not feeling any of the craziness other guys have told me about (at least, not yet). Like wanting to spend your whole life with her, or that tightness in your chest that makes you think you're having a heart attack, or the mad urge to go out walking alone in the moonlight (or under the streetlights, if there is no moon). No, that's not my case. I had an incredibly good time doing exactly what I wanted, no chest pain whatsoever, just this very major lust, truly a first in my long years of existence. She really wanted me too (and how!), and she had absolutely no qualms about showing it, which I also appreciated. Of course, there's that other problem: all those doubts she has about what she is, versus what she could be. My feeling is, there's probably no going back. Creature comforts have a way of getting to you, big time. Why, even I can get nostalgic about that whatcha-ma-callit at her place, and the rug, especially the rug! And that's not all. There are those people who stop her on the street, and stare at her, and point her out, and ask her for autographs. She says she doesn't care about any of that, but she likes it too, and it gets to her too. Now, don't get me wrong; I'm not judging her. I understand how she must feel. I bet if I were famous, and girls were always stopping me on the street and looking at me with their mouths hanging open, I'd have more hangups than she does. Maybe vanity and talent go together, and the only reason I'm not vain is that there's nothing I'm good at. Nothing at all? Maybe I'm not good at anything now, but someday I will be. Right now being young is all I can handle; but later on, like when I'm a relic of thirty-five, maybe I'll try to be good at something. The problem is, can you get good at things by just trying hard enough? It must not be that simple. Because I know a few characters who could bust a gut trying, and they still wouldn't be any good. Anyway, why would I want to be good at something *now*? It's just a lot of inconvenience, a lot of responsibility, and a lot of work. Besides, when you're too good at stuff (like Dionisio, for instance, who's a real brain), you probably can't help getting upset about what's going on around here. And if you want to stay young, you can't let anything upset you. So I don't want anything to upset me. But will I be able to pull that off?

15

I wait for her after rehearsal, and this time she does wave to me from a distance; when she gets closer, she gives me a peck on the cheek, and introduces me to her colleagues, starting with a big woman, who, of course, plays all the wise matrons. And then the director, and the guy who does the lighting, and the set designer. And this ambiguous-looking young guy who doesn't take his eyes off me. And she says, "This is Eduardo," so naturally that before long, she even has me convinced my name's Eduardo. But it's not. Besides, if she wanted to give me a new name, why couldn't she come up with something that would make a good alias, like Asdrúbal or Eusebio or Saúl? "*Che*, Eduardo," yells the guy who does the lighting and naturally, I'm oblivious, so I don't answer. And the guy gets insulted and turns his back to me; but then it dawns on me that I'm Eduardo, so I ask him does he want me for something, and he says what a quick comeback.

The whole gang goes out to dinner. I don't eat anything, because "I've already eaten." The problem is, if I eat, it stands to reason I'll have to pay, and these folks pick a place like Edelweiss, where they even charge for the toothpicks. So I watch trays of food go by, in front of me, in back of me, on all sides—salads, brochettes, rabbit *a la cacciatore, gnocchis a la bolognese*; meanwhile, there I sit pretending to be stuffed, but hungry as hell, and salivating like it's going out of style. To make my misery complete, not only am I sitting far away from Let's–Call–Her–Isabel (when I thought I had a date with her, not with this carnival troupe), but it seems I've hit the jackpot: I'm stuck between the ambiguous-looking guy and the actress who plays

the matrons, and I don't know what the hell to talk about. Everything
I can think of has to do with digestion, or menus, or seasoning,
etc., and I'm afraid to even mention any of that, because I may end
up with no saliva at all, which can be dangerous.

Way down at the other end of the table, Let's–Call–Her–Isabel
is laughing her head off, as the lighting technician sits there gossiping
away. I don't like the way she's shaking her wig. I don't like how she
looks with that lighting technician either. Suddenly, she catches sight
of me; and she winks and purses her lips. I don't react. Maybe being
so hungry is making me irritable. Then she opens her bag, takes
out a piece of paper, scribbles something on it, folds it into quarters,
and asks the waiter to hand it to me: "In a little while, we'll go home.
Just you and me." I fold it up again, and stick it in my pocket. I look
right back at her, but without sending any signals.

Then the set designer starts talking politics: he's heard they're
torturing people. And it's true; they are. But as far as he's concerned,
that's just fine. If those kids are so anxious to change everything;
and they want to do away with all our Western and Christian
traditions, he says; and they're so opposed to private property, even
though for the founding fathers, Rivadavia and Saavedra, for
instance, private property was sacred; and they're against all the
good things this generation inherited, including the family,
motherhood, Christmas, even those beautiful cows of ours, well,
che, they can just pay the price. And if the price is torture, *che*, they'll
just have to be tortured. And if they are, *che*, you can be very sure
his hair won't stand on end. The actress who plays all the matrons
whispers in my ear: "Naturally; he's bald as a cue ball."

I think about Vicky and Dionisio. But that kind of repression is
a different story. Or is it? As I listen to the set designer talk, I can't
stop picturing Vicky getting raped right in front of Dionisio; then
as a living corpse, stuck for good in that isolation cell she's built
around herself. And I can't stand it. So, I say goodbye to the actress
who plays the matrons and the ambiguous-looking guy ("I have a
long day ahead"), and glance at the other end of the table where
Let's–Call–Her–Isabel has stopped shaking her wig by now; and
maybe that's why she can see me stand up, and say a short, sweet

goodbye and start to leave. Just as I'm about to step out the door, I turn around for one last look at them all, as they sit there in a thick, smoky haze, chomping away.

16

How much longer will I be able to go on writing this? What happened today has me wondering. I'm walking down Rivadavia on my way home from work, and I notice something strange going on near the corner of Billinghurst. I don't turn back; that always looks suspicious. Hundreds of guys are standing there with their hands up and their faces to the wall. But the soldiers aren't frisking them; they're just keeping an eye on them. Then these four Ford Falcons come tearing over, and a bunch of hooligans with machine guns leap out while they're still moving. Apparently they're after a certain couple: he's tall and dark, with a moustache and a black briefcase; and she's a redhead, who's wearing a light-colored coat and carrying a woolen bag. The attack takes them both by surprise. She falls down in the mud. He tries to protect her, but two members of the commando knock him down with four or five sharp, definitive punches. The man gets back up and again, he tries to defy them. But this time they knock him out cold. As three of them hold the woman down, she screams at the top of her lungs: "We are Luis and Norma Sierra! We are Luis and Norma Sierra! Tell everyone we're being kidnapped!" The butt of a rifle smashes into her mouth; and then, all I can hear are a few faint moans that could be the music to her lyrics of a moment ago. I'm standing maybe thirty yards away, on the corner. The soldiers keep the guys against the wall under surveillance, until the whole thing is over. Nobody makes the slightest attempt to defend the couple. Neither do I. I've never in my life felt so helpless, or so insignificant. Two of the goons drag the guy, who's still unconscious, into the first Falcon, and the woman, all bloody and covered with mud, into the third. Then the four cars speed up Rivadavia toward the Parliament Building like bats out of hell. The guys against the wall are allowed to lower their arms and move on. I move on too, by way of Billinghurst. I'd be ashamed to be seen on Rivadavia. I miss those dogs from the other night.

17

I haven't seen any more of Let's–Call–Her–Isabel. Since that night at Edelweiss, I haven't felt like it. She doesn't know where to call me. I know her address and phone number, and besides, I can always go by for her after rehearsal. But I don't want to. What for? I know all theater people aren't like that set designer. I know for a fact that lots of actors and actresses take chances: they go onstage knowing they can be shot down at any time because up there, they're moving (and sometimes stationary) targets. Yeah, I know lots of them go from factory to factory, improvising skits in each place on the problems there; and that's a big help, because when an actor puts what everyone is thinking into words, the audience understands it better. I know that. Even Let's–Call–Her–Isabel told me, a little enviously, of course, because she's afraid to do it. That's all true, and I really wouldn't mind talking to those people. But, what do I have in common with the group that had dinner at Edelweiss? With that smart-assed glibness of theirs, that wears thin so fast, and leaves you in such a terrible mood? With all their sarcasm, and their blatant envy, and their constant wisecracks at everyone else's expense? Let's–Call–Her–Isabel's not so bad; with a little effort and a little nudging, she might really shape up. But I'm not anxious to take on any great patriotic causes these days. It's hard enough just trying to stay alive.

Dionisio is feeling better. He got a letter from his people in Monte. And for the first time, they're feeling hopeful about Vicky; since last Thursday she's been crying a lot, sometimes for hours; and her face has some expression, although nobody's sure what it means. The doctors are sounding a little more optimistic now. If she improves enough to get through it, they'll try for an abortion. That would be the best solution. Vicky's father writes that last Sunday somebody mentioned Dionisio, and Vicky smiled. Just barely, but she smiled. So now Dionisio's hanging on to that smile for dear life.

We meet at a café across from Plaza Italia. Dionisio shows me the letter, and I make encouraging noises:

"It'll all be O.K., you'll see. As soon as she gets here, you'll both start living again."

"You really think so?" Sure, I do. We've got to; there's no other alternative.

I go to the men's room. Just as I'm washing my hands, in runs this kid—a real kid (can't be more than twelve or thirteen)—with his face all flushed, and he blurts out:

"Your friend says to tell you he had to split. The goons are around."

"Here?"

"No, on the corner." I don't even thank him. I just tear out of the bathroom with my hands still soapy, and head for the door. The waiter notices what a big hurry I'm in and naturally, thinks I'm trying to get out without paying; so he starts yelling at me from a distance. I slap some money down on the counter (enough to cover the tab and a tip) and run like mad. But that waiter's voice has alerted the goons. "There he goes!" yells one of them. "It's that one!" bellows another. I'm not the least bit proud of all the attention I'm getting. I'm running like a scared rabbit, like two rabbits, three rabbits. With a whole army behind me. I haven't figured out what to do yet. But one thing I know: this time I won't get caught like an idiot. Or like anything else. I won't let them catch me. I cut through a line of seven or eight buses that are about to turn onto Las Heras. I'm so determined to get away, I almost end up under their wheels. But when I feel myself slipping, I get my balance by hopping onto a #60 bus. Neither the driver nor any of the passengers say a word, though I'm obviously not on my way home from a wedding. The goons are all over the place, and they're frantic. They're stopping the buses, looking inside, sometimes climbing on, maybe checking I.D.'s. A man in a tie and jacket gets up and warns me, "You'd better sit down." I catch on, and I do. While I'm at it, I slick back my hair.

Now I look presentable. A goon stops the bus. "Did somebody just jump on here in a big hurry?" The driver wrinkles his brow. "I did," answers the guardian angel who just gave me his seat. "Damn...," says the goon, impatient and exhausted. "O.K.! Keep moving!" he orders the driver. Mister Angel doesn't even look at me. Neither does anyone else. When we get to Laprida, I jump off the bus and run into a supermarket. I stand on line for twenty minutes and blow my last few pesos on six boxes of matches. The cashier looks so rattled, I might as well be Nero. I wonder if she's planning to call the fire department.

18

Around Plaza Once, life has gotten impossible. I never go out anymore without my passport, some money, and this notebook. You never know. Dionisio got away by the skin of his teeth. He says it was thanks to the flap I caused. All because of that suspicious waiter. "You're blacklisted," Dionisio tells me, and I don't doubt it. Each one of those bastards that shouted "Get that guy!" must have my face tattooed on his brain. "No," Dionisio says, "You were blacklisted before that. In the files down on Calle Moreno. Diego told me. That guy always has his contacts, you know. Well, one of them got a look at the list in the Uruguayan section. Diego's not on it yet. But he's laying low, just in case. He says to call him tomorrow, you know where."

O.K. I'm really not surprised. I go to back to the *pensión*. Or I should say, I almost do. Two blocks away, I run into the sonorous lady's husband. He grabs me by the arm: "Doña Rosa says not to even come near the place. They came looking for you this morning. We've been waiting on all four streets around the house, so whoever saw you first could warn you." He hands me a bag, my Pluna Airlines bag. "Here are your things. Doña Rosa says to call her someday, but not to use your name. Say you're Servando." Finally, a name that sounds like an alias: Servando.

145

19

Diego found me a place to sleep for a week. "You've got to pull a vanishing act. After this week, we'll see where else we can hide you." He's already notified my boss at the publishing house; they'll understand, I'm sure they will.

"But tell me, Diego, why?"

"Why what?"

"Why a vanishing act here, too?"

"Because they're looking for you, you idiot, or do you want them to nab you? Remember, in this town they mean business. They do away with you, and that's that; then they claim you were trying to escape."

"O.K., but I still don't understand why...."

"Don't be a jerk! "

"The only political thing I've done in my whole life is carry a rose."

"And you don't think that's enough?"

I look up Let's–Call–Her–Isabel in my address book. I call her from a café. "Who-o-o-o?" answers the set designer's voice, so I hang up. I'm not feeling any chest pain, so obviously, I'm not having a heart attack, and I'm not in love. Lucky for me.

Having to go into hiding pisses me off, but what can you do? I walk a few blocks along Vicente López (with all those mansions, the Barrio Norte is still pretty safe). Before I disappear, I've got to get to a Post Office. I stop in a bookstore, buy a nice manila envelope, and address it using Let's–Call–Her–Isabel's real name. Before I put this notebook into it, my green marker prints in big letters on the cover: "I have to split. Love and kisses. Here's something for you to read on that great big, comfortable whatcha-ma-callit of yours. I'm sending it, because maybe there's still hope for you."

1976

Translated by Maria and Matthew Proser and Louise Popkin

Just like Greenwich

"You're not from Mallorca, are you?" asks the teenage girl at the next table.

"Huh? What did you say?" Quiñones is so startled, he almost chokes on his dry sherry.

"Did I startle you?" Her tone didn't seem teasing, just amused.

"You surprised me, I'll admit that much. Nobody knows me here in Palma. I'm just passing through."

"That means you're not a *mallorquino*. Or even a Spaniard."

"Let's get the third degree over with, O.K.? I'm Argentine."

"I thought so."

"How did you know?" Quiñones takes a closer look at the girl, with her dark slacks and white blouse, and her childish but promising figure.

"I'm not sure. By the crease in your pants, I guess, and the way you strike a match, and the way you look at women."

"Now that's what I call progress. People used to recognize us by our accent."

"I'd say you're about forty-three."

"Forty-one."

"You wouldn't be lying about your age, would you?"

There is something refreshing about the girl's impudence. Quiñones feels at ease.

"I'm Uruguayan, and I'm fourteen," she says.

"That's nice."

"Doesn't it interest you?"

"Sure, why not? But to tell you the truth, these days meeting Argentines and Uruguayans in Europe is nothing new."

"My name is Susana. What's yours?"

"Quiñones."

147

Susana had ordered a lemonade, which she still hadn't tasted.

"Your lemonade's going to get warm. Remember, it's August."

"Ice cold drinks don't agree with me."

She wraps her fingers around the glass to see how cold it is, and decides to wait a little longer.

"Do you like all those Swedish and Dutch and German girls parading up and down the boulevard? You seem fascinated by them."

"That depends. There are Dutch girls and Dutch girls."

"Which kind do you prefer? The ones with the dainty little boobs, or the ones with cellulitis?"

Quiñones looks at her, intrigued.

"Who taught you that kind of language?"

"Oh, so now we're getting personal. How nice."

"As you like."

"Let's just say I'm not illiterate."

"I'd say you're a little too literate for a fourteen-year-old."

Susana stares at her thin arms in silence, as if to inspect her skin pore by pore.

"Whenever I get too much sun, I end up with freckles."

"Me too," says Quiñones, just to keep the conversation going.

"The Freckle Face Duo. Can you sing?"

"My voice is squeakier than a deaf rooster's. And yours?"

"Mine is scratchier than a violin."

"You shouldn't generalize. There are violins that..."

"Never mind. They're all scratchy. I ought to know. My uncle was a violinist, and he did nothing but scrape away all day long. Well, I guess we can forget about the Duo."

"Why do you say he *was* a violinist? Doesn't your uncle play anymore?"

"He's a carpenter now. These days his saw does all the scraping. That's exile for you."

"Oh, so you're in exile."

"Obviously."

"What's so obvious about it? Not all Uruguayans and Argentines are exiles."

"At least half of them are."

"Well, what about the other half?"

"They're the children of the first ones. I really belong to that second group. How about you?"

"To the first."

"How long ago did you leave Buenos Aires?"

"Tucumán. Buenos Aires isn't the whole country, you know."

"O.K., O.K."

"Four years ago."

"And what are you doing in Palma?

"Right now I'm on vacation, but usually I'm a salesman. I sell advertising. All over Spain."

"That's interesting. I live in Germany."

"And how do you like it there?"

"It's O.K., I guess. Germans are Germans."

Quiñones smiles and swallows a little of his sherry.

"Tell me something, what made you decide to come talk to me?"

"I'm not sure. Maybe the fact that you're a stranger."

"Or maybe you just felt like talking."

"Not exactly. To tell you the truth, I needed to tell someone I'm planning to kill myself. That's pretty heavy stuff to deal with alone."

Suddenly, the girl seemed in deadly earnest Quiñones took another swallow, but this time it was just saliva.

"Are you here in Palma on your own?"

"No. I'm with my dad."

"That's a good thing."

"And with his girl friend too. They'll come looking for me pretty soon."

"Where's your mom?"

"Back in Germany. She and my dad have been separated for quite a while now. She has a friend too, or a lover, or whatever he is."

"Is that why you want to kill yourself?"

"Oh, so you believed me."

"Were you kidding?"

"Not at all. I just didn't think anyone would believe me. No, that's not the reason."

He looked back at the parade of tourists. As a rule, he would sit here, at the tables outside the Miami Café, waiting for the truck to arrive with the papers from Madrid. Then he'd cross over to the newsstand and buy two dailies and some magazines, so as not to lose touch with the rest of the world.

"Well, are you going to tell me any more?"

"Maybe. You seem like a pretty nice guy. In spite of that awful name, Quiñones."

"You don't like it?"

"To tell you the truth, I think it's disgusting. Of course, what matters about people isn't their name. Are you a nice guy or not?

"I think I am."

"Then you are. If you weren't, you would have said you were sure."

"You've certainly got your own way of going about things."

"Mmmm. We all do the best we can."

The waiter comes by with his empty tray, and Quiñones stops him to order another sherry.

"That guy must think I'm some pervert out to corrupt minors."

"Or that I'm a pervert out to corrupt grownups."

"There are a few of those around too."

"For sure. Were you in prison in Argentina?"

Again her question startles him. Trying to appear unfazed, he takes off his glasses and wipes them with a dirty handkerchief.

"For three years."

"Are you alone here in Spain?"

"All alone."

"Don't you have a wife or kids?

"I have a wife. But remember, you were the one who was talking about suicide, not me."

"That's true. But I don't think you're taking me very seriously."

"I'm dead serious. To be honest with you, I wish I weren't. That would be easier. But I am."

"Doesn't it surprise you to hear someone this young talking about suicide?"

"I'd appreciate it if you'd stop sounding like a journalist. No, it doesn't surprise me."

"Nobody knows about it."

"What do you mean, 'nobody'? I do."

"But you won't tell on me, will you? At least, I don't think you will."

"Why don't you talk to your father?"

"He just wouldn't get it."

"And I will?"

"I'm not sure. I'm checking you out, that's all. You're a little old, but you have young eyes. So, maybe...."

"Thanks for the benefit of the doubt."

"What are my eyes like?"

"They look confused."

"I see you've got your way of going about things, too."

"Mmmm. We all do the best we can."

She wipes her hands on her pant legs in a spontaneous, almost ritual, gesture.

"Have you ever tried drugs?" Quiñones inquires matter-of-factly.

"Yeah, but they're no good. They didn't take to me, and I didn't take to them. I guess we're just incompatible."

"Lucky for you."

"Or unlucky, who knows. Anyhow, they didn't do anything for me."

Quiñones sees the truck arrive and drop off the papers from Madrid, but he makes no move to get up; he'll have time for that later. For now he stays right where he is, next to the girl.

"Was your father in prison, too?"

"Yeah."

"Did they give him a rough time?"

"Yeah. Besides, my name isn't Susana."

"You don't say."

151

"It's Elena."

"Well, well...."

"I wasn't sure I could trust you."

"And now?"

"Now, I think I can."

"Well I hate to tell you this, but my name is still Quiñones."

"What a shame. I was really hoping it wasn't."

"Sorry about that."

"Don't you believe in being careful?"

"Sure I do. But you don't exactly look like you're with the C.I.A."

Here, Quiñones proceeds to attack his second glass of sherry.

"How is it? Any good?"

"Great."

"I've never tried sherry."

"Would you like me to order you some?"

"No. Alcohol gives me a rash. Tangos too."

"Tell me, am I supposed to ask you why you propose to kill yourself?"

"It's not a question of proposing. I've made up my mind."

"We usually make up our minds for a reason."

"Well, what's it going to be? Are you going to ask me, or not?"

"Fine, so what made you decide to do it?"

"All sorts of things. My old man, my old lady, his girl friend, her boyfriend, what they and others say about things back there, what life is like for me and others over here."

"Where's over here?"

"Germany, Europe, this whole campground. Do you like to read?"

"Yeah, but I'm no bookworm."

"How about music?"

"Ditto. And you?"

"Ditto, ditto. What of it?"

"Where are you going to start?"

"At the beginning, like a proper storyteller. When we had to split for Europe, like bats out of hell, I was eight. But my brother was only two."

152

"So, you have a brother.... I'm surprised to hear that."

"What's so surprising about it?"

"I would have sworn you were an only child."

"I do act like one, don't I. But I happen to have a brother, too. He was so little then, he doesn't remember a thing. But I do. We lived in this cute little house, two stories high, with a yard, in Punta Carretas. Do you know Montevideo?"

"I've only been there twice, a long time ago. But I know where Punta Carretas is. The lighthouse and all."

"Well, from our place you couldn't see the lighthouse, but you could see the prison."

"Knock wood."

"When we got to Germany my folks were still together. Together, but touchy as all getout. Every little thing was an argument. But at least, each night they would make love."

"No kidding. Did you make that up, or did you spy on them?"

"I could tell from the way the bed creaked. It meant a lot to me, not because I was precocious, or all that curious about sex (don't get the wrong idea), but as proof that they still needed each other. I'm a pretty normal kid, so maybe that's why I didn't like the idea of them splitting up."

"But they split up anyway."

"They would fight over everything, but especially politics. They're both pretty far to the left.... What made it so messy is that they didn't belong to the same group. So each one would blame the other for the clobbering they all took. I didn't understand a whole lot, but it was definitely nasty. Sometimes, I could hear them even when I covered my ears. But my brother would scream his head off, and finally they'd have to stop so he would calm down."

"Is your brother in Palma, too?"

"No. He stayed with my mother. We split up evenly. The boy with mom, the girl with dad."

"And then what?"

"We went along like that for a while until suddenly one night, I didn't hear the bed creak and I realized they were at the end of their rope. So I wasn't surprised, when they got up the nerve one afternoon to say look, kid, you've gotta understand, sometimes these things just happen, your mom and dad are splitting up, etc. The worst part was the etcetera."

Elena, *a.k.a.* Susana, finally drinks half of her lemonade, and Quiñones tries unsuccessfully to stifle a yawn.

"Am I boring you?"

"No, kiddo, it's just the heat."

"Look, if I'm boring you, we can forget it. You know why I'm telling you this whole national saga? Because we'll never see each other again."

"What makes you so sure?"

"You figure it out. We're leaving here the day after tomorrow, and I'll be gone just a few days after that. The only reason I'm not doing it here is that the paperwork would be even more complicated for my dad. Besides, I don't want to ruin his vacation. Anyhow, this little chat is my goodbye to the world."

"I don't know that I've ever been called a world before."

"Anyhow, then my dad got involved with his girl friend, or mistress, or whatever she is, who's even Uruguayan, what else? And my mom got involved with her boyfriend, or lover; he's Uruguayan too, how about that? Nothing like keeping it all in the family. Homeland or Death. Well, they can have the Homeland, and I'll take the rest."

"And are there many Uruguayans in Germany?"

"A fair number. They're always getting together to talk about how things are back in Uruguay. How there's poverty and unemployment; how they're shutting down papers; how they're banning songs; how they're confiscating books; how they're terrorizing, torturing, killing."

"That's all true."

"I know. But it's like a broken record, especially when you keep hearing about it but you haven't lived through any of it. Little by little we're learning to hate everything about Uruguay. I mean, those of us who came here as kids. Remember, in Germany my dad doesn't have to worry about losing his job, and neither does my mom.

Nobody's killing them or torturing them, and we kids can go to school and have our friends."

"And what do all those marvelous advantages have to do with your plans?"

"Just be patient, Quiñones."

"I'm listening."

"One day my brother, who's eight now just like I was when we got here, stood up to my old man and told him he was never going back; how's that for nerve? My old man all but fell on his ass. Then, before anyone could ask him why, my brother added that Uruguay was a real chickenshit place, and that's when the 'all but' disappeared and my old man wound up on the floor. I'll summarize it for you, so you won't get bored: it was my folks themselves, and the rest of their Uruguayan clan, that had convinced my brother of all those things. You know what it is? They all go on and on, and argue and yell as if we didn't exist, or we were stones instead of sponges. But we're exactly like sponges. We soak things up."

"Are you a sponge too?"

"Yeah, except for me it's a little different. I was older than my brother when I got here, so at least I can remember our house and our yard in Punta Carretas. But I understand him, and I know what he means."

The girl's speech is hurried now, she's perked up and her green eyes sparkle in a way Quiñones finds appealing. He feels compelled to address the point.

"Can I tell you something? If by any chance you should decide not to kill yourself, five years from now you're going to wreak havoc on the young male population."

She snickers in amusement.

"You mean the young males of the G.F.R.?"

"Any young males you happen to meet."

"I just now realized what a line that is. You aren't falling in love with me, are you?"

"No, my dear, you don't have to worry. Just go on."

"You see, remembering our little yard isn't enough. It isn't as clear-cut for me as it is for my brother. But I really wouldn't fit in back there, either. Well, maybe in Punta Carretas I would, but not in Uruguay, or even in Montevideo."

"In other words, you feel German."

"Forget it. Do I look like I belong in that big *Kartoffelnsalat*?"

"Excuse me, but I happen to like it."

"That's different; you're from Buenos Aires."

"Tucumán."

"Anyway, you guys are different."

"And what's keeping you from feeling German? Haven't you made any good friends yet?"

"*Jawohl*. I'm good friends with boys, girls, puppies, kittens; but even the kittens realize I'll never be German."

"Do you talk with an accent?"

"My German is better than Willy Brandt's. What I'm missing is a different kind of accent."

"What kind? Spiritual?

"Oh, gimme a break! That's so corny, I could puke."

"O.K., sorry. But what kind of accent do you mean?"

"A different kind, period. Why does it have to have a name? You see, that proves you're over forty even if your eyes do look young. You're from a generation that's always labeling things."

"Exactly. The dictionary generation. What else?"

"It's a complicated story."

"I can see that."

"Sometimes, I live with my mother and her boyfriend. The guy has his good points. He's a little bossy, maybe, but honest. Other times, I live with my father and that lady of his, Rosalba. Let's just say I'm not as fond of her. I admit I'm prejudiced."

"I guess so."

"But between one part-time place and another, it's like I don't have any place to go."

"So, is that the real reason?"

"Be patient, will you, Quiñones? Whenever two of them are away, I stay with the other two, and vice versa. But once all four of them left town at the same time, or I should say all five, because my brother left also. Two of them went East, and three went West. And there I was in the middle, just like Greenwich. With a great big city all to myself. For the first time. And that's when it happened."

Quiñones notices a change in the girl, who suddenly looks less like a twentieth-century Diana.

"When what happened?"

"Nothing much," she says in a lifeless voice. "I got raped."

"What did you say?"

"I got raped, Quiñones. I'm walking home alone one night, when this enormous guy jumps out of the shadows, and drags me over to a construction site. Just like in the movies. It was classic. He had his huge hand over my mouth, which really wasn't necessary since I was so terrified, it didn't even occur to me to scream for help. Then he proceeded to do his thing; he was obviously experienced. For me, it was a really crummy début. And get this. The whole time that fat slob was on top of me all I could think about was the way my folks' bed used to squeak. Isn't that a riot? Besides, he was saying things I couldn't understand. He wasn't German."

"What was he?"

"I couldn't tell. He kept making these guttural sounds. Hoarse ones. I can't describe it. It was pretty awful."

"You're making yourself very clear. What did you do afterwards?"

"When this person had had enough, he punched me really hard and took off. Somehow, I managed to get back on my feet. I was all bruised and bloody, but it wasn't serious; so I was able to make it back to one of my part-time places—my mom's—that was only two blocks away and of course, there was no one there. So no one found out. No one knows to this day, except you. You're the first person I've told."

"But, how come you didn't even tell your mother?"

"What for?"

"You should have seen a doctor."

"Maybe, but I hate being examined. For a while I was afraid I might be pregnant. And that was when I decided. To kill myself, I mean."

"But you weren't pregnant."

"Of course not. That's what clinched it. I figured if I was pregnant, I'd have to stay alive. You know, for the kid's sake and all that. In that case, it wouldn't have mattered what my family or society thought. But if I wasn't pregnant, then I had to end it."

"I don't understand a thing."

"I guess not. That's why I haven't told anyone. I thought maybe you, with your young eyes and all.... Well, I was wrong."

"But Susana, Elena, or whatever your name is, listen to me."

"I don't know if you've noticed, but I'm not crying. That's just so they won't arrest you, for molesting a minor."

"Thank you. You have no idea how grateful I am. But I really wish you'd listen."

"It shouldn't be that hard to understand. I don't fit in here. I don't fit in there. And on top of that, I get beaten up and raped by some guy who isn't from here or there. For all I know, he's a Martian. And he doesn't even give me a baby, who at least would be from here. Or from there. Or from Turdville, to give a name to wherever that animal came from. As you can probably tell, it's got me all tied up in knots."

"What if we began by untying the knots?"

"That's impossible. Or maybe at this point, I don't want to."

"We could at least try."

"But don't you understand? Since that night, it's like I'm a total outsider, a misfit. You see all those bored, red-faced Swedes, Dutchmen, and Germans parading up and down the boulevard? Well, I don't give a shit about any of them."

"Neither do I. And nobody raped me."

"O.K., I'll admit that was a weak argument. But I look at my mother and my mother's boyfriend, my father and my father's girl friend, and even my brother and my Uruguayan friends and my German friends, and none of them matter to me either. Because I'm out in the cold. Just dumped there, like a piece of junk. Some useless, broken down object that can never be fixed."

"Remember, you said you weren't going to cry."

"That's so they won't arrest you. I just hope you appreciate the effort I'm making, because right now I'd give anything to cry."

"Still, I think there's a lesson to be learned here. The mere fact that your lip is trembling, that you feel so much like crying, proves you're no misfit. If you were the outsider you say you are, you'd feel empty, totally drained."

"And just how do you know?"

Quiñones pulls out a cigarette and tries to light up; but it takes him a while to accomplish that, because the match is shaking inexplicably.

"How do I know? I know because I've been there."

Her lip trembles again, only this time she looks more like she's five years old than fourteen. Fighting back tears for the second time, she finally finishes her lemonade. Then, just as she is about to say something, Quiñones sees her expression change abruptly, as if she had put on a mask.

"Look out, here they come."

What an anticlimax: the girl's father and a woman that must be Rosalba are fast approaching with the long, useless strides of people who know they're late for an appointment.

"Oh, I'm so glad you're still here," says Rosalba, struggling to catch her breath. We were afraid you'd get tired of waiting."

"It's gotten very late," the father declares. "There isn't even time to sit down and have a cold drink. We have a date back at the hotel with the Elguetas, those Chileans we met the other night in Barcelona, remember?

"This is my dad, and this is Rosalba," says the girl as she gathers up her things. "And this is Señor Quiñones. He's an Argentine from Tucumán."

"Pleased to meet you," her dad, Rosalba and Quiñones say in unison.

"Señor Quiñones has been very nice," she adds. Not only has he kept me company all this time, but he's convinced me not to kill myself."

Rosalba smiles a little absentmindedly, but the girl's father lets out a guffaw.

"Señor what-did-you-say-your-name-was...."

"Quiñones."

"Señor Quiñones, you'll have to forgive my daughter. These youngsters say some of the darndest things."

"I've found her bright and quite charming."

"That's very kind of you," adds the father. "But now that we're taking her with us, I'm sure it'll be a lot quieter around here."

"Thanks, Quiñones," says the girl.

As her old man and Rosalba scan the street in search of a taxi, she puts two fingers to her lips and blows Quiñones a quick kiss.

"Please, we really have to go now," her old man urges, this time a little anxiously.

"Yes," says Rosalba. "Your father is right. Come along, Inés."

1982

Translated by Louise Popkin

A Note for Paula

As he gets up from the sand, carefully folds his towel, takes several deep breaths, walks down to the water's edge and wades slowly into the sea, he's sure he hasn't left a single detail to chance. Back in town, on his pillow in room 512 at the Hotel Condor is a note, in an envelope with five words written on it in red: Please deliver to Paula Acosta. The chambermaid will find it when she gets there, as usual, at noon. He's taken three whole months to make up his mind, but at this point there's no turning back. Frankly, he's had as much of himself as he can take, so it's time to end it. Still, there's no point in rushing things.

As the water cools his ankles, he knows the last chapter has begun. A flashback to an earlier chapter puts him on another beach, across the Atlantic at Portezuelo, where his mother and stepfather Victor stroll arm in arm along the tightly packed sands, while Joaquín picks out some *milonga* on his harmonica and the damp, diminutive Brutus yaps as usual, determined to live up to his name. A time of innocence or isolation, purity or pride, he's not sure which. A time of discovery, as his robust ten or twelve years of existence settle into that solid sense of well-being, amid shafts of sunlight salty breezes, clean white rocks. His mother and Victor, so young then, yet (to him) so ancient. And the father nobody mentions, the father he never knew, although he did manage to piece together a few fragments of that puzzling story from conversations with his cousin, José Carlos. The sudden, almost criminal, escape to an unknown destination abroad that cut him off shamelessly from his wife and child, with no explanation, no letters, no direct news of any kind. Images of his mother crying for days and weeks on end, but also memories of her recovery six years later, thanks to Victor, who's a pretty good athlete and a nice guy, but so ancient. The fact

161

is, in those days everyone seemed ancient except his peers, José Carlos and Paula.

He wants to take a careful, conscientious look at his life. Why wait for the traditional high-speed version that's presumably a feature of the average death by drowning? After all, there's plenty of time to go over the whole story calmly. So when he's up to his knees in the Mediterranean, he zooms in on his adolescence, on brilliant grades and balmy summers and Victor, as thrilled as any father when he outruns the other high-school participants in the 800-meter race, hanging back until the 600 mark, then—in a final display of stamina—sprinting past the others, as easily as if they were poles in the ground, and across the finish line. A time for reading, his first great books, the ones that would leave their mark on him. And Paula. Walking her home from school, their late afternoons in the park, discovering the Milky Way together.

He gets to select the images, and even to do the editing. There he is standing barefoot on the smooth stones of the ocean floor, the water up to his thighs, there he is, relentlessly choosing the scenes. For instance, his falling out with Joaquín, who no longer plays *milongas* on his harmonica because he's too busy justifying the first faint stirrings of repression; who falls in with a gang of ultra-right-wing thugs and puts the finger on his classmates. And Paula. Organic Chemistry and kisses. Inorganic Chemistry and making out. Physiology and the whole works. Meanwhile, not even a whole cosmetic factory can hide his mother's wrinkles and Victor, for all his inner calm, has gotten himself a duodenal ulcer. Time marches on. Some people open their eyes, and others close them.

The gentle but treacherous ripples splash against his testicles, causing them to contract. It's a long walk out to where it's deep enough to lose his footing. The ripples touch his penis. Paula too, and she stayed with him after that. He thought it was forever, and so did she. Now, it turns out, she's kept to her commitment, and he's the one who's leaving. He's leaving her for the vastness of the sea, its unfathomable peace. Paula is a body he watched grow, take shape, blossom, ripen, take on character. And much more. Paula is the lure of life. That's hard to resist. But he's made his choice. Still more sorrow when Victor dies in that accident on the road to Punta del Este, and his mother is left devastated, alone again, more ancient than ever.

But it's only when the clear water reaches his stomach that his memory really explodes. He doesn't think in terms of shoot-outs because he hates the jargon in those TV serials from the States, yet that's exactly how it feels: like a hail of bullets, machine guns going off, heavy crossfire. When did the whole nightmare start? Maybe when they began arresting students. How could he just sit there doing nothing, safe in his little corner? And Paula. A different kind of love, almost a communal orgasm. How could he fail to do something, be a part of it somehow? And Paula. How marvelous, how exciting to embrace that young body, so familiar, yet so changed. What perilous bliss to enter her, share a cigarette, make their plans, and enter her again. Then go out to those secret meetings, where even the shouting was muted. What an incredible, cautious, bold, congenial, lovable city, and how changed, how full of solidarity. A password, a buzzer pressed twice, and doors opening, beer, coffee, *mate*, maps drawn in an almost childish hand, who has some matches, burn it, that's that. And Paula. Luckily, she wasn't around when they were captured at that bungalow in Atlántida. It was high noon, and the place was crawling with tourists, and bicycles, and street vendors. There was no way out. They had thought of everything except the time of day: all those rotten lunch time rituals made rounding them up a snap.

His outstretched arms seem to caress the water, as the ripples finally lap at the gooseflesh underneath. Of course, he had prepared himself mentally for torture, mustered his defenses, reaffirmed his principles. But when it really happened.... Seven days and seven nights spent searching for something he could tell them, something convincing, even more or less true, but that wouldn't give anything away. Something, just so they'd let him catch his breath. And he came up with that address, of an apartment where no one lived anymore, because by a week earlier everyone had left, gone off in different directions. But even then they kept at him, in long, rough sessions lasting four more days and nights: for once they had that detail, they wanted corroboration, sequels, postscripts. That old apartment where no one lived anymore. But someone did. Damn it all, someone did. Shit, someone did. And thanks to him, thanks to his unforgivable blunder, they took Omar by surprise—just Omar—and when he resisted, they shot him to pieces. It's been eight long years since then. And never for a moment....

The water, colder and colder, is a noose around his neck. He had found it impossible to forgive himself. Even though no one else knew. Because no one did, except Paula. He had told her himself, here in Europe, supposedly a free man now, because a past like that was too much for one memory to bear. And he was grateful when she didn't excuse him, or absolve him or justify him, or ask but what can you do about it, it's done; he was grateful when she just held him and said you poor thing. Because that's more or less what he was. A poor slob dragging Omar's memory around. Omar, whom he had never seen, but had unwittingly helped to eliminate. And Paula. Their relationship changed after his confession. Because she understands, she knows why he feels this way. She knows that night after night, he leans against the towering wall of that needless death he's come to think of as his own private property, that insurmountable barrier that stands between him and others, between him and life. And she snuggles up and leans back with him against that grim wall, never doubting its existence. She helps him look for solutions, not false alibis, but real ways out. Only there are none. Except this long, slow walk into the sea. He doesn't foresee any surprises once his head and with it, his past, present and future, are under the water for good. After all, he had come so close to drowning when they dunked him head first into gallons of filth, held him there until he thought his lungs would burst. To a survivor of the "submarine," that feeling of suffocation is hardly new. And say what they will about pollution, the Mediterranean is a lot cleaner than the shit-filled tank in the barracks. In other words, it's like he's rewarding himself, claiming some kind of prize, by choosing to drown in clean water, pure and purifying. And Paula. She seemed pretty calm when he left her back in Barcelona, saying he had to come talk to Tito and Beatrice about the Solidarity Group while they were here on vacation. But it's really the sea he's come to talk to—this deep blue Mediterranean, without Paula.

The same Mediterranean that laps at his chin now, bringing a familiar, briny taste to his lips. And now too, a shrill, desperate scream reaches his ears. Then only the sound of the water, and again that shattering scream, soaring into the air and out to sea. He has no time, no right, to stop and think: at most, just one or two seconds to act. Once more the scream—it could be help, or save me, or simply a cry—pierces the silence, invades the unfathomable peace about to receive him. And he has no choice but to kick off from the bottom, gather his wits, tread water while he locates the sound, then swim, swim, swim as hard as his strength and experience allow. The terrified little girl bobs up and down, up and down, then up again; and before she can go back under, he grabs her by her blond hair to keep her afloat as he maneuvers one arm around her neck and propels himself toward land with the other, purposefully, without losing his head as he swims, swims, swims, with a renewed, heightened, powerful obsession.

Everything seems to happen in a single long instant. At last the girl is stretched out on the sand, and he looks on with a watery and distant gaze as two or three hefty strangers apply what they know about artificial respiration. About fifty spectators have formed a circle around her motionless body and every so often someone breaks free of the group to come over and touch his shoulder, or smile or say you were great, or thanks to you, or that really took guts or pal, you sure saved the day. Because suddenly he notices that they're treating him like an old friend and the little girl is sitting up now, and she's gotten her color back and she asks where's the man who brought her in. Then, just as everything is getting back to normal, someone happens to mention that it's eleven-thirty. And totally unfazed, without missing a step, he realizes he'd better run back up to the hotel, and see if he can make it to room 512 before the chambermaid finds that note.

1983

Translated by Louise Popkin

Just Kidding

At first he refused to believe it. Then he decided it was true, but couldn't get himself to take it seriously. To anyone with a trained ear, that faint sound (at times, like coins clinking in a slot; at others, just a dull drone) was a giveaway. Armando didn't know why; but the fact was, his phone was tapped. He didn't feel particularly honored or oppressed; the whole thing simply struck him as absurd. He had never managed to understand what the weighty, mysterious, terrifying connotations of the word "surveillance" had to do with an insignificant little country like his that had no oil, no tin, no copper, just several varieties of fruit that no one north of the Rio Grande cared much about, plus some meat and hides their economists regarded as foreign competition.

Surveillance here, in this 1965, middle-class bureaucrat's Uruguay? They've got to be kidding! Nevertheless, there was a tap on his phone. What a drag! After all, nothing he said on the phone was much more of a secret than what he wrote in his articles. To be sure, his phone style was somewhat less refined; he was even guilty of an occasional obscenity. "What do you mean, 'guilty'?" Barreiro would retort vehemently. "Remember, obscenity can border on the sublime."

Since the very idea of surveillance—at least right there—struck him as ridiculous, Armando proceeded to indulge in a little reckless mischief. Whenever he got a call from Barreiro, the only other person who was in on the secret, the two of them made sure they took a few cheap shots at the U.S., Johnson, or the C.I.A.

"Take it easy," Barreiro would say. "When you talk that fast, it's impossible to keep up with you. You want to get some poor stenographer fired?"

"Come again?" Armando would reply. "Is that a stenographer listening in, or a tape recorder?"

"Usually it's a tape recorder, but it seems theirs overheated on them and broke down, so they replaced it with a stenographer. The good thing about stenographers is, their motors don't overheat."

"Hey, do you think we should give the guy some top secret information, so he can get a little recognition?"

"Like tell him about the plans for a riot?"

"No, *che*, it's a little soon for that."

And that's how they'd carry on. Later, after they'd had a good laugh together at the café, they'd get to work on the next day's episode.

"How about if we started using names?"

"You mean make some up?"

"Sure. Or better yet, use theirs. You know, we could say Rodríguez Larreta when we mean Pedro, and Aguerrondo instead of Aníbal; Andrés could be Tejera, and Juan Carlos, Beltrán."

But just a few days after they began using their new code, in the middle of a totally innocent conversation to boot, there was a new development. Maruja had called, and she was talking about all the things fiancées talk about when they're feeling neglected and in need of attention: "You couldn't care less about me"; "When's the last time you took me to a movie?"; "I'll bet your brother takes better care of Celia," and so on. For a few seconds, Armando forgot about phone taps.

"I can't go today, either. You see, I've got a meeting."

"Is it political?" she asked.

With that, a series of three sounds came over the wires—the first and last longer than the second: somebody cleared his throat once, then twice more.

"Was that you clearing your throat?" Maruja asked.

Armando did some fast thinking.

"Yeah," he answered.

Actually, those three sounds in a row were the first exciting thing that had happened to him since they began tapping his phone.

"So," she insisted, "you still haven't answered my question: is that meeting of yours political, or not?"

"No. It's a stag party."

"Well, I can just imagine the filthy stuff you'll all be talking about," she muttered; and she hung up.

Maruja was right. His brother did take good care of Celia. But then, Tito was a special kind of guy. Armando had always admired him...his sense of discipline; his self-restraint; the methodical way he went about his business, his impeccable manners. Celia, on the other hand, often made fun of him for being too fussy: "Bring me his baby pictures," she would demand jokingly, "so I can see if he wore a necktie when he was six months old."

Tito wasn't interested in politics. "It's such nasty business," was the way he liked to put it. (Armando had no problem admitting that politics was nasty business; but even so, he was interested.) With his brand-new diploma, his sizeable income, his big, bright office, his sacrosanct weekends off, his Sunday masses, and his devotion to their mother, Tito was idolized by his family, held up by the entire clan as a shining example, from the time he and Armando were in grade school together.

Although Armando joked with Barreiro about his tapped phone, he never broached the subject with Tito. The brothers had stopped talking politics some time before, after one final, telling conversation, which Tito had ended with a scathing observation: "I don't see how you can associate with the likes of those characters. Can't you see how unscrupulous they all are? Left, right, middle-of-the-road, they're all the same." Oh yes, Tito was even impartial where contempt was concerned. And that too Armando admired, since he didn't feel he could be anything like that independent himself. It takes tremendous courage not to get riled up no matter what, he thought; and maybe that explained how Tito always stayed so calm.

He heard those same three sounds (long, short, long) on a few other occasions. Some kind of warning, maybe? Just in case, Armando decided he wouldn't mention it to a soul—not to Tito, not to his father (though he was sure his old man could be trusted), not even to Barreiro, who was unquestionably his best friend.

"Let's quit joking around on the phone, O.K.?"

"Why?"

"It's just getting to be a bore."

Barreiro was still finding it pretty funny, but he didn't argue.

The night Armando was arrested, there hadn't been any trouble—not from the students, not from the unions, not even from the rowdier soccer fans. Montevideo was quiet, after one of those rare April days that are neither too hot, too cold nor too windy. As he made his way down Ciudadela Street some time after midnight, he was stopped near the main square by two plainclothesmen demanding to see his papers. Armando handed over his national I.D. card.

One of the agents pointed out that it had expired. That was true. He had been meaning to renew it for at least six months.

As they led him away, Armando hoped it was all a big nuisance; he chewed himself out for being so careless, and that was that. It'll be O.K., he reassured himself, halfway optimistic and halfway resigned.

But it wasn't O.K. That same night he was interrogated by two guys, each a specialist of sorts: the first one was courteous, chummy, and laid back; the other boorish and sinister-seeming.

"Why do you say all those silly things on the phone?" the friendly guy asked, throwing him the kind of look usually reserved for a naughty child.

But the other one got right to the point.

"Who is Beltrán?"

"The President of the Council of State."

"I wouldn't play dumb, if I were you. I want the name of the person you and that pal of yours keep referring to as Beltrán."

Armando didn't answer. Soon they would stick pins under his fingernails, or burn his back with lighted cigarettes, or apply a cattle prod to his testicles. These guys meant business. Scared as he was, Armando wasn't too rattled to muse about how respectable that insignificant little country of his had become—a full-fledged State, torture and all. Naturally, he wasn't sure how much of it he, personally, could take.

"It was just a joke."

"Oh, it was, was it?" said the boorish one. "Well, what we're going to do to you is no joke."

That fist landed squarely on his nose. Armando felt something burst inside him, and he couldn't keep his eyes from filling with tears. When the second punch landed on his ear, his head jerked to the right.

"There's no such person," he stammered. "Those names were there for the heck of it; we were just kidding."

Blood was streaming down his shirt. He rubbed his nose with his fist, and the pain was excruciating.

"Just kidding, were you?"

This time the guy slapped him, even harder than he had punched him before. Armando's lower lip blew up like a balloon.

"Well, isn't that nice!"

Then a knee rammed into the small of his back.

"Ever heard of a cattle prod?"

Each time the other guy mentioned that word, Armando felt his testicles contract. "I've got to insult him, so he'll keep hitting me," he thought. "That way, maybe he'll forget about the rest." He couldn't manage too many words at once, so mustering all his strength he just said, "You shit."

The other guy reacted as if Armando had spit right in his face; but then immediately, he smiled.

"If you think you can throw me off that easily, you're pretty wet behind the ears. I'm not forgetting what you hope I'll forget."

"That's enough," the friendly guy interrupted. "Lay off now; he's probably telling the truth." His voice sounded decisive; he had made up his mind. Armando took a deep breath. But just then his strength gave out, and he fainted.

In a way, Maruja was the indirect beneficiary of that outrageous affair. Now she could spend all day with Armando, dressing his wounds, doting on him, kissing him, wearing him out with all her plans. Armando did more than his share of whining because in fact, he didn't mind her pampering. He even considered marrying Maruja sometime soon, but he was very wary of his own idea: "The way those guys worked me over, I'll bet they did something to my head."

Maruja's gentle hand suddenly stopped its stroking. When Armando opened his eyes, there they all were: his father, his mother, Barreiro, Tito, Celia.

"How did you manage to keep from talking?" Barreiro asked over and over. And Armando gave his standard explanation: all they had done was rough him up, though pretty hard, to be sure; the worst part was when they kneed him in the back.

"I don't know what would have happened if they had used that cattle prod."

His mother was in tears; all she had done for about three days was cry.

"Down at the paper," his father said, "they told me the Union is planning to issue a statement of protest."

"They can issue their statements from here to kingdom come," Barreiro grumbled. "He still took one hell of a beating."

Celia had laid a gloved hand on his arm, and Maruja was kissing the one tiny section of forehead that was visible among the bandages. As sore as he was, Armando was just about in seventh heaven.

Behind Barreiro stood Tito, quieter than usual. Suddenly Maruja noticed him there.

"And what do you have to say about this? Are you still feeling impartial?"

Tito smiled before answering deliberately: "I keep telling my little brother what nasty business politics is."

With that, he cleared his throat. Three times in a row. Long, short, long.

1966

Translated by Louise Popkin

Post Mortem

He would have preferred it if no one had stayed around, if they had taken all their shock, their anger, their false cheerfulness home with them, breathing sighs of relief because it wasn't their problem, so they had nothing to lose by talking about her death with their wives, their children, their servants; about the corpse he had provided for their contemplation, young enough to warrant references to the Romantics or hackneyed quotes about the democracy of the grave, and beautiful enough to provoke a vigorous thrust or two in their tired marriage beds (once they had checked the local paper for that day's crimes); for he, Jaime Abal, had presented his dead wife with no apologies, scarcely needing to hold on to her, the way one offers friends a cocktail; and they, after a long look at her sharply-chiseled nose, her dried out lips the color of cardboard, her prominent cheekbones (as striking as ever), immediately accepted her absence, got used to it, all but replenished it; they came filing past him, muttering their condolences, squeezing his hand, and one unusually sincere soul (who was it?), sensing that nothing could comfort him, even said so; and with that, his two standard responses—"It's really awful," "Thanks so much," "It's really awful," "Thanks so much," regardless of what anyone said to him—gave way to a kind of relief, to the realization that he could breathe at last, because someone had uttered his only truth, the single applicable statute in a harsh new set of laws he would have to adapt to and live with as if it were a flesh and blood presence, an elusive, yet enormously powerful companion; because her death was precisely that—her uncertain, faltering young death that refused to go by name, refused to heed her timid pleas—because it was simply inconceivable; because even she herself seemed to find her attitude pathetic—her pitiful pursuit of the end—as if there still existed in the past an unyielding, inextinguishable hope, a possibility that neither advanced nor receded, but might perhaps be attainable in that incessantly fanatical game of pure chance that pits the superstitious against their own awareness; as if there were still a trip in the future, or a party to look forward to, or an accident—anything that might crack open his stifling present, let in some light, free it of compulsory and compelling desires, of that fake and familiar despair—freeing him, freeing her (and why not?) from Jaime Abal; and that suspicion stood between him and whatever might have comforted him; for we really don't know a thing; for wrestling with a bad conscience is always a sorry task; for nothing would have seemed any clearer if no one had stayed around.

2

"Well, that's that," thought Jaime Abal. "But why? I'm just one more vulnerable guy now, with no more illusions. I've had a wife amputated, and that's that. But why? I kept hoping she'd decide to settle down and be as much a part of my world as I once was of hers. The frustrations of youth? That could be. But it's not so easy to work your way up in the world, come out on top, make a name for yourself; not everybody manages to be somebody. Maybe she was wrong about love. But at some point, ours made sense."

Everyone had left except his mother and Ramona. He had asked all the others to go. From right there behind his desk, he could hear his mother bustling around, breezing through the housework *she* had always dawdled over reluctantly.

Not a thing was stirring in that wretched space. By the time they reached the fifteenth floor, the street noises were nothing but a dense, gloomy undertone; only the blare of an occasional car horn, no doubt jarring down below, stood out like some distant shout, some faint, remorseful cry.

Anytime now, his mother would be coming in with tea. She had sent Ramona ahead to tell him: "Mrs. Abal senior says you've got to eat something; you can't go on like this." On the servant's dark face, a little splotchy from all that tearful kitchen talk about Señora Marta and other women who had died, Jaime glimpsed her submissive smile, the stark whiteness of her teeth; but immediately her simple, compassionate expression gave way to another fit of uncontrollable weeping.

He looked over at his bookshelves, at all the thick volumes bound in leather. They too were a thing of the past. Whenever he got back from the office, with the smell of the street clinging to his clothes, face, hands as if the whole world had it in for him, feeling cornered, wiped out, humanly incapable of facing even one more setback, then the sheer physical presence of those books—those worlds where anything was possible—awaiting his return gave him all the relief he needed, helped him forget the rigors of his day. He would spend all evening in his study reading. He always planned to turn in before midnight; in fact, he always knew he wouldn't. And when he finally got to bed, she was always fast asleep. Was that the crime for which he was being punished? Exactly what was this death, anyway? A reprimand? An acquittal? Just a form of silence?

From behind his left shoulder came his mother's familiar voice: "It's time for tea. You've got to eat something, Jaime; you can't go on like this."

3

"But who is he? What's he like?" Jaime asked.

"His name is Pablo Pierri, and he says you don't know him."

"I don't know him?"

"That's what he said. And that he wants to talk to you about poor Señora Marta."

"Who on earth...? Oh well, show him in."

As Ramona went to get Pierri, it struck Jaime that this unwelcome guest was about to lead him into dark, forbidden territory; and he was somewhat repulsed by his own unavoidable curiosity.

But the man who showed up wasn't altogether unappealing. He was a little shorter than Jaime, maybe thirty to thirty-five years old, dark-eyed, blond, with a full head of hair. He had on a gray off-the-rack suit and an inexpensive white shirt; his brown shoes could have used a shine. But surprisingly enough, he didn't look all that chintzy. Wrapped carelessly in clothes that were the antithesis of his slick charm, Pierri was capable of instant rapport, even with somebody as withdrawn and ill-at-ease as Jaime. At the same time, Jaime suspected that the shaky equilibrium they managed as they introduced themselves, exchanged the customary niceties, and sized one another up, would have broken down willy-nilly with Marta's mere impossible presence. Her death so eradicated any thought of violence, so numbed his feelings, that he could even put up with some totally ordinary guy—some stranger named Pierri—supplying him with a past he never knew about, a secondhand life, a whole new Marta.

"You never expected to suffer like this," Pierri was saying, "and that's why you're feeling so helpless—a mixture of miserable and afraid. Or maybe I can be more specific: afraid of being lonely. Am I wrong about that?"

"Yes, you are," Jaime replied with some effort. "You're dead wrong. It's true I haven't managed to get Marta out of my life yet; she's a habit I keep coming up against when I least expect it. Still, I can assure you I'm not the least bit miserable or afraid. You see, loneliness is no longer an issue, since I have nobody to relate it to. Shaken up is what I am."

"That's just another way of being afraid, or maybe a first taste of fear. When the shock wears off and you can be calm again instead of miserable; when a sense of relief comes over you and you're feeling comforted, don't lash out at yourself in anger. Because you still won't be done with her, or with the way you were when she was around. Your fear will stay with you—no more shock, just that constant, abiding fear."

"But fear of what? What's there to be afraid of?"

"You say loneliness isn't an issue. Naturally, you'd say that, when you've lost all your drive. This sudden break in your routine has filled you with a stoicism you aren't used to, so you feel stronger than you ever imagined you could, and in the midst of it all, you see yourself as calm and unruffled. But once you get past this stage of what you might call 'euphoric depression,' you'll discover that you're sliding inevitably toward the future; and no amount of willpower in the world can ever change that."

Jaime felt a sudden rush of anger at the whole absurd situation. How preposterous that someone he didn't know should venture to scold him, give him advice, warn him about how he might eventually feel, leave him with no excuses, cut through all his normal defenses! But what angered him most was the realization that little by little, without meaning to, he had begun to take this stranger's words seriously. "O.K.," he said crossly; "but don't we all slide inevitably toward the future?"

"Sure," Pierri countered; "but the future can sometimes be a living hell. Just when you feel as though you've come back to life, you may discover that feeling alive again can mean reliving all the misery life entails, intensely, over and over. And that's when the fear of loneliness will hit you; because once you've loved a woman and she's nevertheless moved on, leaving you with no one to relate your loneliness to, you've also discovered that every new woman you love will eventually move on and leave you with no one to relate your loneliness to. Or maybe you think there's an even lonelier loneliness, more endlessly anchored in the future? As a matter of fact," he added with a smile, "there's a lot to be afraid of."

The short silence that followed gave Jaime just enough time to look for another way out. "You.... You knew Marta?" As soon as he spoke, he realized his impatience was a sure sign that he felt humiliated; he should never have asked. But it was too late, for Pierri was already answering:

"I met your wife many years ago."

"I see."

"But I never lost track of her after that." The guy's manner was smoother than ever; there was no getting rid of him.

"Please..." said Jaime. Perched haughtily on the sofa, he turned as red as if he had fallen on his knees and his eyes were a mere two inches from Pierri's scuffed shoes. "Please, talk to me about her."

"Gladly," said the unwelcome guest, in full control of himself, the situation, Jaime, the past. "But before I talk about Marta, I have to tell you about Gerardo."

4

"Gerardo used to bully me," said Pierri, "but to my mind, that was no reason to dislike him. He was two years older than I was, and a lot more worldly. He smoked, had a huge repertoire of dirty jokes, and was up on all the latest swearwords. In spite of all that, I took a mild interest in what he said about his day-to-day plans. I often felt he was covering up his innocence, like it was one of those little raw spots that never quite heals and eventually becomes an obsession. I remember one time we'd gone down to the side of the road; the bus from Montevideo was due by at seven, and Gerardo was supposed to pick up a package of books. I was happy just lying there in the grass. One of my legs had gone to sleep and I could feel the edge of the embankment digging into the small of my back, but the dusky sky looked almost close enough to touch. Naturally, Gerardo felt like talking; and that day, without any warning he started getting personal. A little annoyed and wishing he wouldn't spoil such a peaceful moment, I listened to him mumble. Then suddenly, his words began to sink in; I realized I was hearing about all his filth, all the nasty things he did in secret, and I couldn't help blushing. With that he looked straight at me, shouted 'You idiot!' and slapped me twice across the face. So I let go of all my inhibitions and burst out laughing. On the one hand, I didn't feel like reacting to what he had just done; on the other, laughing seemed like the easiest and best way out. Soon the bus came, and we picked up the books and left. At that point, neither of us was in the mood to talk; all we wanted was to get away from one another. I didn't feel particularly resentful towards Gerardo. I simply understood that I had let him down. He had tried to show me a private, guilty part of his life, and I had made the double mistake of getting embarrassed and embarrassing him. So I had earned those slaps; I figured they evened the score. But I suspect he never forgave me. Another time the conversation was about my mother. My mother was a tall woman, naturally a bit stoop-shouldered and bent; and I'd feel a sort of tender uneasiness as I watched her bend even further over the flowerbeds in our little garden, where she used to say she was killing time when in fact, time was killing her. Gerardo, who had no mother, felt a somewhat begrudging admiration toward mine. So I was quick to tell him what I remembered about her, my most vivid memories—of that morning, that noontime, that very afternoon— while they still had a life of their own, before they merged with all the others to become part and parcel of my attachment to her. 'I don't understand,' he said. So, I tried to go into more detail: how I had spied on my mother from the tool shed through a crack in the wall; how she, thinking she was alone, had stopped in front of some drooping roses and looked at them, just looked. 'I don't understand,' he repeated. Then, drawing on some unconscious sadistic streak, I subdivided the details even further: how she had looked those roses over one by one, how there was a certain bitterness about her, a strangely depressed quality as she contemplated their sudden lack of pain, of beauty, of life. Suddenly Gerardo lunged at me, beside himself, capable of almost anything, and I realized he had finally caught on. But the worst time of all was with Marta. Marta and I were about the same age, though she sometimes seemed older because of that way she had of lowering her eyelids and just barely moving her lips—as if to articulate ideas instead of words. Sometimes all three of us would go out on our bicycles. Marta was a very nervous girl; and whenever she spotted anything coming in the opposite direction, her bike would start wobbling as if she couldn't decide whether to throw herself under the wheels of the oncoming vehicle, or into the ditch at the side of the road. When I saw her do that, I always knew what to do: I would start passing her on the left and get between her and whatever was coming toward us, so I could either keep her from falling or, if worse came to worse, push her over to the right. That's exactly what happened the afternoon in question. The bus coming towards us was too close to the center line, and that made Marta more nervous than usual. Twice I watched her wobble dangerously. When the bus was almost on top of us, she threw up her arms in a panic. Since there was no way to keep her from falling, I pushed her into the ditch. Gerardo, who was riding up ahead and had turned to look back, managed to catch what I did but not why I did it. He got off his bike and took a good look at the two of us: Marta with her knees all bloody, covered with mud; and me, standing there gawking like an idiot instead of helping. Then he walked over, wiped off Marta's knees as best he could, and coming up to me, without a word, almost casually, slammed his fist into my temple. I don't know what Marta did or what, if anything, she said. If I remember correctly, they got back on their bikes and pedaled off slowly, without even looking at me. The whole thing left me feeling a little dazed, like it was all a misunderstanding. I couldn't hate anyone because of a misunderstanding, something that was sure to be cleared up later on. But it never was. They never knew that I sat there, bewildered and in tears, until it was dark out and I was numb from the cold."

5

"My house was right across from where the train stopped," Pierri was saying now, "and Gerardo's was about three and a half miles away from mine. Only Marta's house overlooked the main road. What brought us together, what we had in common, was lots of free time and very little to do with it. We were no good at conversation, we had nothing to talk about, and there was nothing we wanted. All we ever did was invent places to go, wander around the countryside, and roughhouse together. To Gerardo and me, Marta was one of the guys. During our school years, we had always walked into town together. Now that our time was our own, what we shared was our reticence, the river, our long walks. Gerardo was living with a well-to-do aunt and uncle, neither of whom paid much attention to him. In those days Marta's family owned a lovely villa (by the time you met her, they had sold it), with a car, two dogs in the yard, and three or four women in the kitchen. But her parents spent weeks at a time in Montevideo, while Marta did as she liked.

179

As for me, I lived with my mother in the house she was kept in by Don Elías, a farmer who by then, was dead and buried in the cemetery out on the ridge, and who everyone claimed was my father. I didn't believe that, first because my mother never mentioned him to me, and second because Don Elías's elderly widow was still living back in Los Arrayanes with her four sons. I didn't know where we got money to live on. Still, we got by with no effort on my mother's part or mine. There was never anything left over; but we always had what we needed. For several years after I quit school, I was the laziest good-for-nothing for miles around. If I wasn't out in the shed reading big fat novels Gerardo lent me, I'd be loafing up in the *ombú* tree outside the kitchen window, or lying in the grass and staring at the sky. My greatest pleasure was riding my bike, stopping by to get Marta or Gerardo, or having them come by for me. After Gerardo got sick, we went to visit him every two or three days; and for reasons I've never understood, he was so mellow we barely recognized him. It was as if his fever had somehow made him look and sound gentle: he was soft-spoken, not the least bit awkward, unusually affectionate, surprisingly placid and imaginative. One afternoon he even took me and Marta by the hand and murmured 'My dear, dear friends!' with a smile so broad, that it left both of us feeling leery and apprehensive. On our way out, Marta remarked that there was something odd about him. I figured it was his fever. We pedaled along for about ten minutes. There was no one else in sight. Behind us, the setting sun was barely visible over the ridge. The trees by the side of the road loomed gray in the dwindling light—dreary, uninspired imitations of their own noontime shadows. Just ahead of me, Marta had begun coasting downhill. For the first time, I was struck by her youth, her light brown hair, her attractiveness as a woman. The sight of her taut, skinny legs bearing down firmly on the pedals was mesmerizing. My newly acquired awareness knocked the wind right out of me; I felt weak in the knees. Just then, Marta glanced back. Caught totally off guard by my look of wonder and amazement, finding me so completely changed, she veered off the road into the ditch. As I stopped to help her, and we muttered something about a broken wheel, and we set off again avoiding one another's eyes, I knew our friendship was over; and she knew it was time for a different kind of antagonism, different arguments, different games. From then on when I went to see Gerardo, I preferred to go alone, early in the morning when I wouldn't meet anyone on the way except, at most, a few workers coming off the night shift at the oil refinery. I was just discovering— or, perhaps, deciding—that there was no excuse for my laziness; and I liked to brood over how little I had done in life, how much I intended to do. As I pedaled along I would think about my mother's relatively secure income (in the light of what I now knew); about Don Elías, who was nothing but a name to me; about my own persistent and tedious loafing. Then I would be overcome by feelings of shame and worthlessness. A phony was what I was, a complete fraud...thanks to my mother, to me, to the nonexistent—dead and buried—Don Elías. I still wasn't strong enough to stop feeling like a victim, or brave enough to try rising above my circumstances. I still thought what it took to get ahead was a modicum of gall, of sheer pushiness. I didn't lose hope, because I wasn't all that set in my ways; there was nothing passionate about my loser's mentality, the sense that I would never amount to much; it was simply a bad habit chosen at random, as if good and evil had contributed in equal shares to that earlier future, so difficult to recapture in all its purity, as if evil had come sneaking up on me, treacherously, from behind, without allowing me even a single question. The evil in this instance was my birth, Don Elías's money, my mother's silence, Gerardo's bullying. Anything that made no sense, or kept on happening, or went wrong, became part of it; it was a crisis in how I related to the world, related to Gerardo, related to Marta. It was wanting to forget about myself, and the self-consciousness that kept me from forgetting. It was my guilty conscience, with its deliberate omissions and restless nights. It was, in other words, exactly what Marta used to say. Yes, Marta—still reachable, though solemn and confused— had thrown back her head, waited for her gesture to awaken my desire, even helped herself to a few more seconds of my image of her, before disappearing, becoming a new Marta, who showed the true colors of the old one. Only then did she say: 'And besides, there's the matter of your mother.' All the rest, then, that list of excuses over half an hour long (her plans for school; the problem of our age; all her parents' objections; my virtual uselessness when it came to anything practical) was a mere by-product of her initial response: *it'll never work*; while the matter of my mother on the other hand, was substantive, serious, true—the brutally honest version of *it'll never work.* 'The matter of my mother' meant me, and Don Elías's money, and the ridiculous notion that the surveyor's daughter and the whore's son could ever hold hands and count each other's fingers, the way fools and lovers do. So, in other words, if I went to see Gerardo early in the morning, under a cloyingly blue sky, telling myself I didn't have to visit if I didn't want to, knowing I preferred the old bully to the candy-coated, feverish Gerardo who greeted me calmly—almost like a sister—when I arrived and pointed to the green armchair, saying: 'Come on in; you can sit here;' if I went to see him it was because I knew that sooner or later, I'd have to tell him; that my secret was bound to come out during some inevitable silence I had yet to choose. But that day, the silence itself did the choosing. I watched it take shape, announce its arrival in the rhythm of the conversation, in all we hinted at but didn't say. Then, just as it was about to disintegrate—as I leaned my arms against the lovebirds smooching on his bedspread; as I was about to say, 'There's something I should tell you about Marta'—just then, he sat himself up, leaned his elbows on the pillow, looked me straight in the face, absolutely calm, scrutinizing each pimple, each tiny pore, and began to say: 'There's something I should tell you about Marta.'"

6

It had been a while since Pierri had said goodbye with a perfunctory handshake. There was nothing friendly, conciliatory or even polite about it; it had simply reaffirmed the non-relationship that preceded their encounter, leaving him just as bewildered and isolated as before. So, she hadn't loved Pierri either. So, Pierri wasn't the enemy. So—at least, according to Pierri—she hadn't loved Gerardo either.

"Little by little, he got back on his feet," Pierri had said; "but I stopped seeing him after that. Marta kept on visiting, although apparently, she didn't care much about him. To tell you the truth, I don't know whether Gerardo ever made love to her, or if so, when. I didn't see them together until about a year later, at a dance in town. As a rule, they didn't go dancing, and neither did I. But that day, I went with two girls."

How different it had been, before they were married, to hear her say he wasn't the first; how different to tell her it didn't matter (the truth is, he was too busy trying to get her clothes off), how different from actually picturing her now with all those men: the short ones, the tall ones, the adolescents with their pudgy baby faces and disgusting acne, the older ones with their cold, greedy eyes, their hands pawing her body with no imagination.

"I left both my dates on the dance floor, because I was bored and anxious to have the evening over with as soon as possible. Then I went into what I assumed was the coatroom and flicked on the light. I turned around so quickly, that they didn't have time to pull apart; there they were in each others' arms, kissing and so close together, they..."

At that, he had jumped to his feet and said, "O.K., I think I've heard enough;" then, in response to Pierri's begrudging silence: "Now, please go." That's when Pierri had shaken his hand. The corners of his lips were turned upwards, as if he couldn't help smiling.

"Don't take it that way. For whatever it's worth, I can assure you she never loved Gerardo. Or let's say she never loved Gerardo any more than she may have loved you. And if that still strikes you as a rash statement, then let's just say she didn't love Gerardo any more than she loved me."

7

"...and all my plans, but now what's going on, what's happening to me? I can't stand that superpolite way he has of putting up with everything; I can't stand his bookishness, or his sickening

183

apologies—the way he never sticks up for himself. Oh, God, why does he have to act like such a wimp? Because he likes being a martyr, that's why—always groveling like a beggar; always watching his step like some criminal on the run. What on earth do those sweaty hands of his, or his bony body, or anything about that whining wretch have to do with me, anyway? I don't want sedatives; I don't want a guy looking at me like some wounded puppy. I want a real man in bed. After all, Ana, we aren't kids anymore; we hardly need fumigating each time we mess with a mortal sin. The way I see it, either I'll get what I want, or I'll go down trying. The question is will I be any match for Jaime, his mother, their friends—that rotten bunch of loners, those meek-mannered sanctimonious bigots, those perfect degenerates? So what if their morals are the opposite of mine; maybe theirs and mine are pretty sleazy. In any case, I can't go on pretending like this. Love is a hit-or-miss proposition; you can't catch it in a trap. And to tell you the truth, I don't even care to try. I hate him so much I could burst and the worst part is, I'm beginning to enjoy it. I like hurting his feelings, showing him how little he knows about me; I like making fun of his petty ambitions, his all but nonexistent urges. You have no idea how many times I've wished he was dead, once and for all, with a bullet in his head, sprawled on the ground, stone cold.... Other times, I wish I had that bullet for myself. I've had really rotten luck, Ana. I don't mean to sound irreverent, but my opinion of God and company is pretty bizarre—downright obscene, in fact. It's true, Ana, I've had rotten luck. And that doesn't make me unhappy, just mad. But what makes me even madder is that he has no idea how rotten it's been; he doesn't have a clue about Gerardo, or Pierri, or Luis María. And unless he knows about them—especially Luis María—he'll never have a clue. Hey, what if I were to..."

1951

Translated by Louise Popkin

Fidelities

At age thirty-five, Ileana Márquez had a husband (Dámaso) and a lover (Marcos). She had no qualms about being loved, or at least desired, by two men; it made her more self-assured, more confident in her dealings with others. What's more, in both appearance and disposition, Dámaso and Marcos were, so to speak, complementary. That's why what attracted her to one didn't make her lose interest in the other. When she was in Dámaso's arms, she never thought of Marcos, and vice versa.

Dámaso and Marcos knew each other. They weren't friends, but they got along well enough. Marcos obviously knew that Ileana had sex with her husband; but Dámaso had no idea how intimate the other relationship had become. Oddly enough, Ileana considered herself faithful to both men, since she had never been interested in anyone else. She was perfectly aware of how attractive her body— so lovely and shapely despite (or perhaps because of) her age—was to both her husband and her lover. Her own smooth skin, with its unique odor, responded just as pleasurably to Marcos's velvety hands as to Dámaso's more rugged touch. She felt fulfilled and in control, of both parts of her sex life.

The warning light came on one night when her husband merely went through the motions; then she felt his indifference for a second time, and a third...until pretty soon, their lovemaking was a rare and perfunctory routine—initiated by her, at that. At first, she suspected a loss of libido, brought on by overwork or stress; but little by little, she began blaming herself. "What's wrong with me?" she wondered, staring at the same old reflection in the same old mirror. "What's wrong with my body?" Eventually, she decided that Dámaso had taken a mistress, and this made her deeply resentful. She wouldn't stand for such an obvious betrayal! Nevertheless, she didn't say a word.

From then on, her only consolation was Marcos, whose services, in the best sense of the word, were still available. She didn't dare tell him about the changes in Dámaso, for fear he might find her less attractive. She had read somewhere that one of the best ways for a married woman to hang on to a lover was to keep her husband interested. The sad part was that one night, the same thing that happened with Dámaso began to happen with Marcos: he said he was tired, and they just lay there next to each other.

It happened again and again. Ileana got terribly depressed, which made things even worse: a certain pallor spread from her cheeks to the rest of her body—from her breasts (once so round and firm, now so out-of-shape and flabby), all the way down to her pubis—she looked sallow and pasty; and with all these changes, which she was the first to see, she felt she had less and less to offer, not just to Dámaso and Marcos, but to any man. Her double alliance had turned out to be a colossal fiasco, and her biggest problem was that she couldn't figure out why. In Marcos's case, loss of libido was less likely than in Dámaso's. Had Marcos decided to trade her in for another mistress? Or did he have a fiancee? Maybe he was about to get married, and afraid to tell her. Strictly speaking, Marcos's indifference hurt her even more than Dámaso's, for all those magazine articles and nineteenth-century novels had taught her that sexual boredom was more common between husband and wife, than between lovers.

One weekend she decided to do something about it. First she would tail Marcos for a while, and then she would tail Dámaso. She had to have an answer; that was the only way out of this rut. She was thoroughly familiar with her men's routines. Marcos left his office at 6:00 PM and usually walked home, since he didn't live far from work. So, on Monday, she parked her car near his office; at a little after six she saw him leave with some friends. They parted ways at the corner, and Marcos hailed a cab. Ileana had to pull away from the curb in a hurry (she had left the engine running, just in case), since she hadn't anticipated that move. The cabbie turned down a few side streets, then took Agraciada and April 19th all the way to Prado Park, where he stopped. Ileana stopped too, a safe distance away. Marcos got out of the cab and set out along a pathway in the park. Ileana gave him a head start, then got out of her car to follow him. She saw Marcos turn right onto another path and walked faster, so she wouldn't lose him.

When she caught up to him again, what she saw in the dwindling light stopped her dead in her tracks. But then, almost magically, all her old self-confidence returned. Marcos and Dámaso wandered off together, hand in hand.

1985

Translated by David Unger

A Bolivian with an Outlet
to the Sea

While I've never been able to confirm it, I'm told that in the thick of the Malvinas War, Borges was asked if he had any ideas about how to end the conflict; with his usual metaphysical irony, he replied: "I think Argentina and Great Britain should come to an agreement and hand over the Malvinas to Bolivia, so Bolivia will finally get its outlet to the sea."

Actually, Borges's irony (assuming the quote is accurate) is based on Bolivia's national obsession: Bolivians always seem to be scanning the horizon for a glimpse of the sea they've been denied. Sure, there's Titicaca; but that huge lake only increases their frustration, since instead of leading to other worlds, it just leads back to itself.

In any case, when a Bolivian reaches the sea, even somebody else's, it's always a Caucasian, never an Indian. However, thanks to an odd stroke of luck, an Indian from somewhere near the Oruro mines once reached that forbidden destination.

He must have been a sweet, well-behaved child, since he was picked up and brought to the capital by a lady from a wealthy La Paz family who happened to be passing through Oruro. This was back inn the fifties. Rebaptized Gualberto Aniceto Morales, he was taught how to read, and trained as a servant. He was so dependable that when his masters traveled to Europe they took him along, not exactly to broaden his horizons, but because they needed someone to help with the daily chores.

And so, the young man (who was past fifteen at the time) stored up in his head a whole collection of impressions of the sea, from the warm blue waters of the Mediterranean to the icy bays of the Baltic. When his masters returned to Bolivia a year later, Gualberto

Aniceto asked for permission to return to his native village to see his family.

There, in the bleak, windswept spot where he was born, amid the astonished gazes and dense silences of his family, the traveler told stories slowly and in great detail, full of steep cliffs, waves, dolphins, shipyards, stevedores, tides, flying fish, tankers, piers, flashing beacons, sharks, gulls, and huge ocean liners.

But one night he ran out of memories and fell silent. His family kept staring at him, waiting for more, huddled together on the dirt floor with wads of coca leaves bulging in their cheeks. They waited and stared at his silence, and from the back of the room came his grandfather's voice, demanding despite his rotten lungs, "What else did you see?"

Gualberto Aniceto felt he couldn't disappoint them. He knew from experience that the yearning for the sea is boundless. So it was then, only then, that he started to tell them about the mermaids.

1986

Translated by David Unger

Isosceles Triangle

Lawyer Arsenio Portales and former actress Fanny Araluce had been married for twelve blissful years. From the start, Arsenio had insisted that Fanny leave the stage. Apparently, he wasn't terribly open-minded, and the thought of his pretty wife in the arms of all those actors night after night was too much for him.

It hadn't been easy for Fanny to accept his terms, which she considered absurd, chauvinistic and totally unprofessional. "Besides," he added by way of justification after she had quit, "I don't think you have what it takes to be an actress. You're too honest, always playing yourself when you should be playing the character. You're too transparent. A true actress is probably a complete mystery in real life; otherwise, she'd never be able to take on new identities, to become someone else. You can dress up all you want as Ophelia, Electra or Mariana Pineda, but you'll always be Fanny Araluce. I'm not saying you don't have an artistic temperament, but you really should try your hand at painting or writing; for painters and writers, transparency is a asset, instead of a liability."

Fanny would hear him out, but he never really convinced her. If she gave up acting, it was out of love. He clearly didn't see it that way. Still, offstage, in everyday life, she was almost the perfect housewife, calm and orderly. Probably too perfect for Portales, Attorney-at-Law. For the past two years, Arsenio had carried on a secret affair with another woman, who was passionate, sexy, unpredictable and, as if all that weren't enough, also quite attractive.

As an appropriate meeting place for the two of them, Portales rented an apartment only eight blocks from his house. He had been careful to come up with a simple alibi: for professional reasons not altogether clear, he had to make a weekly trip to Buenos Aires. Since he was only gone Tuesday nights, he would tell Fanny not to bother to call but just in case, he had given her the phone number of an Argentine colleague, who had clear instructions: "Arsenio? He's at a meeting that won't be over till very late." Fanny never called.

Since his wife knew his likes and dislikes better than anyone else, she would pack his suitcase and call the cab. Portales would get out eight blocks away from the house, go up to his little lovenest, get comfortable, prepare drinks, and put on the TV, while he waited for Raquel, who was also married and who, therefore, had to wait for her husband to leave for his weekly inspection of their place in the country. Actually, if they got together on Tuesdays, it was to please Raquel, since that was the day her husband had chosen for tending to his fields. "Which leaves the whole playing field to us," Arsenio would quip.

When Raquel finally got there, they would eat at home, since they couldn't risk being seen together at a restaurant or at the movies. Then they would make love playfully, almost like two frisky teenagers. Each Tuesday, Portales felt like a new man. Each Wednesday, it was hard to go back to the respectability of his real, orderly, legitimate home.

On his trip back—he wasn't sure just why—he was always over-cautious. He'd have a cab drop him off at the airport; then, after a while, he'd take another cab from Carrasco to his house. Fanny played her role by asking him how everything had gone, whereupon he would go into great detail about his meetings with those boring Argentine clients, always making it his business to say, of course, how great it was to be home.

For the Tuesday that marked the second anniversary of his exhilarating and devious affair with Raquel, Portales got her a necklace made out of Florentine beads. He had asked a client—this time a real one, who owed him a favor—to bring it back from Italy. Settling into his posh little pad, Portales put the champagne on ice, took out two goblets, sat down in the rocking chair and waited, more impatiently than usual, for his mistress.

Raquel got there later than usual—justifiably, since she too, had decided to buy him a little gift in honor of their secret anniversary: a silk tie, with blue stripes on a grey background. That was when

Arsenio Portales gave her the box with the necklace. She loved it. "I'll be right back," she said, on her way to the bathroom; "I want to see how it looks on me." And as a foretaste of the reward he had coming, she gave him a tender, passionate kiss. Understandably, he took that to mean that a glorious night lay ahead.

But Raquel took her time in the bathroom, and he started feeling restless. He got up, went over to the closed door and asked: "What's up? Are you okay?"

"Absolutely," she answered. "I'll be right with you."

Reassured, but still eager to get on with things, Portales went back to his rocker. Five minutes later, the bathroom door opened. To his great surprise, it was his wife, Fanny Araluce, and not Raquel, who stepped out wearing the Florentine beads.

Dumbfounded, Portales blurted out: "Fanny, what are you doing here?"

"Here?" she repeated. "Why, the same thing we do every Tuesday, darling. I'm here to see you, go to bed with you, make love to you and be made love to." And as her husband sat there speechless, Fanny added: "You see, Arsenio, I'm both Fanny and Raquel. At home I'm Mrs. Portales, but here I'm former actress Fanny Araluce. Or rather at home, I'm transparent, but here I'm a complete mystery, with the help of a little makeup, of course, plus a wig and a good script."

"You're Raquel?" Arsenio Portales stammered.

"Yes, I'm Raquel. Get it? You've been cheating on me with me. Now, after two years of leading two lives, it's time to choose. Either you divorce me, or you marry me, because I'm not about to stand for any more of this ambiguity. And that's not all: now that I've made such a success of this show by keeping it running for two years, I'm notifying you officially of my decision to return to the theater."

"But your voice," murmured Arsenio. "There was something so strange about your voice. And even your eyes are a different color."

"Of course. That's what green contacts are for. I've always heard you say that green-eyed brunettes really turned you on."

"And your skin. Your skin was different too."

"Oh no, darling; I'm sorry to disappoint you. Here and at home, I've always had exactly the same skin. The difference was all in your hands. They put different skin on me. And at this point, even I'm not sure which skin I really belong in: Fanny's or Raquel's. So your hands will have to decide."

Portales clenched his fists, more flustered than furious, more embarrassed than angry.

"You've been deceiving me," he gasped.

"Of course," answered Fanny/Raquel.

1986

Translated by David Unger

Maison Lucrèce

"Hey, listen," said Medardo Robles at about two in the morning down at the Double Jeopardy, as he sat there savoring his fifth or sixth whiskey. "Why don't you write a story about the hookers from my hometown? I'll even give you a title: 'The Paramours of San Pascual.' Not bad, eh? If I had your talent I'd take on the project personally.... But to be honest, pal, I'm so sure I'll never write it that I'm happy to pass on the basic facts to you. Consider it proof of our friendship; nowadays, good friends are hard to come by. Like I told you, I'm from San Pascual, an average-sized town in the Interior near the Uruguay River; it's nothing spectacular, but no run-of-the-mill place either, an unusual spot, where people are on the conservative side and fairly well-read. An especially energetic teacher from the local high school (hey, yeah, we've even got our own high school in San Pascual) once spent several years collecting the names of authors who were born in our town. And guess what? He came up with a grand total of fifteen poets and nine prose writers. Of course, all of them eventually left for Montevideo. Now, I'm sure no other town can boast of anything like our *hetaerae* (how's that for class?), because our locals have always had a culture all their own, and when it comes to fancy new angles or exotic shortcuts, they've never needed any lessons from those know-it-all city-slickers who come around spouting their venerable gibberish. Back where I come from, people usually just listen; they don't ask a lot of questions. Once they do speak up though, they can really put a lecturer on the spot. I'll never forget the time a poet showed up in a pink shirt and multicolored tie, to deliver a longwinded lecture at the local dance hall on the structure of violence in Dante's *Inferno*. He had asked for a blackboard and on it, he wrote the words 'Umano, Spoglia, Rinnova,' explaining that those were the three states of the soul corresponding to Hell, Purgatory and Paradise. He followed that with an hour of highbrow interpretations, then concluded by declaring Francesca da Rimini to be Dante's greatest character and the First Woman of Modern Times. After a few seconds of polite applause, he offered to take questions from the audience. And that's when this bald guy Freirías got up to say that he had no questions, but he did have several comments: (a) that *umano*, the first state of the soul on the blackboard, was missing an 'h'; (b) that in his humble opinion, the First Woman of Modern Times wasn't that Francesca lady at all, but Doña Luisa, who had seventeen kids, all of them alive and working in San Pascual (his suggestion was applauded roundly); and (c) could he please hear the speaker's arguments in support of Francesca, and then he would offer his own in favor of Doña Luisa. After making it clear that *umano* had no 'h' because it was spelled that way in Italian, the poor lecturer tried to get off the hook by making it just as clear that his opinion about Francesca da Rimini really belonged to Francesco de Sanctis, the distinguished Italian critic and scholar; so then Freirías asked him courteously why, in that case, he had passed it off as his own. In other words, Doña Luisa won the contest by default. I'm telling you all this so you'll realize how impossible it would have been to intimidate those folks with a lot of pedantic jargon. They respected knowledge, but only when it was offered unpretentiously. Anyway, getting back to what I said I'd tell you, on the outskirts of San Pascual stood (and still stands) what used to be the only two-story house in town; a pretty little sign over the door identifies it as Maison Lucrèce, a brothel unlike any other. The origins of the Maison go all the way back to 1919, the year its founders landed in Uruguay as an unforeseen consequence of World War One. From the word go, Madame Lucrèce instilled in her pupils the pluralistic, quasi-ecumenical style that would be their hallmark even after her death in 1939 (coincidentally, just two days before the Wehrmacht invaded Poland). In other words, the career of that illustrious emissary of Eros (as Deputy Inclán once called her) spanned almost to the day, the twenty years between the two World Wars. Her philosophy was quite simple: bear in mind, my dear ladies, that what we're running here is not a den of iniquity, but a temple of culture. So, it's imperative that all our customers feel comfortable, if not fulfilled—from the pharmacist to the Justice of the Peace, from the Chief of Police to the wealthiest rancher, from the cattle-broker to the parish priest. It was Madame Lucrèce who brought culture to San Pascual. Each girl had a bookcase in her working quarters; and when business was slow, that is, before the regular patrons arrived or after they abandoned that haven of wholesome pleasures, Madame Lucrèce would hold veritable seminars for her pupils on matters directly or vaguely cultural. You're probably wondering what ever led a woman of such stature to come bury herself and her professional accomplishments in a one-horse town and a country as stingy with sex as ours. I admit I once asked her that, at the end of an evening we spent exchanging opinions on Schopenhauer, the supposedly scientific roots of Symbolism and the influence of Breuer's cathartic method on Freud. Her incisive and revealing reply was that in the uncharted territory of nontraditional sexual practices, she had always considered rustic simplicity preferable to urban sophistication; and from the perspective of her unorthodox ideology, the most suitable working environment was not just out in the country, but as far away from civilization as she could get. Here I should mention another detail: back in San Pascual we always addressed each other formally as *usted*. I attribute that to a strange admiration for the Anglo-Saxon world, where the only time they use anything like the familiar *tú* is when they're sweet talking God. Well, it was an unequivocal sign of Madame Lucrèce's adaptability that at the Maison, no one ever used *tú*. That custom set a definite tone for human relations, whether dressed or in the raw. And here's something else: even as they performed their amorous rituals, the girls were engrossed in their books. I'll never forget how it boggled my mind as a novice to see Augusta, the whore I had chosen for my initiation into that sacred order, leafing through *Selections from the Reader's Digest* while I attempted to assert my masculinity. Later, I learned that to the others, Augusta was barely literate. Even in a bordello, the *Reader's Digest* was considered lowbrow. As time passed, I was to discover what the rest of them liked to read. Renata would let you make love to her with her nose buried in *Fortunata y Jacinta*; Marielle was a fan of Romain Rolland; Colette, an admirer of Colette (who ever would have guessed?); Brunhilde, a devotee of Thomas Mann. You may find it strange but in retrospect, I realize that not once, in all my years of boisterous escapades, have I matched the exquisite, uplifting and succulent orgasm I had at Maison Lucrèce, the night I performed my amorous acrobatics on a splendiferous whore named Ondine, with voluptuous curves and lips like daggers: while her left hand displayed an exceptional understanding of the male epidermis and the hypersensitivity of its tiniest pores, her right hand roamed lackadaisically through the *Confessions* of Saint Augustine. Well, what do you think? I trust I've briefed you thoroughly enough. Now that I've supplied you with a subject, and told you about the idiosyncrasies of that first-class whorehouse, the atmosphere there, and the astonishing proclivities of the woman who founded it, all you have to do is write down the story (which, you'll admit, is the easiest part). Oh, and one more thing. Will you think I'm very bold if I ask you, when you do get around to writing it, to dedicate it to yours truly? You see, that might give me a little extra pull with the girls who work there now. I confess that every so often, I can still muster the energy and the hormones for a quick trip to San Pascual; and of course, I make a courtesy call each time I go. Unfortunately, these days they're reading Bukowski.... And I'm sure you'll agree that it's just not the same: there's no comparison between Bukowski's venereal basics and the culpable carnality of the *Confessions*, especially where the honorable bishop and Doctor of the Church describes the quagmire of his lust and the dark distress of impure love (sic). There's simply no comparison. Well, I'm just about through, now. But if I can add a final fillip to this folksy piece, here's one more bit of wisdom for you, straight from the horse's mouth: only a saint can ever hope to be a tried and true lecher."

1987

Translated by Louise Popkin

The Williamses and the Peabodys

For the second August in a row, the Williamses and the Peabodys were back in Port Pollença. Like so many of their English, French, and Scandinavian counterparts, they preferred that resort, with its relatively calm seas and good weather, to others along the coast of Mallorca. Three years earlier, the Peabodys had planned on vacationing in Arenal; but daunted by the raucous nightlife there, and the crowds forever milling about on the beach (there were days when you couldn't even spread out a towel), they had promptly gone in search of a more inviting spot.

They adored the Mediterranean, but they needed a little peace and quiet. Hugh Peabody was an engineer; he worked in Liverpool and by summer, he was totally exhausted. So his number one priority was a good rest, with lots of invigorating Spanish *siestas* and light reading; enough mussels, shrimp, and sole to give him a full year's supply of phosphorus; and long swims in the gorgeous natural pool known as Pollença Bay, with its festive array of private yachts and all those topless Scandinavian girls, cooking themselves to a crisp in the sun.

The cabbie who drove them in from the airport in Palma turned out to be quite the amateur sociologist: upon discovering that the Peabodys knew some Spanish, he had felt called upon to argue at length that, whereas the French and Germans flocked to the beaches of Mallorca simply to stock up on fitness, the English and the Scandinavians came looking for status. Why else would they spend their whole vacation out in the sun, tanning their well-greased hides? When they got back to London, or Copenhagen, or Oslo, their laboriously acquired tans would serve as unequivocal proof that they had actually been to the Mediterranean, thus guaranteeing them both the envy and the admiration of their less affluent neighbors.

Hugh responded with a reticent—that is, a typically British— chuckle to the cabbie's analysis; but his limited Spanish precluded any inquiry into its origins. At which point, sensing doubt was in the air, the garrulous theoretician asked his audience please, not to think he was making the whole thing up; why, just yesterday afternoon he had heard it from an expert on the tourist trade who had his own program on a local FM station.

Later on in their hotel, Hugh remarked to his wife, Diana, and their son, Peter, that now he knew why Mallorca had always attracted so many foreign writers: the Mediterranean, with its crystal-clear water, slow-moving, fluffy clouds, and bright sunlight, undoubtedly fired the imagination. If a mere local cabbie could come up with such a superb piece of "gossip-fiction," he argued (the part about the radio program couldn't possibly be true), there was simply no saying what the island's climate may have done for the art of a George Sand or a Robert Graves.

The Williamses were in a different league from the Peabodys— in fact, a different class. They never stayed at the resort hotels along the waterfront, but in a magnificent house in the neighboring town of Pollença, some twelve miles inland. Still, since their daughter, Mary Ann, and the Peabody boy had become such good friends the year before, the two couples generally got together twice a week.

If Peabody, the engineer, was pro-Labor, his fellow Englishman was no ordinary Tory: Fred Williams' politics were, to put it mildly, somewhere to the right of Margaret Thatcher's. The owner of "a factory and a half" (the other half belonged to his cousin Harold, which was hardly a problem since Harold was much more given to hunting foxes and women, than in looking after the business), he had been spending July and August in Pollença with his family for a number of years.

As the owners of that gorgeous house with a pool, the Williamses never came down to Port Pollença to sunbathe, much less to swim; that was what the fancy pool was for. "I could never go swimming in the same water as that hotel bunch," Mary Ann's mother Kate would say, her face the picture of revulsion. "Why, it's full of their urine, spit, and excrement." Unlike her parents, Mary

Ann had jet black hair, and a pair of green eyes Peter found irresistible from the moment he saw her.

That comment of Kate's was a little too direct for Hugh and Diana who, themselves, were part of the "hotel bunch"; although they never said as much, even to one another, it inevitably evoked an image of their own urine, spit and excrement. At times, it seemed to Hugh as if the Williamses had too much class to bother with body functions at all; those were for the workers in their "factory and a half."

Inasmuch as Mary Ann (seventeen), and Peter (a mere fifteen), were such good friends, at those family get-togethers the adults favored small talk over politics. Sometimes Hugh and Fred had to go out of their way to avoid capital gains, social security and the right to strike, but they did manage to steer clear of those forbidden areas.

Among the Williams family's many possessions was a lovely, fashionable yacht, the *Karen*, which they always berthed in Port Pollença, just opposite the restaurant in the old Fish Exchange on the pier; and sometimes the three of them would go out for a sail, with Peter in tow. And Peter could tell that the differences between Mary Ann and her parents went beyond complexion and coloring. While they acted pretty much like a normal family, there was a not quite invisible wall between the girl and her elders. To be sure, the same was true of him and his parents; but in their case (although he had yet to give it a name), the distance was just part of the "generation gap." Something else was going on between the Williamses. He would often detect a flash of steeliness in Kate's blue eyes when she looked at Mary Ann; and in Mary Ann's green eyes, a glimmer of fear, or at least of misgiving.

"I hope you'll always come with us when we go sailing," was the way Mary Ann would put her invitation to Peter, making sure her parents were there to hear it. Fred and Kate were noncommital, but they usually took him along. Of course, that made Peter positively ecstatic, since by then, predictably, he was head over heels in love with Mary Ann. He would spend all day waiting for her to show up in Port Pollença; and when she did—not necessarily with her parents (sometimes, the chauffeur would bring her down in the gray Mercedes), and despite Kate's reservations—then they'd go for a swim, and stretch out together in the sun. Try as he would, Peter could never take his eager eyes off Mary Ann's bare, suntanned breasts; he'd barely notice the daredevil stunts those U.S. Air Force planes were forever practicing over the calm waters of the bay.

During the preceding week, a newcomer had unexpectedly joined the Williams clan. Instead of going to see them at home, he would meet them on the pier in Port Pollença; and when Mary Ann and Peter wandered off past the boat slips, he, Kate and Fred would have a few drinks together in the restaurant. At first, Peter was afraid this interloper (who looked about twenty-five and, by the way, not the least bit British) might be an admirer of Mary Ann's—even a prospective fiance—but he soon concluded otherwise. He asked Mary Ann who the newcomer was:

"Who? Oh, him.... He's just a guy my parents met last year in Southampton. I think it has to do with some business deal." The indifference Peter sensed in the girl's voice cheered him and relieved his anxiety.

One day after lunch, Peter and Mary Ann went out for a sail on the *Karen*; but as soon as they lost sight of land, they turned off the motor and lay down on the deck to sunbathe. Mary Ann took off her blouse; and at the sight of those small breasts, familiar from the year before and now ripened to near perfection, Peter felt a bit woozy, though not exactly because the boat was rocking.

Mary Ann smiled, which, of course, did little to restore Peter's composure. Then she simply asked, "Don't you feel well?"

"As a matter of fact, I feel unbearably well. It's just that you're so beautiful." And as he uttered those totally conventional words, his eyes were riveted on his friend's carefree bosom.

"You like them?" she asked. Silently, he shook his head yes. He really didn't feel up to saying a word.

"Would you like to touch them?" Slowly, Peter stretched out his hand; helpfully, she guided it to its destination. For him, it was as if the yacht, the bay, the hotels along the waterfront, the windsurfers' sails, the rest of the world, had vanished. There was nothing but him and Mary Ann....

"We'd better go downstairs," she said, her smile gone and her tone more solemn. So, down they went. Since the bunk was narrow, they stretched out on the floor. But first she slipped off her shorts and then, to make it all easier, helped Peter out of his. "You've never done it before, have you?" she asked. Peter shook his head no. "Good. Neither have I, so we can learn together." Admittedly, in this connection the movement of the boat was quite useful; it even allowed them to improvise, use their imaginations.

After resting a while in silence, they did it a second time. Then Mary Ann lit up a cigarette, and he wanted one too. "No, not yet," she said. "You're still a kid...although I must say you've certainly changed in a year!" Then, as he rested his blond head on that so newly discovered belly, she added, "Just don't go getting any ideas, O.K.? I wanted us do it together, so we did. I really wanted my first time to be with you, because I think you're terrific; that's the honest truth. But it's nowhere near the whole story; there's a lot about me I can't tell you."

"What's that supposed to mean? That you're older than I am?"

"No, Peter. It's not my age.... Look, I can't say any more. Besides, I don't think Fred and Kate are planning to bring me with them next year."

"Can I ask you a question? How come you're a brunette, when they're both blond and blue-eyed?"

"Oh, genes are funny things.... You know what genes are, Peter?" He didn't, of course. A long silence followed. Then she said, "We'd better head back. I don't want the chauffeur looking for me before we get to the pier. Remember, none of them even know we go sailing together." Nevertheless, as they steered the *Karen* into its berth, they spotted the chauffeur's grey, somewhat sinister-looking figure.

"*Señorita*," he said, before they had had time to disembark, "I've been waiting for you for twenty minutes."

Three days later, Peter was standing on the terrace at his hotel; with the German binoculars Hugh had lent him, he could survey

202

Port Pollença inch by inch. It was ten in the morning. As he focused in on the old Fish Exchange, he happened to spot the grey Mercedes. Next to it stood the chauffeur. Further out on the pier he could see the three Williamses walking toward their yacht, where the interloper was waiting for them, apparently ready to set sail. And set sail they did. The yacht glided slowly out to sea; but Peter managed to keep track of it with his binoculars. At about eleven, it stopped moving and simply floated on the horizon. For hours Peter's eyes were glued to that spot, as if his very life depended on it. When Hugh and Diana called him for lunch, he said he wasn't hungry.

Finally, the yacht began moving again and headed back toward land. When he figured it was about twenty minutes out of port, Peter went down to his room, put the binoculars back in their case, and ran off anxiously to meet it. When it docked, he was standing there waiting. Only Fred, Kate and the interloper got off. Kate, who spotted him walking toward them, greeted him with her usual "Hello, Peter," then stood there, waiting for his question:

"Where's Mary Ann?"

"Oh, we ran into some old friends on their yacht, and Mary Ann decided to join them."

"And when will she be back?"

"I don't know. They're so much fun, I'm sure they'll keep her busy for at least a week, if not more."

Peter tried to seem nonchalant, or only understandably upset about his friend's not being there. Then saying goodbye, he walked slowly away, while the chauffeur, the Williamses, and this time the interloper as well, climbed into the grey Mercedes and sped off towards town.

Peter returned to the hotel and phoned his father from the lobby. Something in his voice worried Hugh, who came downstairs to see what was the matter. That's when Peter told him about the Williamses' yacht—how it sailed out to sea; how he tracked it with the binoculars; how it had come back to the pier without Mary Ann; how Kate had explained her absence.

"What a shame," said Hugh. "Mary Ann is such a pretty girl, and the two of you are really good friends. But maybe she likes being with old friends too. Now, that's not the end of the world, is it?" White as a sheet, Peter felt his throat tighten.

"The trouble is," he managed to say, "I was watching through the binoculars the entire time, and I can tell you for a fact that no other boat came anywhere near the *Karen*."

1987

Translated by Louise Popkin

Blood Pact

My name is Octavio, but no one ever calls me that anymore. Now that I'm eighty-four, even my own daughter calls me grandpa. At my age, what else can you expect? I expect nothing. I'm just as proud as I ever was. But after all these years, I'm used to being confined to my bed and my rocking chair. I never say a word. The others don't think I can talk; even the doctor doesn't. But I can talk, alright. At night, I talk to myself, in a whisper, of course, so they won't hear me. Just to reassure myself that I can. What do I have to gab about, anyway? Luckily, I can still make it to the bathroom on my own. It's only seven steps from here to the sink or the toilet, and I can walk that far. I can't take a shower, though, at least not without help. So for my personal care, there's an aide who comes in once a week to give me a sponge bath (I wish it were more often, but they say he's expensive). He's pretty good at it. I let him do his job, anyhow I have no choice. It's more comfortable that way and besides, his technique is superb. At the end when he goes over my testicles with a damp towel, the cold feels good, except in the middle of winter. Real good, even though naturally, nothing could bring those dead things back to life. Sometimes when I'm in the bathroom I take a peek at my private parts in the mirror, and private is definitely how they should stay. Private parts.... Mine look just like a goat's beard. But I'll admit that cold towel makes me feel better. It's as close as I've come to the *sitzbath* a hydrotherapist prescribed for me about sixty years ago—"revitalizing," he called it. A skinny old fellow (him, I mean, not me), white-haired, with a know-it-all look in his pale blue eyes and an impersonal, but kind voice. He sat me down in front of him, looked me over for what couldn't have been more than a minute, and immediately began typing on a big old Remington as clumsy as a streetcar. I was a new patient, so he was taking a history. As he typed away he read it aloud to me, probably to see if I disagreed with any of his observations. It was incredible. Everything he said was absolutely true. Childhood diseases: measles, German measles, scarlet fever, diphtheria, typhus; athletic as a boy, lucky for me because otherwise, now I'd probably have breathing problems; premature varicose veins, a reduced inguinal hernia, good teeth, etc. I didn't realize until that day how many quirks I had managed to accumulate. But thanks to that guy and his advice, gradually I got into better shape. The bad part came later, as the years started piling up. Years. That's one thing no hydrotherapist or quack doctor can cure you of. Now that all I'm good for is sitting around in silence (sitting, by necessity; in silence, by choice), I spend my time reminiscing: rummaging through my memories for details I think I've forgotten, until they turn up in some corner of my brain. With my eyes almost always teary (not from weeping, but old age), I study the palms of my hands. They've forgotten the feel of a woman's flesh, but my mind remembers; it can wander like the eye of a camera over the bodies of the women I loved, stopping at will to notice a neck that always thrilled me (was that Ana's?), a pair of breasts (weren't they Luisa's?) that had me believing in God for a year, a tiny waist (was it Carmen's?) that cried out for my strong arms. And that silky blond pubis I used to call my golden fleece (wasn't it Ema's?), that cropped up so often in my daydreams (as a lustful underbrush) and my nightmares (as a kind of Moloch, swallowing me up for good). It's odd how often I can recall particular details of a body, but no face and no name, and how other times a name pops into my mind, but I can't match it to a body. I wonder what's become of all those women.... Are they still alive? Do people call them grandma, just plain old grandma, or does anybody call them by name? Because old age plunges us into a kind of anonymity. In Spain, the newspapers say (or used to): an elderly man of sixty died in such-and-such a place. Those morons.... I wonder what label they've got left to describe us poor octogenarians. Museum piece? Junk heap? Pile of debris? When I was sixty, I was anything but elderly. At the beach, if I played racquetball with my kids and their friends, I'd beat them every time. In bed, when a woman contributed her fair share to our physical dialogue, I'd contribute more than mine. At work, I may not have been number one, but I certainly pulled my weight. I had my share of fun too—naturally, without upsetting Teresa. Now, there's a name I associate with a body. Of course, that body belongs to my wife. We were together so many times, and things weren't always perfect between us, but most of the time they were fine. For as long as she could, Teresa made sure of that. She probably figured I had my adventures here and there; but she never acted jealous, or said any of those nasty things that make living together so miserable. In exchange, I was always careful not to hurt her, embarrass her, or make her look ridiculous (a good husband's first responsibility), because she never would have forgiven me for that. I loved her dearly, in a different way, of course. In a sense, she was my other half, someone to lean on when the going got rough. And I gave her three sons and a daughter. Neither of us could have asked for more. The asthma attack that killed her was the prelude to my coronary. She was sixty-eight at the time, and I was seventy. So that would be fourteen years ago. Not very long. The tide went out for me when Teresa died, and it's never come back in. Who am I supposed to talk to? I know I'm dead weight to my daughter and son-in-law. Not that they don't love me, but I might as well be an antique table, or a cuckoo clock, or (these days) a microwave oven. And I really wouldn't mind it so much, if they'd just let me be. But my daughter comes in early each morning and she doesn't say how's it going, Papa, but how's it going, Grandpa, as if she weren't a product of my prehistoric sperm bank. At lunchtime it's my son-in-law's turn to say how's it going, Grandpa. Coming from him that's not a misstatement, but a sign of affection which I value accordingly, because he's here compliments of some other guy's sperm (probably Italian, since his name is Aldo Cagnoli). Wow, I got his whole name right. Whenever either of them shows up, I smile, nod my head, and give them one of my weepy, but intelligent looks. I'm only saying that to myself, so I'm not being vain, or presumptuous, or coy like so many old fogeys are these days. I say intelligent, because it happens to be true. I also suspect they're delighted that I can't talk (so they think, anyway). I can just imagine what goes through their minds: Thank God we don't have to put up with a lot of senile babbling. But the truth is, they don't know what they're missing. Only I know how many interesting stories I could tell them, how much history I actually saw happen. What do they know about the First and Second World Wars, or the first Model-T Fords, or the soccer medal we won in the 1924 Olympics, or the death of Batlle y Ordóñez, or the send-off they gave Rodó when he left for Italy, or the 1930 Centennial celebrations? It's a good thing I only talk about those things to myself; that way I don't have to keep them in chronological order. Anyhow, what do they know? They may have seen a footnote, or heard them mentioned in some longwinded political speech. But the atmosphere, the crowds in the streets, the sadness or joy on peoples' faces, the blazing sun or the pouring rain, the roof of umbrellas over Plaza Cagancha when Uruguay beat Italy three to two in the Amsterdam semifinals and there was no play-by-play via satellite like there is today, just telegrams (Uruguay attacks; corner against Italy; Italy puts pressure on Mazali's goal; Scarone shoots and misses)....They don't know about any of that, and it's their loss. When my daughter comes in and says how's it going, Grandpa, I should answer remember how you used to bury your head in my lap and cry because the neighbor's boy had called you *Negrita*, and you thought that was an insult because you knew you had light-colored skin, and I'd explain to you that the neighbor's boy only called you that because of your dark hair, but that anyhow, even if your skin had been darker that would have been nothing to be ashamed of, because people with dark skin are like us in every other way, and they can be just as good or just as bad as the whitest people around. And then you'd stop crying (and my lap would be all wet, but I'd say don't worry, my child, tears don't leave a stain) and you'd run off again to play with the other kids and the next time the neighbor's boy called you *Negrita*, you'd sneer at him the way only a seven-year-old can and embarrass the hell out of him by yelling, yeah, Paleface? I could remind you of all that, but what for? Maybe you'd say, oh, Grandpa, stop talking nonsense. Or maybe you wouldn't, but I don't want to take a chance because if you did, I'd be mortified. It's not nonsense,

Teresita (you're named after your mother; obviously, imagination wasn't our strong suit), I taught you a few things, and so did she. So then, why is it that when you talk about her, you say when Mama was alive, but when you talk to me it's how's it going, Grandpa? Maybe if I had died first, right now you'd be saying when Papa was alive. The trouble is that for better or for worse, your papa is alive, and maybe he doesn't talk, but he has a brain; maybe he doesn't talk, but he has feelings.

The only one who has every right to call me grandpa, of course, is my grandson, who's name is Octavio too (apparently, imagination wasn't his parents' strong suit, either). And there's the key. When I can say his name, Octavio. Yes, say it. Because my grandson is the one human being I talk to, except for myself, of course. It all began a year ago, when Octavio was seven. One day I was lying there with my eyes closed and, thinking I was alone, I said goddammit, my back hurts, in a voice just loud enough to be heard. But I wasn't alone. I hadn't heard my grandson come in. Hey, Grandpa, you're talking, he said, so surprised and delighted it brought tears to my eyes. I asked him if anyone else was home and when he said no, the others were out, I proposed we make a deal. If he didn't tell anyone I could talk, I would tell him stories no one else had ever heard. Sure, he said, but we have to make a blood pact. He went out of the room and came back almost immediately with a razor blade, a bottle of alcohol and a package of cotton. He knew exactly what to do; in fact, since he had that series of injections for his allergies, he's even something of an expert. Calm as could be, he made a tiny nick on my wrist and one on his own, just big enough to draw a few drops of blood, then we pressed our secret wounds together and we hugged. Finally, Octavio put a little alcohol on a piece of cotton, held it against both cuts until they stopped bleeding, and ran out to put everything back in the medicine cabinet. Since then, whenever we're alone in the house (as we often are), it's time for me to hold up my end of the bargain and come up with some brand-new stories. Each time my daughter and son-in-law go out, they say now, you take good care of Grandpa, and he answers don't worry, I will, pretending to be annoyed so they won't get suspicious, but winking at me knowingly; then as soon as he hears the door shut and he's sure we won't be interrupted, he pulls a chair over to my rocker or my bed and sits there waiting for me to comply with the terms of our blood pact and tell him a story no one else has ever heard. And that's the hard part: all those hours I spend sitting or lying around with my eyes shut, as if I were asleep, what I'm really doing is working out the next story right down to the tiniest details, because if the fox hurts his paw in a trap one day and the next day he runs around chasing chickens, Octavio immediately reminds me that it's too soon for his paw to have healed; so then I have to do a little editing and change "runs" to "limps." And if I have the old Wizard of the Mountain whipping the Gnomes of the Forest every day until his hair falls out, and then I have him combing his hair while he gazes at his reflection in a lake, Octavio immediately comes out with, I thought you said he was bald. Talking my way out of that kind of fix is a little easier since by definition, wizards have magical powers they can use to grow their hair back. So then my grandson asks whether he can grow his hair back too, if he ever goes bald. No, not you, I say, setting him straight, because you'll never be a wizard. And he says too bad, and in a way he has a point since if I had been a wizard, I certainly would have used my magical powers to grow my hair back when it fell out before I was fifty. I'm not the only storyteller either; Octavio tells me what happens in school, and out in the street, and on TV, and at the soccer stadium. He's a Danubio fan, and he can't believe that I'm for Wanderers. I keep trying to convert him, but it's obvious he's not about to defect. So then I tell him about great games and spectacular plays I remember, like when Piendibeni scored his famous goal against the divine Zamora; or all the times that sneaky one-armed player Castro advanced the ball illegally in the penalty area using his stump; or when that skinny guy García went for a whole round and a half without a single goal against him (of course, the backs were none other than Nazassi and Domingos da Guía), or when Ghiggia scored this winning goal at Maracaná, or when, or when, or when.... And Octavio listens as if I were some kind of genius, and I think how lucky I am that I can still talk, and tell him all that, and see the excitement on his face, and give myself so much pleasure.

The truth is, I don't remember what my own kids were like at Octavio's age. Simón, the oldest one, died. How long ago was that? It was after Teresa's death. Anyhow, who cares what day it was? He's dead, and that's all there is to it. I don't think he had any kids, or maybe I've just forgotten them. I'm never sure where I'll find a hole in my memory—or even a crater. My second boy, Braulio, did have kids, but they're all in Denver, what ever made him decide to go there? The truth is, I can't remember. Sometimes they send a few snapshots, taken with that marvelous Polaroid of theirs, or even a postcard saying give the old man a hug. That's me. He calls me old man, instead of grandpa. I'll be damned if that's any better. I'll admit that once, he sent me a transistor radio. I still have it, and I turn it on sometimes. But the batteries keep running out, and I'd have to ask for new ones. And I expect nothing. I never ask anybody for anything. I know I'm a proud S.O.B. but at this stage I'm not about to change, right? In any case, the only one I'm spiting is myself, because if I always had batteries for my radio, I could listen to a game once in a while, not too often, though, because most of the sportscasters wear me out with all their phony enthusiasm and awful grammar. And I could listen to classical music, which is the only kind I can stomach. I was so happy that afternoon I heard them play Beethoven's Septet. I had a recording of it a long time ago, but who knows where it ended up. Maybe there's some way for me to get those batteries after all without sacrificing my stinking pride, like telling my grandson I need them, and he could just to go to my daughter and say, look, Grandpa's radio is out of batteries; he wouldn't have to violate the terms of our pact or anything, or give our secret away. They'd send him down to the corner hardware store to get them, and that would be that. I know how to put them in; although sometimes I get them in backwards, so the radio doesn't work. It's taken me as long as fifteen minutes to find the right position for four 1.5 volt batteries, but even that gives me something to do for a while. I can't read anymore. Or watch TV. But I can listen to the radio, or change the batteries. My youngest boy's name is Diego and he's in Europe; I think he teaches in Zurich, and he even speaks German. He has two girls that speak German too, but they don't speak any Spanish. Isn't that the damnedest mess? Diego doesn't write as often as Braulio, even though he teaches literature (Swiss literature, naturally). I get a card from him too, for Christmas, with a few words from the girls, but in German. I don't know any German, just the little bit of English I needed to handle business letters, like the ones I used to write personally when I was manager of that shipping company, South Atlantic Imports and Exports, Ltd. Little phrases like we acknowledge receipt of your kind letter, or Very truly yours, enough so the folks up north would know they could answer with Dear Sirs, or Gentlemen. My youngest boy sometimes sends me little things too, like an eighteen-carat-gold Swiss key ring. I smiled when I got it, as if to say how pretty, but I was really thinking what a stupid jerk, what does he expect me to do with an eighteen-carat-gold key ring, when I'm almost flat on my back?

In other words, my only contact with the outside world is through my daughter, when she comes in and says how's it going, Grandpa, my son-in-law, ditto, the doctor every so often, and the aide when he comes to wash my long-retired balls, together with the rest of this *corpus delicti*. Last but not least, there's my grandson, and I think he's what keeps me going. Or I should say, what used to. Because yesterday morning he came in, kissed me and said, Grandpa, I'm going to spend a couple of weeks with Uncle Braulio in Denver, I got really good grades this year, so now I get a vacation. I couldn't talk (and maybe I couldn't have anyway, because of the lump in my throat) since my daughter and my son-in-law were in the room, and neither I nor my grandson was about to violate our pact. So I kissed him back, squeezed his hand, and pressed my wrist against his for a second as a sign of what we both knew; and I know he understood perfectly how much I was going to miss having somebody to tell my brand-new stories to. Then they left. But three or four hours later, Aldo came back in, just Aldo, and said, look Grandpa, Octavio didn't leave for just a couple of weeks, he'll be gone a whole year, maybe more; we want him to go to school in the States, that way he'll learn the language while he's young and get an education he can really use later on. The reason he didn't tell you, is that he didn't know it either. We were afraid he'd start crying, because he loves you so much, Grandpa, he always tells me that; and you love him too, right? We plan to break it to him in a letter, after my brother-in-law has a chance to prepare him. Oh, and one more thing. As he was heading for the plane, he turned around and said, give Grandpa a kiss for me, and tell him I'll be honoring our pact. Then he ran off. What pact is that, Grandpa? I closed my eyes so he wouldn't see my tears (even though they're always so weepy now, that it's impossible to tell when I'm crying) and I gestured, as if to say: just kid stuff. He accepted that and left me there, left me alone with my loneliness, because now I really have nobody, and nobody to talk to either. All this has taken me by surprise. But maybe it's for the best. Because now I really want to die. As any eighty-four year old junk heap should. At my age wanting to live is a bad thing because you die anyway, only it takes you by surprise. But not me. Because I want to go now, and take along this whole world I have in my head, plus the dozen or so stories I had ready for my grandson, Octavio. I don't have to kill myself (with what?), because there's nothing surer than wanting to die. I've always known that. You die when you really want to. It may take another day or two. Not much longer. No one will know. Not the doctor (who never even realized I could talk), not the aide, not Teresita, not Aldo. They'll only catch on five minutes before it happens. Maybe then Teresita will call me papa but by then, it will be too late. As for me, I won't even say goodbye, just a faint "so long" with my eyes at the end. No, I won't say goodbye, because I want my grandson Octavio to know someday, that even in that trickiest of moments, I never stopped honoring our blood pact. And I'll go tell my stories elsewhere. Or nowhere at all.

1988

Translated by Louise Popkin

MARIO BENEDETTI, one of Latin America's best-known and most beloved authors, was born in 1920 in Paso de los Toros, Uruguay. He grew up in Montevideo, where his family moved when he was four years old. Trained as an accountant, he published his first story at the age of 27. In the late fifties and sixties, he traveled extensively in Latin America, Europe and the U.S. While in Cuba, he founded the world famous Centro de Investigaciones Literarias at Casa de las Americas; he directed that Center from 1969 to 1971. Returning to Uruguay in 1971, he opposed increasing government repression through his writing and participation in the leftist coalition known as the Frente Amplio, which he helped organize. Following the coup of June 1973, his work was banned by the Uruguayan Military. From that moment until the return of civilian government in 1985, he lived in exile in Argentina, Peru, Cuba and Spain. Writing for an international audience, he denounced the tragic events in his country. To date, Benedetti's more than fifty books of poetry, fiction, drama, literary and cultural criticism, and his political journalism are known around the globe. His poetic texts, some of them set to music and frequently performed at folk concerts, are familiar to the generations of Latin Americans who flock to hear him whenever he appears in public. Several of his novels have been made into films, and two have been published in English: *The Truce* (New York, 1969) and *Juan Angel's Birthday* (Amherst, MA, 1974). Currently he resides in Montevideo and Madrid, and devotes himself full time to his writing.

Curbstone Press, Inc.
is a non-profit publishing house dedicated to literature that reflects
a commitment to social change, with an emphasis on contemporary
writing from Latin America and Latino communities in the United
States. Curbstone presents writers who give voice to the unheard in a
language that goes beyond denunciation to celebrate, honor and teach.
Curbstone builds bridges between its writers and the public – from
inner-city to rural areas, colleges to community centers, children to
adults. Curbstone seeks out the highest aesthetic expression of the
dedication to human rights and intercultural understanding: poetry,
testimonials, novels, stories, photography.

This mission requires more than just producing books. It requires
ensuring that as many people as possible know about these books and
read them. To achieve this, a large portion of Curbstone's schedule is
dedicated to arranging tours and programs for its authors, working
with public school and university teachers to enrich curricula, reaching
out to underserved audiences by donating books and conducting
readings and community programs, and promoting discussion in the
media. It is only through these combined efforts that literature can truly
make a difference.

Curbstone Press, like all non-profit presses, depends on the support
of individuals, foundations, and government agencies to bring you, the
reader, works of literary merit and social significance which might not
find a place in profit-driven publishing channels. Our sincere thanks to
the many individuals who support this endeavor and to the following
organizations, foundations and government agencies: ADCO
Foundation, Witter Bynner Foundation for Poetry, Connecticut
Commission on the Arts, Connecticut Arts Endowment Fund, Ford
Foundation, Greater Hartford Arts Council, Junior League of Hartford,
Lawson Valentine Foundation, LEF Foundation, Lila Wallace-Reader's
Digest Fund, The Andrew W. Mellon Foundation, National Endowment
for the Arts, Samuel Rubin Foundation and the Puffin Foundation.

Please support Curbstone's efforts to present the diverse voices and
views that make our culture richer. Tax-deductible donations can be
made by check or credit card to Curbstone Press, 321 Jackson St.,
Willimantic, CT 06226 Tel: (860) 423-5110.